MOONLIGHT& MISADVENTURE

---

20 STORIES OF MYSTERY & SUSPENSE

Edited by
JUDY PENZ SHELUK

Superior Shores Press

PRAISE FOR MOONLIGHT & MISADVENTURE
20 STORIES OF MYSTERY & SUSPENSE

"What a bunch of misadventures. These twenty authors have created stories where dialog snaps, characters carom, and plots surprise all under the ever-present moon."—*James Blakey, DERRINGER award-winning author*

"Twenty moonlit escapades in an outstanding, action-packed collection, showing the short story genre at its sparkling best."—*CRIME FICTION LOVER*

"Twenty tasty crime fiction bites in a variety of sub-genres: neo-noir, police procedural, mystery, caper, and historical. Laced with moonlit suspense, twisty turns, and dark humor, readers will be checking the shadows for murderers and miscreants."—*Rosemary McCracken, DEBUT DAGGER and DERRINGER finalist, and author of the PAT TIERNEY mystery series*

"You cannot go wrong with this book. It is a collection to be read again and again. Savored. It is simply wonderful."—*Joan Leotta, author and story performer*

"These individual stories flow together like notes in a phrase of music."—*Joanna Vander Vlugt, podcaster and author of THE UNRAVELLING, a CANADIAN BOOK CLUB AWARDS finalist*

"From the complicated and powerful opening tale to the twist ending in the last one, the twenty stories in *Moonlight & Misadventure* are all good ones. Moonlight, misadventure, and in many cases a hint of madness, are all at work in this highly entertaining read. Every tale selected for this anthology is well worth your time." *Kevin Tipple, Book Reviewer, Kevin's Corner*

PRAISE FOR THE SUPERIOR SHORES ANTHOLOGIES

The Best Laid Plans: 21 Stories of Mystery & Suspense

"Crime doesn't pay, especially for criminals who think they've found a loophole...The Best Laid Plans should be read by anyone who loves this genre." —*LONG AND SHORT REVIEWS*

"Killer acting and get-rich schemes...the clever twists are endless."—*Catherine Astolfo, bestselling author and two-time winner of the ARTHUR ELLIS AWARD for Best Crime Short Story*

"A dazzling collection of twenty-one short tales of mayhem, leaving both the reader and the corpses breathless. A five-star read."—*Kate Thornton, DERRINGER-nominated short story author*

Praise for Heartbreaks & Half-truths: 22 Stories of Mystery & Suspense

"A memorable collection. Yes, there's heartbreak, but those half-truths will get you every time."—*CRIME FICTION LOVER*

"This book is a real orthopedic workout. There are stories that will shiver your spine, tickle your funny bone, and, in a few cases, drop your jaw."—*Robert Lopresti, winner of the DERRINGER and BLACK ORCHID NOVELLA awards*

"Twenty-two writers explore the theme and deliver 22 strikingly different viewpoints. Prepare yourself for an entertaining journey. A satisfying literary adventure awaits."— *J. R. Lindermuth, author of THE BARTERED BODY.*

Moonlight & Misadventure: 20 Stories of Mystery & Suspense

Compilation Copyright © 2021 Judy Penz Sheluk

Story Copyrights © 2021 by Individual Authors:

K.L. Abrahamson

Sharon Hart Addy

C.W. Blackwell

Clark Boyd

M.H. Callway

Michael A. Clark

*Susan Daly

Buzz Dixon

Jeanne DuBois

Elizabeth Elwood

Tracy Falenwolfe

Kate Fellowes

*John M. Floyd

Billy Houston

Bethany Maines

Judy Penz Sheluk

KM Rockwood

Joseph S. Walker

Robert Weibezahl

Susan Jane Wright

*My Night with the Duke of Edinburgh by Susan Daly originally appeared in *Fishy Business*, the Fifth Guppy Anthology (Wildside Press, 2019)

*Reunions by John M. Floyd originally appeared in *The Strand Magazine* (Feb-May 2010 issue) and *Deception* (Dogwood Press, 2013)

All stories compiled and edited by Judy Penz Sheluk, www.judypenzsheluk.com, with the exception of "Strawberry Moon," edited by Jennifer Grybowski

Editorial assistance by Jennifer Grybowski

Cover Art by Hunter Martin

Published by Superior Shores Press

ISBN Trade Paperback: 978-1-989495-39-1

ISBN e-Book: 978-1-989495-40-7

First Edition: June 2021

"Don't tell me the moon is shining; show me the glint of light on broken glass."—Anton Chekhov

CONTENTS

INTRODUCTION

I've been captivated by the moon since childhood, when a friend informed me that wishes made on the full moon were guaranteed to come true. Naturally, there was a ritual to follow: I had to stare at the moon while making my wish—never to be revealed to anyone—and then tap the tips of my right index and middle fingers against my left wrist. What finger tapping has to do with anything remains a mystery to me, but all these years later, I find myself doing it.

My mother, on the other hand, believed it was unlucky to view the full moon through glass—a superstition, I might add, that has also stuck with me until present day. Interestingly, the Irish believe it's viewing the new moon through glass that should be avoided, and that even the position of the new moon is important; for luck the new moon should be seen over the right shoulder, never the left. Still others believe that the new moon is a time to set worthwhile intentions. I do that when I remember.

The Farmers' Almanac also weighs in with advice on planting crops. Crops that grow above the earth, such as corn and wheat, the *Almanac* tells us, should be planted while the moon is waxing, so the moon can pull them out of the ground as it grows bigger. Conversely, root crops, such as turnips, carrots, and yams, should be planted while the moon is waning, allowing vegetables to grow deep into the ground.

Of course, And so, it seemed a natural fit to combine my fascination with the moon with my passion for short stories of mystery and suspense. I thought Moonlight & Misadventure had a nice ring to it.

The Call for Submissions went out October 1, 2020. Ninety-three submissions were received, representing twenty-six U.S. states, four Canadian provinces, as well as the U.K., the Netherlands, India, Austria, and New Zealand. Cutting the field in half, and then by more than half again, is never easy, and I am grateful to Jennifer Grybowski, my friend, co-editor, and fellow Cancerian, for her invaluable insights and input.

The twenty authors represented in this collection have interpreted the underlying theme of moonlight and misadventure in their own inimitable fashion, where only one thing is assured: Waxing, waning, gibbous, or full, the moon is always there, illuminating people and places better left in the dark.

Judy Penz Sheluk

JOSEPH S. WALKER

Joseph S. Walker is a teacher living in Indiana. His fiction has appeared in *Alfred Hitchcock Mystery Magazine*, *Ellery Queen Mystery Magazine*, *Mystery Weekly*, *Tough*, and a number of collections, including *Heartbreaks and Half-Truths*, the second Superior Shores anthology. An Edgar nominee, Joseph has won the Al Blanchard Award and the Bill Crider Prize for Short Fiction, and is a member of Mystery Writers of America, Sisters in Crime, Private Eye Writers of America, and the Short Mystery Fiction Society. Find him at https://jsw47408.wixsite.com/website.

CROWN JEWEL

JOSEPH S. WALKER

GIVEN A CHOICE, Keenan Beech wouldn't have committed his first felony on the night of a full moon. He particularly would not have picked a night just after a big snowfall, when the lunar glow on the unbroken whiteness of the fields turned night into another day. Driving toward his brother's ramshackle house, out in the endless miles of flat, glowing farmland surrounding town, Keenan felt exposed. Vulnerable. The moon was an eye, hanging in space to witness his crime, and he was an ant, dashing across a clean kitchen floor, hoping to reach shelter before some karmic boot came down on him. Hard.

Of course, he didn't have a choice. His brother had seen to that. Xavier had taken something that was rightfully his. He'd been cheated. The pristine expanses of white around him might make him feel uncomfortably visible, but they also reminded him of what was at stake.

Xavier had his White Album, and that could not stand.

It didn't matter that Keenan had others, 348 others, to be exact, and Keenan was always exact. More than 300 copies of the first American pressing of the 1968 double album properly titled *The Beatles*, but universally referred to as the White Album for the blank white cover broken only by the embossed words "The Beatles" and, in the lower right corner of the first few million copies, a stamped serial number.

It was the serial number that burned itself into some people's brains, and Keenan was firmly of their ranks. He was already a wax fanatic, a collector of vintage vinyl ten years back, when he picked up a copy of the White Album at a flea market and casually added it to his stack of purchases. It wasn't until he got home that he noticed the number, A1423679, on the cover. Curious, he turned to Google and fell into a rabbit hole he was yet to come out of. American pressings. American pressings *from different pressing plants.* British pressings. Variant numbering styles. Error printings. Tax stamps. This wasn't like collecting other albums, having exactly the same thing everybody else had. Every copy of *The Beatles* announced its unique identity right up front.

Keenan was hooked. Soon, he was obsessed. His 348 copies were the fruit of ten years of online auctions and garage sale eurekas, road trips to record stores stinking of incense, and furtive trades with unshaven men in strip mall parking lots. Most were flawed in various ways, documented in painstaking detail in his database. The black inner sleeves or the pictures of the band members or the lyric poster were missing. The record itself was scratched. The cover was discolored or stained. But he did have a few that seemed unblemished, though their value was limited by their high serial numbers. Also, he had A1590000, the kind of round number his tribe prized. Still rarer was his run of three consecutive numbers, A0894345 through A0894347, acquired in three different deals. All in all, he was sure he had one of the best collections in the Midwest.

Of course, not everyone found that impressive. Two years ago, Keenan brought a woman he'd seen a few times home and took her to a spare bedroom converted into an audiophile's dream, the walls lined with racks of records, the turntable hooked up to an exquisitely balanced sound system. He showed her the three bins filled with copies of the White Album, each lovingly sheathed in its protective plastic sleeve. She pulled one out at random, turned it over in her hands, and looked at him in utter confusion.

"Don't they have this on CD?" she'd asked. "It would save a lot of room."

That was the last time he saw her.

For several years, the crown jewel of Keenan's collection had been A0009304, the only copy he'd ever personally seen numbered under ten thousand. Then, a few days ago, a Milwaukee record store where he'd made many purchases emailed. They had A0001521. The record itself was lightly scratched, but it still had the original poster, the four pictures of the band members, and the correct sleeves. They were charging $5,000. Was he interested?

Keenan should have called them immediately and had the record shipped. Instead, he simply responded that he would make the three-hour drive and be there Saturday, after the New Year holiday. He would make a weekend of it, stay in a good hotel, and treat himself to an extravagant meal to celebrate. And then he made the real mistake: he told Xavier. Oh, he knew why he did it. It was another move in the endless, often vicious competition the two of them had been engaged in since they came into the world, seven minutes apart. He wanted his little brother (seven minutes was seven minutes) to know that, yes, he could drop five grand on a record he would never listen to, a record he would keep in his big, completely paid off home while Xavier scrambled for gig work and temp jobs.

The following day Xavier played his own gambit: a text message saying, "You mean this record?" with a picture of himself holding the album and giving a thumbs up. The man standing beside him was the owner of the Milwaukee record store. His stomach lurching, Keenan called the store. Xavier had come in, claimed to be Keenan, and paid cash for the album that morning.

Sometimes there were real downsides to being a twin.

Keenan had the sense to close his office door before giving vent to his rage, picking up one of the wooden chairs in front of his desk and slamming it onto the concrete floor until he could feel the joints starting to give way. He also had the sense not to respond to the text or call Xavier. Why give him the chance to gloat? He sat down and put his hands flat on the desk and forced himself to take long, deep, shuddering breaths.

Where in the hell had Xavier, whose picture could be in the dictionary under *slacker*, gotten five thousand dollars in cash? The only explanation was that he had stolen or borrowed it. Therefore, he was probably going to need it back, which meant he was going to have to sell the record, and the logical person to sell it to was Keenan. Which meant he would probably get the record after all, but only at whatever markup Xavier decided to demand, and at the further cost of having this humiliation forever hung over his head.

Unacceptable.

There was another, obvious alternative. Steal it. Xavier would know it was Keenan, of course, but what proof would he have? Being Xavier, he probably hadn't even kept the receipt to prove he ever possessed the record in the first place. As far as the record store knew, Keenan had bought it, so what would be odd about it being in his collection? What cop or DA would believe an obviously embittered man, jealous of his more affluent sibling?

He considered the ethical objections to theft and dismissed them. Xavier had, in effect, stolen from him. Balancing the scales was simply a permissible correction. Moreover, in Xavier's possession the album was nothing, merely a marker of spite. In Keenan's collection it would have context and meaning as the prized centerpiece of a carefully curated cultural assemblage, something to be left to posterity. If anything, a higher morality demanded that Keenan act.

He hesitated longer over practical concerns, the actual mechanics and risks inherent to reclaiming the thing. It should be easy enough to find. He couldn't think of any place in the world Xavier could keep the album other than his home, which wouldn't take more than half an hour to search. Furthermore, Keenan knew just when it would be safe to go. Today was December 30. Xavier hadn't stayed in on New Year's Eve since he was fourteen. He'd go out partying with whatever waitress or slumming elementary-school teacher he was dating this week, stagger home in the wee hours and be hung over all the next day. He probably wouldn't even notice the record was missing until days later.

Sitting at his office desk, it all seemed simple and clear. Thirty hours later, as he made the turn up Xavier's (unplowed, of course) drive under the moon's unblinking scrutiny, it was nerve-wracking.

There was no garage, just a broad, flat empty space in front of the house. As he'd guessed, Xavier's car was nowhere to be seen. Keenan powered through the snow, turned so the car was facing out, and killed the engine.

The silence was immediate and total, the muffled un-noise of a world smothered in snow. The sounds of the car door and his own shoes, the squeaking noise of compressed snow that brought him back to childhood, would surely carry for miles. More than ever, he had the sense of being not just watched, but on display, the moon bright enough that he cast an actual shadow on the snow in front of him. He fought down panic. Xavier was probably halfway to passed out in some bar back in town. There was nothing out here to fear.

The house was a small gray structure, once a modest farmhouse before the surrounding fields were absorbed by a sprawling corporate farm. When Xavier bought it, during a period of relative peace between the brothers, Keenan had helped with the finances and paid for a lot of the necessary repairs, including the new lock on the front door. In the process he acquired his own copy of the key. It still fit. Keenan opened the door and went inside, flicking on the light. There was no point stumbling around in the dark. Nobody was going to see the lights who wouldn't also see his car parked out front.

The small front room was cramped, with an oversized sofa facing a big TV mounted on the wall. Not as messy as Keenan had expected, though there were beer bottles clustered on the coffee table and the TV tray. Keenan got on his knees and looked under the furniture, then, grimacing, ran his hands under the cushions. He couldn't see anywhere else in this room the record could be hidden.

He went through to the back room, wrinkling his nose at the twin bed with mismatched, stained sheets. A battered bureau stood against the wall. On top of it was a big plastic bag with the logo of the Milwaukee record store.

He can't be making it this easy.

Keenan picked up the bag and looked inside. The White Album was there, snug inside one of the clear plastic clamshells used to protect especially valuable records. He knew he should grab it and go, but a decade of obsession was begging for a close inspection of the prize. He was starting to reach into the bag when he heard an engine outside.

He froze. Someone passing on the road? No. Tires were coming up the snowy drive. He ground his teeth in frustration. No choice now. Xavier had caught him, but he was damned if he was going to leave here tonight without this album. He'd just have to pay whatever exorbitant price his brother decided to demand. Keenan walked back out to the front room, the bag dangling from his hand. He waited for the engine outside to cut out, for his smug little brother to come through the door.

That didn't happen. The engine kept running. A car door opened, and then a deep voice he didn't know yelled. "Get your ass out here, Beech. Don't make us come in after you."

Keenan went to the window and peered around the edge. The car was pointed directly at the front of the house, its headlights so bright that he couldn't make out anything about it. Standing in front of the car was the silhouette of a large man, much larger than Xavier, standing with his hands hanging loosely by his side.

Only one thing made sense. The police. In a flash Keenan saw the whole thing, clear as day. Xavier hadn't just bought the record. He'd bought some kind of alarm or camera that would send an alert to his phone when someone came into the house. Then all he had to do was call the cops and tell them that his brother was breaking and entering. It was a trap, and one he should have anticipated since he could easily imagine doing the same thing to Xavier, if only he'd thought of it first.

There was no point lingering here. He couldn't get to his car, and trying to flee across miles of snow-covered fields would likely be suicide. Besides, they knew who he was. His stomach lurching, he stepped out onto the stoop, pulling the door shut behind him.

"Good boy." The big shadow stepped forward. Keenan saw to his shock that there was a gun dangling from his right hand. Surely they didn't think he was dangerous? Before he could process the thought the man had reached out and grabbed him by the front of his jacket, pulling him roughly down the stairs. Almost falling, Keenan registered that the man was wearing a heavy plaid coat, not the uniform he'd been expecting. The man put a massive hand on the back of Keenan's neck and marched him toward the car. He heard the driver's door open. They went past the burning headlights. It was a big, dark car, not a police cruiser. A woman had gotten out of the driver's seat, and as they approached she opened the trunk. The hand on his neck spun him around and pushed hard. The next thing Keenan knew he was in the trunk, looking up at the two of them. The man's face was rough and scarred. The woman seemed younger, but her expression was as flat and empty as a mannequin.

"You're not cops," Keenan said.

The man made a sound like a screwdriver scraping against concrete. It might have been a laugh. The woman's mouth twitched.

"Good guess," she said.

The man pointed the gun at Keenan and held out his hand. "Phone," he said.

Keenan stared, not processing.

The woman cocked her head. "Do you want me to tell you what happened to the last person Tony had to ask twice?"

Keenan pulled out his phone and handed it over. Tony shoved it into the pocket of his coat.

Then the trunk closed and Keenan was alone in the dark.

BY THE TIME he fought down his terror and tried to take stock of what was happening, the car was moving. He felt the jounce as it reached the bottom of Xavier's drive, heard the whine of the tires on wet asphalt as it turned onto the road. He thought about yelling, but the only people who might hear him were already perfectly aware of his plight.

How many movies had he seen where characters were shoved into trunks and pulled off a miraculous escape?

Probably not as many as movies where characters were shoved into trunks and, shortly afterward, gruesomely killed.

He tried to remember all the clever things those characters had done. He couldn't find a latch on the inside of the trunk or any way to push through into the back seat. He was supposed to keep track of the turns and speed to figure out where he was, but he gave that up as useless. The turns, when they came, slammed him back and forth in disorienting confusion, and all he could tell about their speed was that, bouncing around loose in an uncomfortable metal box, it seemed terrifyingly fast.

He had no idea how much time passed before the car slowed, turned, and stopped, the engine cutting out. The doors up front opened, and a moment later the trunk lid popped up. Tony and the woman were there but, blinded after his time in the dark, that was all Keenan could tell at first. Tony used both hands to pull him out, Keenan almost falling as he tried to get his balance.

They were parked in the middle slot of a three-car garage. There were shelves against one wall filled with tools and bags of gravel and other miscellaneous garage things, but the space was otherwise empty, and the overhead doors were closed. The woman walked toward a door to the side of the shelves. Tony took Keenan's elbow and shoved him along to follow.

They went through the door and down a flight of stairs into a furnished basement, passing through a room with a pool table and into another, smaller room set up as an office. The man behind the desk was working on a laptop. He looked up as they came in, grunted, and closed it, nodding to the chair across from him. Tony shoved Keenan down roughly into it. Instead of taking the other chairs, he and the woman stood against the wall to the side of the room, their arms crossed.

The man behind the desk was wearing a black T-shirt and

hadn't shaved in a couple of days. He was trim, with brown hair that hung down almost to his eyes. Keenan guessed he was around forty. He stared at Keenan and cracked the knuckles on both hands. The look on his face suggested he'd just been brought something at a restaurant and didn't care for the smell.

"Bring me a present, X?" he said.

Keenan opened his mouth, but nothing came out. He shook his head, baffled, and the man pointed at his side. Looking down, Keenan saw that he was still carrying the bag from the record store. He realized he'd clutched it to his chest the entire time he was in the trunk, trying to keep the record from being damaged.

"No," he said. "This is mine." That much he was sure of.

"I'm finding it a little odd that you haven't started begging yet," the man said.

"Begging?" Keenan said. The *X* caught up with him. "You think I'm Xavier."

"I *think* you're Xavier? Sure that's the game you want to play here, X?"

"My name is Keenan. Keenan Beech. I'm Xavier's twin brother."

"Twin brother," the man said flatly. He looked at Tony and the woman. "Lena, dear, did you bring me the wrong man, or is X here trying the ballsiest bluff I've ever seen?"

Lena's expression didn't change. "You gave me an address, said bring me Beech. I went to the address. Here's a Beech."

The man grunted. "X has a raven tattooed on the back of his right shoulder. Tony."

Tony stepped forward off the wall. He yanked Keenan out of the chair, stripped off his jacket, and spun him, pulling up his shirt to expose the blank skin of his back.

"All right," the man said. "Enough."

Tony stepped back to the wall. Keenan pulled his shirt down and sat. "I could have shown you myself." He hated the whine in his voice.

"So," the man said. "Xavier and Keenan Beech."

Don't say it, Keenan thought.

"The Beech boys."

Keenan groaned out loud. "We hated being called that," he said. He remembered hating it before he was even old enough to know what it was a reference to. He didn't want to be one of the Beech boys, forever part of a duo. It was one of the few things he and Xavier ever agreed on. Neither of them wanted to be associated with the other. Even today, Keenan's vinyl collection didn't include a single album by the Beach Boys.

"I'm not interested in what you hate," the man said. "I'm interested in your brother. Where is he?"

"At a party somewhere, I assume," Keenan said. "It's New Year's."

"When's the last time you saw him?"

"In person?" Keenan had to think. "Months ago. Maybe a year or more. We text sometimes if we have big news."

The man drummed his fingers. "You didn't see your own brother at Christmas last week?"

"We don't get along," Keenan said. He thought it was important that the man understand this. "We fought like demons from the time we were babies. Broke each other's toys. Stole each other's girlfriends. He once destroyed a car of mine with a sledgehammer." He licked his lips. "Of course, it's true that was after I set his on fire. We make up sometimes, but mostly—"

The man broke in. "So, what were you doing at his house tonight?"

Keenan swallowed. "That's kind of a long story."

"Is it?" The man looked at his watch. "I'll tell you what. It's 11:49. I'll give you the rest of the year to tell me."

Keenan told him. The man listened, closed his eyes and leaned back in his chair.

"Five thousand dollars," he said. "X spent five thousand dollars on a record."

"Ringo Starr's personal copy went for almost eight hundred grand at auction last year," Keenan said. "Number 0000001."

"That's endlessly fascinating," the man said. He opened his eyes and sat forward. "Do you know who I am?"

"No. I don't think I want to."

"I'm no more interested in what you want than I was in what you hate. My name is Drake. Your brother has worked for me, off and on, for a few years." Drake's hands were clutched into fists, the knuckles white. "Last week I gave him a hundred thousand dollars in cash to purchase certain goods for me. He didn't show up at the buy. Nobody's seen him since. And now I find out that he took part of that money and bought..." Drake closed his eyes, apparently unable to complete the thought. "I'm out a hundred grand because the Beech boys are fighting over a Beatles album."

Keenan's mouth was dry. "I'm sorry, Mr. Drake," he said. "Xavier has done some crazy things, but never this crazy. I'm sure he'll turn up. He probably intended to sell the record to me and return your money. Look, I'll let you know the next time I hear from him."

"I don't think so," Drake said. "X has screwed up before, but nothing like this. He's always stayed just on this side of irritating me too much. He's well over that line now. I don't think he'll be coming back. It would be suicidal. Do you think your brother is suicidal, Keenan?"

"No. But that's between you and him. Just let me walk out of here and I'll forget all about it."

"I don't think you're understanding me. Somebody owes me two hundred thousand dollars." Drake propped his chin on his fist and raised his eyebrows.

Keenan had to try a couple of times before he could talk. "Mr. Drake—"

"Just Drake."

"Drake. I'm sorry. I hope my brother pays you every dime he owes, but this has nothing to do with me."

Drake nodded thoughtfully. "K, I want you to do me a favor. Look at Lena. Look her right in the eye."

Keenan didn't want to, but he turned his head and looked. Lena looked back at him and there was nothing at all in her expression. Keenan could only hold her eyes for a few seconds before he had to look back at Drake.

"There's a room in this house that Lena uses when I let her talk to somebody on her own," Drake said. "Do you want to go to that room with her?"

Keenan's voice was a dry rustle of leaves, barely a whisper. "No. Please."

"Smart. I think we understand each other. If I say you owe me two hundred thousand dollars, then we're all agreed that I'm right about that."

"You said you gave him a hundred thousand." Keenan fought to keep a rising note of panic out of his voice. He knew he didn't succeed.

"I'm not just out what I gave him. I'm also out the profit I would have made selling the package he was supposed to bring me. Two hundred."

"I don't have that," Keenan said.

"What do you have?"

Keenan glanced down at the bag he was holding, and Drake made an impatient noise. "I don't want your damned record. It's not worth the time it would take me to figure out where to sell it. Come on, Beech. Start the new year right. Come up with something good."

Keenan hung his head. "There's a wall safe at my house," he said. "I keep thirty thousand in cash there. You can have that."

"Now we're talking," Drake said. "But I'm not sure I believe you. Why would you keep that kind of money around?"

Keenan threw up his hands and let them drop at his side. "Because of Xavier, of course. Twice he's gone into banks and convinced them he's me and walked out with big chunks of my money. Last time I called the cops and got him to return it, but I don't trust him. Do you blame me?"

"No," Drake said. "All right. Thirty. And what are we going to do about the other one seventy?"

Keenan felt close to tears. "I can't make money out of nothing."

"Sure you can. They do it on Wall Street every day. Lemme ask you, K. You own your house?"

"No," Keenan lied. "The bank does." Inspiration struck. "I can work for you."

Drake laughed. "You don't exactly look like you'd fit into my line of work."

"That's not what I mean," Keenan said. "Listen, I work for Coastal Trucking. You know them? You see the trucks all over the place."

"Sure."

"Okay. I'm a router. I sit at a computer all day, get the info on where we need to make pickups and deliveries, and give the drivers their plans. Get it?"

Drake was nodding slowly. "All right, K. This is getting close to interesting."

"The drivers do whatever their route sheets say. Drop off here, pick up there. They don't know what they're hauling. Half the time they don't even get out of the truck." Keenan held his hands in front of him, shaping the idea. "I don't have to know what they're hauling either. But if you need a package moved from A to B, I can do that. The trucks never get searched. Even if they get a speeding ticket or they're overweight at a weigh station, so what? Your package is safe. And no risk to you or anybody who works for you. No records I can't delete."

Drake held up his hand to stop Keenan. "I get it. Lemme think a minute." He drummed his fingers on the desk again and looked at Lena, raising an eyebrow.

"Would have kept that mess in Winnetka from happening," she said.

Nobody asked what Tony thought.

Drake looked back at Keenan. "Okay. We'll give it a try. We can do a test run in the next couple of weeks. If it works out and I keep using you, I'll knock two grand off the one seventy every month."

Keenan had always been good at math. "That's more than seven years."

"Look who knows numbers. And here's the other part of the deal. You screw up once, cause me a problem once, and I'm gonna start charging interest. High interest. We clear?"

Keenan bit his lip. "What if Xavier does turn up? What if you get the money back?"

"Neither one of us really thinks that's going to happen, do we?" Drake held out his hand. "Give me your wallet."

Keenan started to protest, glanced at Lena, and got his wallet out. Drake took it and spread Keenan's driver's license, social security, Coastal employee ID, and credit cards on the desk. He took pictures of each with his phone, swept everything into a loose pile and tossed it on the edge of the desk close to Keenan. "I know where to find you, K." Keenan was already hating being called that. "I'll be in touch. Soon. Lena, Tony, take Mr. Beech to his house and get my thirty thousand dollar down payment."

Keenan stood up uncertainly. "I can keep the album?"

Drake shook his head. "Yeah. You can keep your album. Now get the hell out of here."

LENA AND TONY let Keenan sit in the back seat this time. Drake's house turned out to be in the town's most affluent suburb, several miles from Keenan's place. He gave Lena directions, only half paying attention. His mind was racing, trying to figure out his next move.

There wasn't thirty thousand in his home safe. There was fifty, pretty much every dime he had that wasn't tied up in the vinyl collection. After Xavier's last impersonation, Keenan had decided to shut that trick down for good.

He had to get the thirty out in such a way that Tony and Lena wouldn't be able to see there was more. If they saw it, they would take it. He couldn't allow that, couldn't allow Xavier's ridiculous antics to leave him completely penniless. If they tried to take it— well, there was one other thing in the safe. A gun.

"This is it," he said as they turned the corner onto his block. "The blue house on the left."

Lena parked in the drive and all three of them got out. "You gonna take me out to my car after this?" Keenan asked as they walked toward the door.

"Call an Uber," Lena said. A few feet from the house she stopped dead, putting her hand on Keenan's chest to hold him in place. "You leave your door open?"

"What? Of course not." But the front door was six inches ajar, light from somewhere inside showing the gap. "What the hell?"

He tried to move forward, but Lena shifted her hand to his wrist and twisted it up painfully behind his back. "You stay with me," she said. "Tony."

The big man had already gotten out his gun again. Holding it in front of him, he walked up to the door and eased inside. Lena twitched Keenan's arm and he muffled a cry and followed.

Inside, the house was quiet and cold. "Where's the room with the safe?" Lena said.

"Upstairs. First door on the right. The audio room."

Tony started up, taking the stairs two at a time, the gun pointed upward. Lena and Keenan stayed a few steps behind. At the top of the stairs Tony swept the hallway with the gun before moving to the door on the right. He stepped inside and a second later the light flicked on. "Okay," he said.

Lena let Keenan go. He pushed past Tony, hovering just inside the door, and moaned wordlessly. Disaster, everywhere he looked. Most of the record bins were empty. The high-end sound system was gone. The vintage Beatles poster that had been in front of the wall safe was lying on the floor, the glass spiderwebbed with cracks.

The safe itself was hanging open. On the floor underneath was a huge, menacing drill, along with a massive hammer and other tools.

Keenan sank to his knees. He put a hand to the floor to keep from collapsing completely.

Lena walked to the safe. She pulled out a folded slip of paper, read it, and shook her head.

"Looks like we're going to be working together a lot longer than seven years, K," she said. Walking back toward the door, she dropped the note beside him. "I wouldn't expect much from the office Christmas parties."

Keenan didn't want to look. He picked up the note.

THANKS FOR TAKING THE BAIT, BIG BROTHER.

P.S. I KNOW YOU'LL PROBABLY BE DOWN ABOUT THIS. JUST KEEP LOOKING AT THE RECORD. IT'S GREAT ADVICE!

The record. He was still carrying the plastic bag. For the first time he pulled the clamshell out and wrenched it open. In the bright light, he saw what he hadn't in a hurried glance at Xavier's: the White Album cover was just a photocopy on a big sheet of paper. It was wrapped around something, something that did feel like a record. He knew it was foolish, but he felt a brief, illogical flicker of hope that the real thing was under there, that Xavier had chosen to leave him this tiny consolation prize. He ripped the paper aside.

Garish colors. A cartoonish storefront.

The Beach Boys.

Smile.

CLARK BOYD

Clark Boyd lives and works in the Netherlands. His fiction and essays have appeared in *High Shelf Press*, *Havok*, *Scare Street*, *Fatal Flaw Magazine*, and various DBND Publishing horror anthologies. He is currently at work on a book about windmills. Or cheese. Maybe both. Find him at www.twitter.com/clark_boyd.

THE BALLAD OF THE JERRELL TWINS

CLARK BOYD

THE SECOND AND final time the Jerrell twins met was at their father's funeral.

"How's it going, Darrell?"

"OK, how about with you, Terrell?"

The boys weren't actually twins. Their father, the late Dr. Harold Jerrell, insisted on calling them that. Court-mandated paternity tests had proven that both were, in fact, the offspring of "Kentuckiana's Premier Provider of Oral Care." But Darrell's mom was Teresa, Harold's wife at the time of conception, while Terrell's was Felicity, Harold's "executive assistant." The former entered the world on the Indiana side of the Ohio River in Madison, while the latter saw first light in Milton, Kentucky. The fact that the two managed to be born on the same night, within minutes of each other no less, convinced Harold they were twins. Or at least should be.

As the two women in Harold Jerrell's life pushed and screamed in different states, he couldn't manage to be with either of them. Instead, he kept driving his red '67 Mustang across the bridge to Kentucky, only to turn around and go back to Indiana. By the third trip, flop sweat had turned his button-down into a limp dishrag. And by the seventh, a full-blown panic attack had left an ominous brown trail down the backside of his khakis. Unable to choose, Harold ultimately hit the brakes in the middle of the bridge and began huffing from the bottle of nitrous oxide he kept in the back seat. He sat there in the light of a waxing gibbous, blocking traffic and giggling, until law enforcement from both sides of the river arrived and found his hands clasped in prayer.

Still, no guidance came.

"I can't decide," he told the Kentucky cops.

Then he turned to the troopers from Indiana. "And I can't decide either."

Harold pitched and yawed between laughter and tears as the officers argued over who was responsible for his incarceration. But after catching a whiff from inside the car, they all decided it was best to just tow him off the bridge and let him go with a warning.

Darrell and Terrell had each heard their father tell this story a hundred times while he was still among the living. In fact, they were thinking about it again as they opened beers and spooned lukewarm potato salad onto their plates after their father's funeral.

"Been a while," Darrell said.

"Twelve years and change. First time we met, right? The infamous barbecue."

Harold's Mustang logged a lot of miles over that bridge during the twins' formative years. Teresa had already divorced him by the time Darrell was born, and Felicity didn't want him living with her and Terrell. So, in a move that both his accountant and therapist deemed "monumentally stupid," Harold kept his office in Indiana, but moved into a small apartment across the river in Kentucky. He told himself this would ensure he'd be a part of both his sons' lives. But instead of dutifully attending basketball games in Kentucky, spelling bees in Indiana, and parent-teacher conferences on both sides of the river, Harold spent all his time driving back and forth, just missing this or that important event. The only quality time he spent with his sons was at their biannual dental check-ups. At least Darrell and Terrell had excellent teeth.

Neither mother gave Harold much quarter. Teresa hated him for cheating on her, Felicity despised him for missing his son's birth, and both women were adamant that they not be reminded of the other's existence. This ensured Darrell and Terrell grew up only vaguely aware of one another.

When the boys turned ten, though, Harold proposed a truce of sorts. A birthday barbecue that promised to finally bring his fractured family together. Reluctantly, all aggrieved parties agreed to give it a try. But repeated tornado warnings and a plethora of cheap vodka quickly turned the event from cookout into cage match. In the confines of Harold's bachelor pad, his ex-wife and former mistress took turns yelling at him and then each other. He dealt with this by retreating to the Mustang and hitting the nitrous while green storm clouds churned and churned until they finally gave way to clear skies and a waning crescent. Harold sat there contemplating the sharp ends until he passed out. Teresa and Felicity fell asleep on the sofa, and the boys swapped out Tom and Jerry cartoons for soft porn on deep cable.

"That was a long night," Terrell said.

"Tom never did catch Jerry, did he?"

They both chuckled, but in distracted ways. Each had adult troubles of his own now.

Darrell worked at two different fast-food restaurants, one in Madison and one in Milton. Those were fronts for what he thought of as his real job, which was running product on both sides of the river for a small-time dope dealer in Carrollton, Kentucky. Things had gotten dicey, though, after the guy found out Darrell was skimming profits and weed. He'd recently made a few trips across the bridge for late-night "business meetings," conducted with the dealer's loaded .38 Special casually placed on the table between them. The younger Jerrell twin needed about $10,000. Fast.

Terrell needed about the same amount. He'd spent five years as a straight-C student and middling fraternity brother at the University of Kentucky. Then, after graduation, he miraculously got a job at the construction company owned by Felicity's brother. His uncle, an unpleasant and thick-headed man with priors, put him in charge of finding and paying the day laborers the company used. In cash. This made it easy for Terrell to take a bit here and there, especially after he discovered how much he loved gambling with money that was not, strictly speaking, his. As the debts mounted, and the workers started to moan, he knew it wouldn't be long until even his dimwitted uncle put two and two together.

So, understandably, the boys were distracted as they sipped their cheap beers. Darrell lit a Swisher Sweet, while Terrell nudged an off-colored deviled egg with his finger.

"You get the message about Dad's 'estate?'" Terrell asked.

"Six thirty this evening at the offices of Melvin J. Shimfissel, Esquire."

"Any idea what Harold left us?"

"All his nitrous?"

Darrell smiled and blew a smoke ring. Terrell glanced around nervously, trying to avoid the stomach-churning fumes. He clocked in on his uncle, who had Felicity pinned in a corner. The two were talking low and looking in his direction.

"If you want, we can go together in my car," Darrell said.

Terrell hesitated, but only briefly. "Sounds good. Thanks."

"Anything for my twin."

An hour later, they were in a beat-up green Datsun headed to the meeting with the lawyer. Darrell had sparked up another Swisher, and Terrell was trying to find the button to lower what he assumed were power windows.

"It's manual," Darrell said, pointing to the hand crank. "But it's broken."

As they came off the bridge, both boys glanced at the "Welcome to Indiana" sign, which was, as always, riddled with small holes made by two or three shotgun blasts.

"Looks just like the Kentucky one, doesn't it?" Darrell mused.

"Indiana is just Kentucky's middle finger. That's what Dad always said."

Darrell nodded. "Music?"

"Sure."

Darrell punched a button and the CD player sprang to life. Creedence Clearwater Revival's *Bad Moon Rising* shot out of the speakers at high volume. "You like this?" he yelled.

"Got anything...newer?"

"Not really. Besides, the disc's stuck in there, and I can't get it out without breaking the whole thing. I haven't got money for a new stereo right now."

"Tell me about it." Terrell shivered.

"Heater's busted too, sorry."

They rode in silence while Darrell puffed away.

"Terrell, seriously. What do you think he left us?"

"No idea. Mom—Felicity, I mean—she always suspected Dad was one set of braces away from bankruptcy."

Eventually, the frigid Datsun shuddered to a stop in front of the lawyer's office. They were ten minutes early. The twins wrapped their jackets tighter and watched big flakes of snow drifting down in the glare of the headlights. Each was secretly hoping their father's will included details of a secret trust fund or a map to buried treasure.

"Time to face the music," Terrell said.

Darrell stubbed out his cigar. "Always sounds the same to me."

When the Jerrells entered the lawyer's office, the waiting room was empty except for a young receptionist talking on the phone. At her feet was the smallest, ugliest dog either of them had ever seen. When Terrell bent to pat it, the animal bared its teeth and yapped.

"I'll call you back," the receptionist said. She hung up. "Dog don't like men."

"Well, it's in luck because we don't qualify," Terrell said.

Darrell snickered but the receptionist did not. She looked them over.

"Mel called you twins, but you don't look like it. Except for the chins, maybe."

"It's complicated," Terrell said.

"We're more like...what do you call them...fraternals?"

"Kind of," Terrell said. "Half-brothers, but born on the same day."

The dog growled softly. The receptionist scratched her head and picked up the phone.

"Mel...Mr. Shimfissel, sorry...the Jerrells are here."

She listened, nodded, and then hung up. "Go on in. Second door on the left."

Shimfissel shook hands with both boys and then sat them down in two big leather chairs. He took a seat behind his big oak desk and shot them a sad smile.

"Your father didn't leave you much."

He reached into his desk and pulled out a single piece of paper and a keychain.

"The title to his Mustang and the keys."

Darrell put his fingers to his temples. Terrell sank in his chair, and a loud farting noise filled the room.

"Boys, let me be honest with you. Your father had nothing else. No cash or stocks. His life insurance barely covered the funeral and burial costs. I guess he did his best."

Harold's sons grimaced.

Shimfissel let the disappointment sink in for a few moments. Then he heard his receptionist on the phone and remembered their weekly "rendezvous" started at 7 p.m. sharp.

"Any other questions for me? No? Okay, here you go."

Darrell took the keys and Terrell grabbed the title.

"The car's parked at your Dad's office."

The Jerrells headed for the door, heads hung low.

"Cheer up," Shimfissel said. "At least this finally brought you two together."

Back in the Datsun, the boys tried to regroup.

Darrell reached into the back seat and tossed aside a tarp, revealing a bottle of nitrous. "You want some? In honor of the old man?"

Terrell shook his head.

Darrell opened the tap, put the mask to his face, and took a long hit. And then another. He started giggling. "Want to go stop in the middle of that bridge?"

"Give me that," Terrell said.

Ten minutes later, as the pair gasped for air between convulsions of laughter, Mel Shimfissel's receptionist came out of the office, dog in tow. The second the beast got onto the sidewalk, it squatted and dropped two tiny turds. She kicked the dog to get it moving, then left the mess behind.

"Dog don't like men," Darrell said.

"And men don't like dog," Terrell shot back.

The car shook with laughter, and then both took another hit.

"How much of this do you think Dad has stashed at his office?" asked Terrell.

"Let's go find out, *brother*. I haven't seen that car in years."

Darrell started the Datsun and they rattled away toward their inheritance.

AS THE NITROUS WORE OFF, the two came clean with each other. Darrell told his brother about his slide into dope dealing, and Terrell admitted he had a gambling problem. They totaled their debts and things faded into a sobering silence that lasted for a few miles.

"There's no way the Mustang's worth that kind of money," Terrell said.

"It's a classic, sure, but I don't think Dad took very good care of it."

Their suspicions were confirmed as they pulled into the parking lot. Harold, forever trying to save money, insisted that the lights in the lot be turned off after working hours. But the skies had cleared, and a full moon lit up the almost empty space. The Mustang sat in a far corner. The boys could see that rust was eating away at most of the body, a problem Harold had tried to fix with brown putty and, in a few places, duct tape.

Darrell got out of the Datsun and opened the driver's side door of the Mustang. He slid into the seat, and then reached over and popped the lock on the passenger side so that Terrell could get in. He put the key in the ignition and turned it. Nothing. On the second try, though, the big V8 sputtered and roared to life.

Terrell plunked down on the passenger side. He opened the glovebox, looking to stow the title. A manila envelope fell onto his lap. He could just make out the words "For my twins" written on the front of it.

"Hit the light, Darrell."

Darrell turned on the dome light, which was yellowed by years of cigarette smoke.

Terrell undid the clasp and reached in. He brought out a stack of loose papers, on top of which was a tape.

"What's that?" asked Darrell.

Terrell took the tape and popped it into the Mustang's cassette deck, the only upgrade their father had ever made to the vehicle. He pressed play.

Their father's cancer-sick voice filled the car.

"Boys, it's your Dad, talking to you from the ether. Haha. Oh, that hurts. Jesus, I loved this car. And I loved both of you. Although it's probably fair to say I never treated any of you with the care and respect you deserved. I hope a little of what I gave to your mothers managed to trickle down to you over the years. Your teeth, anyway, are perfect. That much I know."

Darrell shivered. He was so fixated on the tape he'd forgotten to close the car door.

"One of you is probably holding two insurance policies. The first is for the car, which isn't worth much as you can see. The other covers the dental practice. All the equipment, materials, records. I didn't tell Mel this, but after I was diagnosed, I changed the policy so that you two are the co-beneficiaries. That means if anything should happen to the building or the equipment inside, God forbid, you two would share the payout."

"Yeah, God forbid," Terrell said.

On the tape, their father took a ragged breath and sighed.

"Boys, I hear through the laughing gas grapevine that you've gotten yourselves into some trouble, financially and legally. You'd be surprised what people will tell you when they're high as kites. That uncle of yours, Terrell, loves to talk. As does a certain "entrepreneur" from Carrollton that you've been working with, Darrell. See, the job's not all porcelain crowns and gum grafts. You know, I've never been one to give either of you advice, but since I'm dead now, why not?"

The twins leaned forward.

"Everyone made fun of me because of that nitrous incident on the bridge. But to be honest, I preferred ether. Yeah, it's a bit old fashioned, but you don't have to deal with the incessant laughter. I had a good stash of that stuff at the office. In fact, the last thing I did before I got too sick was move it all to the reception area. You know, so that after I died they could cart it away easily. But the stuff's very unstable. Hazardous, even."

The Jerrell twins' brains were working as hard as they ever had.

"You know, I spent hours sitting here in this parking lot after work, staring at my poorly lit business and wishing I had the guts to burn it down. My entire life felt like I was stuck in the middle of that bridge, waiting for a sign. Hoping someone or something would give me a hint about what to do and how to do it. But it's too late for me now. I don't get another shot, so I'm giving it to you. Listen to me carefully. As I said, ether's extremely flammable. Also, those security cameras around the building? They're all fakes. I couldn't afford real ones. Just be sure to do it before they come and empty the place out. I love you both, okay? Goodbye."

Darrell ejected the tape.

The boys looked at each other and grinned.

THEY SAT in the Mustang for an hour, discussing the hows but not the whys.

In the end, it was Darrell's "two birds, one stone" idea that won out.

Neither of them wanted the decrepit Mustang, and both needed cash. So why not send the car through the front of their father's office and let the crash ignite the ether? They argued for a little while over who would pilot the Mustang on its final run and who would man the getaway car. But, in the end, that decision was easy. The Datsun was a stick, and Terrell had never learned. So, the older twin would take the Mustang, bailing out once he was sure it was headed in the right direction at an appropriately destructive speed. Darrell would drive the Datsun and pick up his half-brother as soon as everything went boom.

The Jerrell twins, who barely knew each other anyway, would escape and go their separate ways again. After someone in a suit handed them a big check, of course.

"Dad gets one last shot at redemption," Darrell said.

"Postmortem," Terrell added. "The poor guy."

The plan, though lacking in detail, had a certain elegance. Or at least they thought so.

Darrell got out of the Mustang, taking all the paperwork and the tape with him. Terrell slid behind the wheel, slamming the door shut and then driving the car out onto the access road. Their father had chosen an office location ten miles outside of town, just off a barely paved two-lane road. When Harold signed the papers in the mid '80s, there was talk of building subdivisions and shopping malls in the area. But those plans, like so many in the life of Harold Jerrell, never quite materialized.

"Guidance," Terrell whispered. In the moonlight, he lined up the center of the car with the door handle of his father's office. How injured would he get when he bailed out and hit the asphalt? The question gave him a moment's pause. But then he thought about what his uncle would do to him if he didn't come up with the money he'd stolen. A few scrapes, even a broken leg, were nothing compared to that.

He looked down and saw he'd fastened his lap belt after he shut the car door. "Idiot," he muttered, unsnapping it. He put the Mustang in neutral and revved the engine twice.

Darrell started the Datsun and turned on the headlights, which trickled out across the parking lot in a half-hearted attempt to help Terrell see where he was going. Darrell glanced at the cassette and the insurance policies next to him on the passenger's seat. He was normally not one to pray, but his mind flashed back to that dope dealer's .38, and he decided it couldn't hurt.

Terrell put the Mustang in drive and floored it. The tires squealed and then bit. The car leapt forward, and the speedometer began to rise. He was about twenty yards out and headed directly for the banner that read "Harold's Happy Smiles" when he reached for the door handle and yanked.

Nothing. It was stuck.

In his panic, Terrell forgot to hit the brakes or turn the wheel. Instead, he yanked harder on the door handle and, in so doing, pushed down on the accelerator.

Darrel was lighting a Swisher Sweet with shaky hands when Terrell failed to exit the Mustang. He watched as both went flying through the office windows.

"What the...?" he screamed.

On instinct, Darrell sank sideways into the Datsun's passenger's seat, ready for the explosion to tear him and the car apart. But it never came. He raised up and saw a trail of glass and chrome in front of the building. A wisp of smoke came from the gaping hole.

"Seriously?" Darrell screamed again.

Cigar still in hand, Darrell jumped out of the Datsun and ran through the broken windows. He couldn't believe what he saw. The Mustang had managed to miss every bottle of ether before plowing through the reception desk and smashing into the back wall. Terrell was slumped over the wheel, his face a mangled mess. Darrell tossed the cigar over his shoulder and tried to open the driver's side door, which was stuck tight. He ran around the car and pulled Terrell out through the passenger-side window.

He laid Terrell's body on the ground. Darrell wiped the back of his hand across his mouth and prepared to give his twin mouth-to-mouth. As he bent over, Terrell sputtered and looked up. "What are you doing?"

"Saving your life," Darrell said.

"Hard pass."

They both laughed. Terrell winced in pain.

"We need to get you to the hospital. I'll see if the office phone still works."

As Darrell stood, Terrell grabbed his arm.

"Dad would've loved to see you kissing me like that, huh?"

"Our Moms not so much, though."

"Always 50-50 with this family."

At that moment, a gust of wind blew through the shattered windows. It caused Darrell's smoldering cigar, which had landed close to the ether bottles, to glow red for an instant. The tiniest bit of hot ash came loose. It tumbled across the floor, until it reached a thin trail of ether leaking from a bottle that Harold had carelessly stacked on its side. The resulting explosion, they say, could be seen forty miles away.

"It was like it was day for a second," said one eyewitness in Eminence, Kentucky.

Only the Datsun survived the blast. In fact, it was still running when the fire department arrived. Mel Shimfissel's younger brother, Sheldon, a detective with the Madison police department, found the cassette and insurance policies on the passenger seat. As he started putting the story together, he made quite a discovery. It turned out the boys had stopped the tape prematurely. After Harold's initial sign-off, he popped back up a few seconds later with an ethery P.S. "Boys, I almost forgot. Don't use the car for this. The driver's side door's been sticking. Probably needs some WD-40. Anyway, boom! Haha. Love you."

"He might've led with that," Sheldon confided to his brother over drinks. "The thing about the door, I mean."

Because of the intensity of the explosion and the fire, positive identification of the boys' bodies proved tricky. Forensics found some teeth in the rubble, but those weren't much help. After all, the twins' dental records were vaporized in the blast. In the end, as they all stood beside two lumpy, misshapen sheets in the county morgue, Detective Shimfissel could only shrug when Teresa and Felicity demanded to know which was which.

United by grief and economic circumstance, the two women managed to swallow some of their hatred of one another. They buried their sons in a shared grave next to their no-account father. Both agreed Harold was still a colossal screw-up, even more so in death than in life. And because money was tight, the mothers decided to mark their sons' final resting place with a single headstone that read: "The Jerrell Twins, 1970-1997."

"At least in death," read their obituary, "no one could tell them apart."

BETHANY MAINES

Bethany Maines the award-winning author of action adventure and fantasy tales that focus on women who know when to apply lipstick and when to apply a foot to someone's hind-end. When she's not traveling to exotic lands, or kicking some serious butt with her black belt in karate, she can be found chasing after her daughter, or glued to the computer working on her next novel. Bethany is a member of the Pacific Northwest Writer's Association and The Stiletto Gang. Find her at www.BethanyMaines.com.

TAMMY LOVES DEREK

BETHANY MAINES

Step One

TAMMY LEE SWANLEY climbed out of the dumpster and walked the three blocks through the salty slush of chemicals, dirt, and snow until she got to the corner across the street from the strip mall that housed Lombard's Jewelry. The early dusk of a winter evening settled into place like a blanket softening the sharp edges of trash and commercialism. Tammy's breath came out in hasty white puffs, triggered by the rapid beating of her heart. She was more nervous than she thought she would be. Tammy took deep inhalations through her nose, trying to slow everything down.

Over the strip mall, the moon hung like a fat yellow wheel of cheese. The owner of the house on the corner didn't come home until after eight on Tuesday's. She'd driven by for six weeks in a row, so she felt confident that no one would be home to notice as she climbed the porch stairs and sat down in the green plastic Adirondack chair. She settled her bag at her feet, watched the moon climb higher in the sky, and waited.

Across the street, Derek Lombard came out of the jewelry store swinging his keys around on his finger and adjusting his crotch with the other hand, while he waited for Jo-Jo to finish locking up. Jo-Jo jiggled the door handle and then walked over to her new Mercedes where Derek was waiting for her. Jo-Jo—or Jo-Ho, as Tammy preferred to call her—giggled at something Derek said and flicked some snow off the hood and onto his jacket. He laughed. Last week Tammy had dripped some water on that same jacket and he'd stomped off to dab it carefully with a sponge, while yelling at her from the bathroom about how she was stupid, clumsy, and careless.

The thing about Derek was that he could fake being a nice person just long enough for someone to get attached to him. He was like fungus. You thought your foot just itched, and then months later you realized the burning desire to tear a toe off was athlete's foot. In essence, Derek was the jock-itch of boyfriends.

Unfortunately, he was also rich. Or at least his daddy was. Tammy wasn't rich, but she wanted to be and at twenty-seven Tammy knew her expiration date was fast approaching. Yeah, she had managed to buy a few extra years by keeping the weight off and not having any kids—big ups to Planned Parenthood—and working at a med-spa kept her skin looking baby fresh. She routinely got carded at clubs, but she knew it was just a matter of time before she went from being young to *still* young. And sadly, the mythical doctor she had been hoping to meet had not materialized. Instead, she'd gotten a Derek. Derek who, at thirty-six, only dated girls who were younger than thirty and who had dumped his previous girlfriend for Tammy because, as she'd heard him say on more than one occasion, Tammy's tits were bigger.

Derek was not a winner. He was the son of a winner. But at the moment he was the closest she was getting to winning. The problem was that rich jerks like Derek knew that a poor girl like Tammy would put up with a lot to get the bank account and the last name. Which meant that there were an endless string of side-chicks and as long as Tammy's tits were bigger, that was going to be the status quo.

Once upon a time, Tammy had believed she wouldn't put up with cheating and disrespect—that she'd demand a guy treat her like a queen. Then she'd grown up and realized that men just saw her as a snack. There is a world of difference between a ruler and something you consume between commercials. So much for fairy tales.

But then, that was why she'd developed her five-step plan to wealth.

Tammy picked up her phone and texted Derek.

I'M GOING TO HIT THE GYM ON MY WAY HOME AND THEN I MIGHT HAVE TO GO OUT FOR DRINKS. SINCLAIR'S BOYFRIEND JUST FOUND OUT THE BABY ISN'T HIS!

Across the parking lot, Derek checked his phone and then tucked it quickly away, still chatting to Jo-Ho. The existence of Jo-Ho was enough to make Tammy blow a gasket for several reasons, not least of which was that Jo-Ho was forty-four. Derek leaned in and kissed her, his hand sliding down into the back of her pants. Jo-Ho swatted at him, but didn't pull back. A minute of ick-inducing tonsil hockey later the two got in her car and drove away. Tammy waited. There was no reason to rush this. Better safe than sorry. Once she was sure they were really not coming back she would move. After that she would have plenty of time. Jo-Ho had a steady supply of Viagra, so Derek probably wouldn't be home for a while. A minute later, she got a response from Derek.

SOUNDS GREAT BABE. GET ALL THE DIRT FOR ME! TEXT ME WHEN YOU'RE HEADING HOME.

Even if she hadn't just watched him leave with another woman that text would have been a sure tip-off. Tammy rolled her eyes, pulled on a pair of latex gloves, hefted her gym bag, and jogged across the street to the jewelry store. She didn't stop to look around. Nothing looked more suspicious than scanning for someone watching. She ran around to the rear of the building, punched in Derek's security code, used the copy of his key she'd made last month, and opened the back door.

STEP TWO

Tammy, still wearing gloves, turned off the security system and carefully deleted her arrival from the camera's storage in the computer. The off-site system would still record that Derek's code had been used, but that was fine. Then she plopped an enormous magnet on top of the security camera computer. That would take care of everything she might have missed.

She made her way through the jewelry store, collecting loose stones, and a few of the un-used settings that looked exactly like fifty-thousand others. Nothing recognizable, nothing traceable. She steered clear of the diamonds; those were all marked. Thanks, Leonardo DiCaprio, for making sure everyone knows about blood diamonds. Now jewel thieves have to work extra hard. Douche.

Once Tammy had safely stowed her haul, she went back through the cases, and pulled out all the traceable items that looked really expensive, along with a few diamonds. Those went in a separate velvet pouch and also got tucked safely in the gym bag.

Then, using the baseball bat that Derek's father, Earl, kept under the cash register, Tammy went to town, smashing everything she could. It didn't really need to be done with that much enthusiasm, but it felt good.

Tammy collected her magnet and her gym bag and left the way she had come in, making sure to leave the door swinging open. The goal was to make it *almost* look like a break-in after all. The moon was now high in the sky and had turned a pale ecru, like Gouda instead of cheddar. Tammy went back across the street and down the block, then climbed onto the ledge of the dumpster and in through the window of the women's locker room at 24-Hour Fitness.

Step Three

Tammy finished her workout and then went out to her car. She drove cautiously in the slushy snow, stopping at the condo she shared with Derek. He liked to act like he was keeping her lavish by bragging that she didn't pay a cent in rent, but he never added the fact that he didn't pay either—his dad owned the condo. Once inside, she stashed the magnet back in Derek's tool chest, along with the second bag of jewelry. She put the jewelry on top of his receipts from the pawnshops. She wasn't sure why he kept those, but if he wanted to be stupid, she was going to take advantage of it. Then she went inside and changed.

On the way out, she took his bag of cash out from behind the pipe under the sink in the downstairs bathroom and moved it to just behind the Lysol Bathroom Cleaner. She didn't want anyone to work that hard to find it. She took one final look around the apartment to make sure there wasn't anything embarrassing to be found. She had already relocated all the sex toys to her storage unit for the weekend. And although she had wanted to hide Derek's collection of boob-shaped shot glasses, she left them where they were. Then she applied a final coat of lip-gloss and went out to meet Sinclair.

At dinner, Tammy got carefully drunk and Ubered home, leaving her car in the bar's parking lot.

STEP FOUR

Derek picked her up after work in his jacked F150. The truck was nice, but climbing up into it was a workout and forget about wearing a skirt. "I can't believe you haven't picked up your car yet," he said, annoyed.

"I didn't have time between work and now."

"Maybe if you hadn't come home wasted last night this wouldn't be a problem. I don't know what you were thinking."

Tammy ignored the barb. "We can stop by and grab the car after we've had dinner with your Dad."

"Yeah, if they haven't eaten already. You are so slow. We were supposed to be there ten minutes ago. You know how much Dad hates to be kept waiting."

"Earl's been out of town all week. I'm sure he won't mind a few extra minutes alone with Jo-Jo. Maybe he'll get some nookie."

"Thanks for the visual but I don't really need to think about my Dad having sex."

"I'm just saying Jo-Jo is hot. If I were him, I'd be hitting that all the time."

"Actually, I don't think they've been getting along that well."

"Really? Did she say something when you two were at work?"

"It's just the feeling I get," Derek said, twitching in his seat. "Just drop it, okay?"

"Consider it dropped," Tammy said, with a shrug, and played with the radio until they parked in front of Earl's house.

"Is that a cop car?" Derek asked, squinting through the windshield.

"It is! Oh no! I hope your Dad's okay!"

Derek was charging up the front walk when Jo-Jo came running out of the house a tissue clutched in her hand. She flung herself into Derek's arms, sobbing.

"Jo-Jo, what is it? Did you tell him?"

"Tell him what?" Tammy asked, adding extra breathlessness to her voice.

"Derek Lombard?"

Everyone turned to see an imposing man in a dark suit, following Jo-Jo out of the house. He looked like he'd been watching too much *NCIS*. Although, Tammy had to admit, he was hot in a Gibbs kind of way, so maybe it was working for him.

"Yes?" Derek looked from the man to Jo-Jo and back.

"Detective Joel Bock. You're under arrest for the theft of assorted stones and jewelry."

"No, that wasn't... We didn't... We were going to put it back. It was just for fun." Derek's voice had gone up about an octave. Tammy out her hand over her mouth to hide her smile and hoped it read as shock.

"You took jewelry from your father's store and sold it to a pawn shop for fun?" Detective Bock asked, his eyebrows telegraphing disbelief that this was the story Derek was going with. Jo-Jo sobbed harder and Derek's lips open and closed like a largemouth bass.

"Dad!" Derek called out to his father who was standing on the porch talking to another police officer. "Dad. Please. Don't let them do this."

But Derek's yelling and Jo-Jo's tears didn't do any good. They still ended up in the back of separate police cars and Tammy, managing to squeeze out a few tears herself, ended up on the porch next to Earl as they pulled away.

STEP FIVE

"I can't believe they really thought I wasn't going to notice them stealing from me," Earl said, as the cop cars turned the corner.

"And I can't believe Derek really thought I wasn't going to notice him cheating on me with his stepmother." Tammy shook her head.

Earl shrugged as if to say cheating was a fact of life. "Meanwhile, I called the insurance company after I called the cops. They'll be sending someone out on Monday to survey the damage. I'll give you the cash when they cut me the check."

"Sounds good."

"Sorry if the cops messed up your place searching it for the 'stolen goods.' You did put the stones in a safe place, right?"

Tammy figured the trunk of her car in the parking lot of the Last Stop Bar and Grill was as safe as anywhere else. "Yes."

"I'll sell those the next time I'm overseas." Earl paused.

"You know, I realize my son's little misadventure is not exactly good news for either of us, but I have to say, it's been real nice doing business with you. Not sure why my son turned out to be such an idiot. Can you believe he started crying there at the end? It's almost enough to make you feel sorry for him."

"Well," Tammy said, "I'd feel a lot sorrier for him if the Alexa hadn't told me he bought Jo-Jo $300 worth of lingerie for Christmas."

Earl clucked his tongue. "What did he get you again?"

"A cookbook," Tammy said, "and a mug that says TAMMY LOVES DEREK."

JEANNE DUBOIS

Jeanne DuBois lives in Florida with two retired greyhounds. Her short stories have appeared in the anthologies *A Murder of Crows*, and *Peace, Love, and Crime: Crime Fiction Inspired by the Songs of the '60s*, as well as online at *Mysterical-E*. Jeanne is a member of the Short Mystery Fiction Society and Sisters in Crime. Find her at jeanne-dubois.com.

MOONSET

JEANNE DUBOIS

THREE TRAIN ROUTES ran from Camden to Atlantic City in July, 1921. Loretta Bremer's late husband helped engineer and maintain the only electric one. Riding it usually reminded her of happier days. Not today. It was hot, the trolley was packed, and the nearest passengers were driving her mad. Her newspaper offered no diversion. Suicide, murder, insurance fraud, police theft. Even the sewing instructions for a "Stylish Apron" seemed a cruel joke. The pictured apron was a nightmare of overlapping flounces.

"Look, Mama, a big hawk!" Eight-year-old Ruthie Bremer stood, pressing her forehead against the glass.

Five-year-old Jack leaned across the aisle and tugged on Loretta's arm. "But you said *I* could have the window after Richland."

"It's not *after* yet," Ruthie said.

"I'll let you use my binoculars." Jack retrieved a battered leather case from his backpack, an Army-issued item altered to fit his smaller size.

"I don't think so." A white bow danced in Ruthie's dark curls. "There's nothing for me to see from the aisle."

Temporarily diverted by the compass on top of the binocular

case, Jack postponed his response until Loretta was immersed in a story about diamonds, worth $100,000, stolen on a train outside Trenton.

"Mama!"

Loretta jumped at Jack's scream, folding the newspaper in a flurry of frustration. "All right. Ruthie, will you—"

"Allow me," a female voice put in. The young woman sitting by the window exchanged seats with Jack, helping him with his backpack and its scattered contents. Loretta remembered her from the station in Glassboro. A dark, round-faced girl, wearing a baggy dress and forgettable hat. She waved aside Loretta's thanks. "I have neephews."

Loretta smiled. She liked the clever combination of "nieces" and "nephews." The tautness in her shoulders lessened as the children quieted, fascinated, for now, by the passing scenery. The young woman offered Loretta a *Good Housekeeping* magazine in exchange for her newspaper. Loretta accepted readily, diving into July's Table of Contents like an Olympic swimmer. She only came up for air when Jack climbed over his seatmate and across the aisle into her lap. He fell asleep, drooling over her dress until the steep incline into the trolley terminal jarred him awake.

A sea of departing passengers swept the young woman down the aisle before Loretta could return her glossy magazine. Loretta slipped it between the folds of her discarded newspaper to protect it, shoved them both into Jack's backpack, and joined the throng heading toward the street. She spied the young woman by an inner wall with a uniformed policeman, but there was no way to cross the crowded terminal to reach her, and no standing still outside.

Loretta entrusted her two labeled suitcases to the driver of an already full seven-seater with a placard in the front window: *Chalfonte-Haddon Hall Only.* Jack refused to give up his backpack, so Loretta steered the children toward the ocean wearing the binocular case to lighten his load.

THE MIX-UP at the hotel was nothing after the noisy confusion of the Boardwalk. Thousands of people moved in mainly two directions there, shouting all the while, up and down and woe to those who chose to go across. Tourists traveled not only on foot, but in wicker rolling chairs, at speeds guaranteed to knock aside distracted children. Or trip them. Ice cream cones eaten at a railing overlooking the beach eased the pain of Jack's skinned knees and Ruthie's bruised elbow.

After a quick descent to the white sand beach to fill packets of newspaper with shells and other treasures, the children allowed themselves to be led back to the boards. A death-defying stroll past the imposing brick Chalfonte and through Haddon Hall's new Boardwalk addition followed. Now the desk clerk was insisting that Loretta had already checked into her room.

"How is that possible?" Loretta asked, exasperated. "I've only just arrived. I'm here to take dictation and type at the convention," she added, hoping to clarify the matter. "Mr. Kern's group?"

The desk clerk wore slicked-back hair and a lofty air. He showed her the register where someone had written *Mr and Mrs Bremer* in a bold hand. "I gave your husband the key."

"But I'm...I'm a widow," she protested, realizing even as she spoke that something about the signature looked familiar.

The clerk sniffed. "He said he was your husband. It's a double room. I assumed..." His gaze traveled downward, to the two wide-eyed children flanking her. "Oh, dear."

"Did he have red hair?" Loretta was thinking of Roger MacNair, a middle-aged junior partner with a college boy's sense of humor.

"I couldn't say, madam, he was wearing a hat. Shall I call Mr. Tomlinson, the house detective, to accompany you?" He sounded less sure of himself now.

"No, thank you. I can handle Roger MacNair. May I have a copy of my room key, please? In case locking me out is part of his latest prank?"

"Of course." The clerk hurried to retrieve it. "Second floor. Your bags were placed in your room when they arrived." He slid a tagged key across the counter and lowered his voice. "Will you telephone the front desk and let us know the matter has been settled?"

Loretta nodded and herded Ruthie and Jack toward the stairs. Thick carpets and high ceilings dampened the sound of their footsteps. They went up one flight, down a long hall, and around a corner where even from thirty yards away it was apparent their door was ajar. After giving strict instructions to the children, Loretta continued on by herself.

She checked the number posted on the door with the one written on the key's tag. They matched. She pushed on the door. It would only open so far. Loretta peered around its edge. Roger MacNair lay on the carpet behind it. His head rested in a puddle of dark blood. Beside him, a coiled wooden snake lifted its painted rattle.

SGT. HARDY QUESTIONED Loretta in Mr. Tomlinson's office on the ground floor of the hotel. Hardy was the survivor of something nasty. Maroon scars ranged across his hands and on his neck above his uniform's banded collar. Loretta felt sad and sorry for him, rather than afraid, which she should have been. He'd sequestered her children, been through her purse, and was now glaring at her over a blood-stained hanky lying crumpled on the table between them.

"I used it to clean off Jack's knees on the Boardwalk," Loretta said. "It's a good thing automobiles aren't allowed on there. You'd need another hospital to treat all the wounded."

The policeman's hawk-like eyes left hers for a moment. Then they flashed back, homing in on his prey. "Why was MacNair in your room? Had you two planned a liaison before your babysitter backed out? Who else knew about your tryst?"

Loretta took an audible breath before answering. "I wouldn't leave my children with anyone for four days. Besides, Mr. MacNair and I barely spoke. I found his pranks juvenile and annoying. You saw the wooden snake. Was that what killed him?" At the sergeant's incredulous look, Loretta amended the question. "Was he hit on the head with it?"

"He hit his head on the edge of the bathtub. What he was doing in there, I couldn't say. There wasn't any water in the tub, and the toilet is in a separate room." Sgt. Hardy's tone insinuated she would know why.

Loretta swallowed her irritation. "Probably hiding the snake. He was always doing stuff like that."

"That why you pushed him?"

She blinked. "I didn't."

Mr. Tomlinson entered the room without knocking and closed the door. His movements were swift, his voice soft. "The desk clerk says the victim isn't the man who signed the register."

Sgt. Hardy turned his attention back to Loretta. "So, who did?"

Her eyes widened. "How should I know?"

The pair stared at her. The burly policeman, brass buttons gleaming. The thin house detective, gray pinstripe, stiff club collar, muted tie.

"I wasn't here," Loretta reminded them.

Mr. Tomlinson leaned against the jamb and crossed his arms. "About your suitcases. It looks like somebody went through them. Could this be a robbery gone wrong?"

"A messy suitcase is what you get when children help with the packing," Loretta said wearily. "I have nothing worth stealing, believe me."

"She's only got coins in her purse, I'll give her that," Sgt. Hardy said.

Loretta's meager supply of banknotes was pinned inside her chemise, thanks to her landlady's warning, delivered in her strong English accent, "Cutpurses on every corner."

"What about the ruby?" Mr. Tomlinson nodded toward the ring on Loretta's left hand.

Loretta glanced down in surprise. "My wedding ring?"

"Bring any matching pieces?"

She shook her head.

Sgt. Hardy leaned forward. "Maybe it'll match one on our reported stolen list."

"Good luck getting it off," Loretta said. "It's been on that finger for thirteen years."

The policeman flicked the hanky across the table with a disgusted look. "Go on. Your kids'll be wanting their supper."

Mr. Tomlinson stepped aside to open the door. "The desk clerk will assign you a new room and see to your suitcases."

"I'll be keeping an eye on you," Sgt. Hardy called after her, somewhat ominously.

"Thank you," Loretta replied, but she didn't mean it.

THE DINING ROOM sent up sandwiches, cake, coffee, and a pitcher of milk at Loretta's request. After supper, Ruthie opened Jack's backpack to retrieve a piece of chalk and made a white circle on the flowered rug. Loretta dumped the contents of the newspaper packets into the empty shoebox she'd brought for that purpose, removed the remaining newspaper pages with their hidden magazine, and separated them to read. The children played marbles until Jack lost his best shooter and cried foul.

Loretta retrieved the plaid flannel pouch from a corner of the rug and dropped it in the center of the circle. "Time to clean up."

Jack swatted it out of his way. "We don't need that."

"Yes, you do," Loretta said. "No more marbles. Put them away now."

He grumbled under his breath, but the rug was clear when she finished stacking their dishes, glasses, cutlery, and soiled napkins on the tray in the hall.

ELECTRIC LIGHTS WERE ABLAZE along the Boardwalk, visible from the window between their beds, though the sun had more than an hour to go before it set. Loretta dropped her room key off at the desk and took the children for a walk on the beach. Jack wore his backpack, Loretta the binoculars. Jack was sure they would need them. Ruthie carried the shoebox.

The children were happy to add weathered clam shells, whelks, slipper snails, and quartz pebbles to their collection. Until Jack picked up a silver quarter, taking it for a shiny bottle cap, and turned the game upside down. Ruthie found a nickel two minutes later. After that, neither child would budge from the beach until the trickle of light from the electric lanterns along the Boardwalk was not enough to show their feet. By then, they'd amassed their first fortune: $2.47.

There was a letter waiting for Loretta at the front desk.

"Oh, and a young woman called for you," the clerk said, handing over Loretta's room key with the envelope. "Something about a borrowed magazine? I gave her your room number and she said she'd call tomorrow."

Loretta thanked him and negotiated the stairs behind the children. Their room was on the fourth floor now and it was a trek. She had to turn the key twice to unlock the door. The children were already inside when she realized the possible significance of that, and there was no stopping Ruthie from running to the toilet. When Loretta discovered no one hiding in that room, behind the bathtub, or under the beds, her fear subsided. She was being a ninny. Why would anyone want to come into her room? Surely not for a twenty-five-cent magazine. And there it was anyway, on the bedside table, reflecting the lamplight, good as new. Loretta plopped on the bed with the envelope, wondering, belatedly, who turned on the lamp. She pondered no more after reading the letter.

"Dear Mrs. Bremer," it began. "We are withdrawing from the convention due to Mr. Rowen's untimely death. Your room is paid until Monday and includes meals. You have your return train tickets. Please accept this letter as your notice of dismissal. We have enjoyed having you in our employ and regret the unfortunate circumstances that impel this action."

It was signed by Mr. Kern.

A GIBBOUS MOON pushed its way up from below the ocean not long after midnight. Loretta marveled at its size on the horizon, watched it shrink as it aged. A metaphor for her life?

"The light grows brighter as it rises," chided the little voice in her head.

By the time the children were awake and running around the next morning, trying to get themselves washed and dressed without tripping one another, Loretta had come to grips with her situation. She'd have to get another job, obviously. In the meantime, she'd request a refund on their remaining three nights in the hotel and see how far that took them.

Someone knocked at the door. Mr. Tomlinson wanted a word. Loretta stepped into the hall.

"Just checking on your plans for the children today," he said. "I didn't see their names on the list for the Nursery."

"Breakfast, Boardwalk, beach, then home," she told him.

He looked taken aback. "What about the convention?"

"Oh, I don't have to work it anymore. Lucky me. Say, did you happen to talk to Mr. Kern about Mr. MacNair's death last night?"

He eyed her warily. "I may have."

"And you told him...?"

"What the police and I think happened."

"And what was that?"

"I think you already know."

"I'm not sure I do."

"A 'friend' of yours..."

Loretta felt her face warm. "Go on."

He seemed to gain confidence from her calm demeanor. "Your 'jealous admirer,' as we call him, caught Mr. MacNair in your room and there was a confrontation that ended in Mr. MacNair's tragic death."

"It would have to be something like that," she said to herself, thinking about her lost job. "Too bad it's all rot."

Mr. Tomlinson said, somewhat defensively, "Mr. MacNair was

pushed. He didn't push himself. You heard the clerk's statement. Mr. MacNair wasn't the one who signed the register. You said yourself you had nothing worth stealing. There's only one other explanation. The man who pushed the victim was waiting there for *you*. Perhaps he didn't know you were bringing—"

Loretta closed the door on him and turned the key, leaned her forehead on the wood and trapped her shaking hands under her arms. Two men fought, one died, and it was her fault. Of *course*, Mr. Kern would listen to the house detective, the hotel's resident expert on crime.

Jack's happy voice brought her back to life. "All dressed, Mama."

Loretta couldn't face the dining room. She took them to the Boardwalk.

"Ice cream for breakfast," Ruthie said. "It's like we're in Heaven."

To be fair, there were waffles, thick and crusty, underneath. As well as grilled sausages and fresh-squeezed orange juice, strained free of pulp.

The children gladly sacrificed a dollar of their found money for a strip of nickel tickets at Steeplechase, an amusement pier not far from the hotel. They worked their way around the place to the airplanes in the back. As the ride ended, Ruthie tumbled out of her plane babbling about ponies. Jack needed some assistance since he had to have his backpack on for every ride. Loretta was, once again, wearing the binocular case.

The ponies trotted on the beach south of the pier. A sign gave the price, impossible to discern at this distance, but it didn't matter, there was no diverting Ruthie. She led Loretta and Jack on a jog through the labyrinth of amusements to the Boardwalk exit, where a sharp left turn took them into a battle against the flow, their target being the next set of steps going down to the beach. Loretta was at the end of their line, a yard behind Jack, holding the binocular case against her midriff to retard its swing, when a man in a brown-checked suit swooped in like a hawk, grabbed Jack, and sped away in the opposite direction.

Stunned, Loretta waited a beat to scream, "Stop!"

Ruthie stopped, turned, then took off after the man and her brother. A minute later, she too was lost in the crowd.

Stay calm. Stay calm. Stay calm. Loretta elbowed apart strolling couples. There was no end to them. Dressed in summer dresses and patterned suits, floppy sun hats and white straw boaters, the tourists swarmed like bees. Loretta pushed them out of her way without apology. She gained some ground behind a rolling chair, spotted the flags atop the next pier, and squeezed to the edge of the Boardwalk. She climbed the railing and scanned the moving mass ahead for Ruthie's bright red hair bow.

Steel Pier jutted even farther than Steeplechase over the ocean. Ruthie was there, on the deck between the buildings and the railing, waving and shouting, her words lost in the cacophony. Yards beyond Ruthie, a man in a brown-checked suit and dark fedora fast-walked with Jack squirming in his arms.

Loretta fussed with a steel gate marked "Exit Only" latched across the walkway. Ruthie hurried to push it open. Loretta flung the binocular case in Ruthie's direction and ran. Between a long building and a column of empty benches, Loretta's shoes pounded the boards. Check-suit ran too, veering left, then right, as the walkway changed direction. Loretta narrowed the gap. The man glanced over his shoulder.

At the next corner, instead of turning left, the man hung Jack over the railing. Loretta froze. A second later, the man stumbled backwards, Jack's backpack in his hands. Regaining his footing, Check-suit sped away. Loretta rushed to the railing. Jack's head bobbed in the swirling water.

Loretta shouted to Ruthie, "Go tell the lifeguards," and jumped off the pier.

The ocean was colder than Loretta expected. She gasped as she went in. Once she surfaced, stopped choking, and caught her breath, she spied Jack easily enough. He was a dark spot on the gray-green water, moving away. Catching up to him was the hard part. Currents pulled her back and under, between the rows of steel pilings. She fought hard. Her oxfords, so good for walking, proved not so good for swimming. She slipped them off. Her bolero jacket went next. Then a clingy half-slip and sagging stockings. Finally, she surged free. Her sleeveless dress swirled like seaweed around her flailing legs.

Stay calm. Stay calm. Stay calm. She switched sides, resting her right arm, pulling at the water with her left. She was well past any other swimmers now. Jack was but another gleam of reflected sunlight riding on the rolling ocean. She kept her eyes glued on him.

After swimming for what seemed like hours, Loretta got a hand on Jack's trailing shirttail and reeled him in. The panic in his eyes eased at the sight of her and he began to cry. She rested on her back, consoling him. He was tired. So was she. It was all she could do to keep them both afloat. Rocked by gentle swells, they drifted.

Water and sky were everywhere now. Loretta wanted to swim toward land. But which way? She craned her head around, desperate for a clue. And there it was. The gibbous moon. Pale, so pale Loretta had to squint to make it out on the daytime horizon. A misshapen globe of gauzy white. Setting in the west. Unnoticed. Like a ghost. Something she didn't plan to be. Not yet anyway. With one arm wrapped around Jack's chest, Loretta set off strongly in its direction.

Eventually, a lifeboat appeared. Two lifeguards jumped in the water. They grappled with mother and son, tried to separate them, ended up lifting them over the gunwale as one. It was a while before Loretta was able to loosen her grip on Jack's arm.

RUTHIE WELCOMED her mother and brother into the First Aid tent on the beach. The nurses there had given her small jobs to perform while she waited. "Such a good girl," they told Loretta. "She ran right up to the lifeguard hut, told them to get the boat launched, didn't stop yelling until they did." One nurse fetched Loretta a pair of canvas beach shoes. Another found a duster to cover her wet, now see-through, dress. The hotel wouldn't admit her, not even through the back door, if she were wet or wore no shoes, they told her. Loretta was too weak to argue. She drank the coffee they handed her, thanked them, and left.

Loretta and her children crossed the small stretch of beach, unaccompanied by choice, and climbed the back stairs to their room. At the last minute, Loretta sent Ruthie to the front desk to retrieve their key. Like a little moonbeam, Ruthie enlightened all along her path, returning not only with the key, but with the house doctor, his wife, a porter, a maid, and three curious hotel guests. The doctor sent the guests away with no explanation, the porter to the dining room for tea, hot soup, and "chocolate eclairs for the little girl with the pretty bow." The maid turned down the beds and ran a warm, fresh-water bath for the swimmers. The doctor's wife bathed Jack and dressed him in pajamas while the doctor checked Loretta's vital signs and pressed a packet of aspirin tablets on her. "You're going to be sore tomorrow." She was *finally* closing the door on her visitors, when Mr. Tomlinson arrived carrying Jack's backpack.

Loretta stepped into the hall to take the empty backpack from the detective's hand. She searched his face for answers. "I don't understand."

"The police found it abandoned in a trash can on the Boardwalk."

"I didn't even report it missing."

Mr. Tomlinson shrugged. "Well, the police, that is, Sgt. Hardy, he, um—"

"He was watching me," Loretta said, with a flash of intuition. "He thought he'd catch me meeting up with my 'jealous admirer' on the Boardwalk, didn't he?"

"He was only trying to verify your statement," Mr. Tomlinson said. "Normal procedure."

"So where was Sgt. Hardy when my boy went in the water?"

"I can't really say, I wasn't—"

"He followed the guy with the backpack, didn't he? Instead of stopping to help save my son from drowning, he followed the guy with the backpack."

Mr. Tomlinson cleared his throat. "The man is a suspect in a death investigation. Of course, the sergeant followed him. He needs to bring him in for questioning."

Loretta regarded the house detective for a long moment. "I wonder."

Mr. Tomlinson's mouth opened and closed like a landed fish.

"Thank you for returning the backpack," Loretta said, before closing the door. "It means a lot to Jack."

As much as Loretta wanted to follow up on the thought that began with her jealous admirer throwing her son into the ocean, the turned-down bed called to her. She dropped the backpack by the door, propped a chair under the doorknob, rinsed off in the tub, donned a soft housedress, and fell asleep between her children.

RUTHIE WAS LINING up seashells on the rug when Loretta's eyes jerked open. She knew what was familiar about the signature at the front desk. No periods on the abbreviations for Mister and Missus. Like the handwritten addresses on all her landlady's postcards. Not just from England, but from Spain, Italy, Egypt, even Australia. Proud of her far-flung friends and relatives, was *Mrs Gerald Whitley*. Loretta glanced at Ruthie and received another jolt. Ruthie was fitting shells into a familiar plaid pouch.

Loretta sat up. "Were the marbles not in the backpack then?"

"They were," Ruthie said. "We put the marbles in the other pouch."

"What other pouch?"

"The black leather one. It was ever so much nicer."

Loretta finished the thought she'd started earlier: If she didn't have a jealous admirer, then she had something to steal. "Was there anything already in the black pouch?"

Ruthie shrugged. "Pebbles. Like the ones we found on the beach. Were they yours, Mama? We put them in the shoebox. Do you want to put them in this pouch? It's not really the right size for shells."

Stay calm. Stay calm. Stay calm. Loretta slipped silently from the bed to avoid waking Jack and peered in the shoebox. There were a lot of similar-looking pebbles among the shells. Small, grayish stones with clear crystals peeking through in some places. Quartz was quite common on the beach. Certainly not a reason to search a room, steal a backpack, and throw a small boy into the ocean. Diamonds were another story. Could some of the stones be diamonds? Like those uncut ones stolen on the train outside Trenton? The estranged wife of the diamond salesman claimed the theft was an insurance fraud, his way of hiding assets from her. But what if it wasn't?

Loretta knelt on the rug and surveyed the stones in the shoebox. The young woman on the trolley could have placed the pouch in Jack's backpack. She boarded the train with them at Glassboro, a large station with train connections not only to competing steam lines between Atlantic City and Camden, but to all the trains between New York and Trenton. And there was that policeman at the Atlantic City terminal. Maybe the young woman was hiding the diamonds from him. Maybe Check-suit was also on the trolley and told her where to stash them. He could've easily gotten to Loretta's hotel ahead of her and waited in the room to ask politely for the return of his pouch. And then Roger MacNair happened.

The pebbles in the box all looked the same. Not exact matches, but similar enough. Perhaps the mythical diamonds had already been retrieved. No, Ruthie took the shoebox to the beach last night. And this morning, Check-suit would've had no reason to steal the backpack.

"Ruthie, I have a very important assignment for you," Loretta said. "Do you know where the hotel library is, that little room across from the front desk? I want you to fetch us some books on rocks, minerals, and shells. Can you do that? Let's see what treasures you and Jack have collected."

Ruthie nodded gravely and set off on her errand. Loretta ventured into the telephone alcove in the hall to call the front desk and ask them to keep an eye out for her daughter. Next, she connected with the dining room and ordered coffee, milk, and sandwiches. Back in a flash, Ruthie was, arms loaded with three volumes. When the food arrived, Ruthie tucked in, oblivious to Loretta's obsession with *A Pocket Handbook of Minerals*.

Loretta was interested to learn about the Hardness Scale, but she certainly didn't want to start scratching at the stones with her ring. Quartz couldn't damage it, but a diamond would. The streak test was useless. Both quartz and diamond were harder than porcelain and would streak clear anyway. Loretta was happy to avoid possible damage to the bathtub. She was starting to believe.

She moved all the pebbles from the shoebox to the lid, carried it into the bathroom with the milk pitcher, which she rinsed and filled with water, and closed the door. After organizing the pebbles into groups by approximate size, she dropped them two at a time into the pitcher. She was looking for the slightest difference in speed to the bottom. According to the chart in the book, diamond had a specific gravity of 3.52, quartz 2.65. Diamond, being denser, would sink faster.

Loretta judged the results and grouped the stones accordingly. After several rounds, they began to sort themselves. It was only then that she began making hesitant scratches. Not with her ruby, but one pebble to another. Until she was sure.

She hid one newspaper packet of stones, tied with string for safekeeping, deep inside the binocular case, the one place Check-suit had never looked. She hid the other in the shoebox, nestled under a pile of shells. Jack was awake now, shoving hunks of bread and cheese into his mouth, watching her every move.

The electric lights along the Boardwalk weren't on yet. But it was time for the Bremers to leave. There were feeble protests from the children, which Loretta ignored. Together they straightened the room, dressed for travel, packed their suitcases, and walked out the back door.

CHECK-SUIT CAUGHT up with them at Newfield, the first of three scheduled stops on the express trolley to Camden. They were riding in the middle one of three cars, the last departure on Friday, when he showed his face at the window on the front end of the car.

"Hello," he said, flipping the leather seat back so he could sit on the bench facing them. He left his hat on. "Glad the lad made out all right. All's well that ends well, ay?"

His vowels were all wrong. Not like her landlady's accent at all.

"Australia?" Loretta said.

Check-suit grinned. "Kiwi."

Loretta had no idea what that meant, but it didn't matter. It wasn't geography he was there to discuss.

"You have something of mine," Check-suit said. "Perhaps we can trade." He pulled a black leather pouch from his pocket and bounced it on his palm. "I think these marbles may belong to your boy."

Jack burrowed closer to Loretta, hugging his backpack. The trolley, meanwhile, had begun its silent journey to Glassboro, only twelve miles away.

Check-suit eyed the binocular case in Loretta's lap and extended a hand for it. Jack made an anguished sound and wrapped his fist around its strap.

"They belonged to his dad," Loretta explained.

"I'll just have a little look inside then." Check-suit tossed the pouch of marbles in Jack's direction. Jack caught it in two hands. The man said to him, "All right?"

Jack, sniffling now, nodded. Loretta delayed handing over the binoculars as the conductor made his way through the car, checking for free-riders and any other illegal activity, which must have been a problem on this route considering the number of passengers it carried. Their car was not packed now, but it wasn't empty either.

Check-suit opened the case, removed the binoculars and the newspaper packet, which went immediately to an inside pocket of his suit jacket.

"For your trouble." He stuffed some banknotes in with the binoculars before closing and snapping the lid. He returned it to Loretta. Then he stood, walked a few steps down the aisle, froze, slowly turned, and strolled back.

"Say, ya haven't got any more stones, do ya?" Check-suit pulled a silver dollar from his pocket and held it up.

Excitedly, Jack said, "They're in our shoebox. Top suitcase." He pointed to the wall rack above their seat and reached for the silver dollar. Beaming, Jack showed it off to Ruthie, who oohed and aahed in delight.

Loretta wiped all emotion from her face. Check-suit unlatched the suitcase, lifted the shoebox lid, retrieved the other newspaper packet, hid it inside his jacket, returned the suitcase to normal, tipped his hat to Loretta, and made a hasty retreat. The train was slowing for Glassboro Station.

Ruthie slid forward in her seat. When the train stopped and Loretta didn't move, she said, "Aren't we getting off here?"

"I thought we'd visit Uncle Hank," Loretta said, watching through the window across the aisle. It was still light enough to see people moving around outside the busy station.

"Oh, boy," Jack said. "We get to ride the ferry."

Check-suit grabbed the arm of a young woman in a baggy dress and pulled her toward the platform where a steam train was boarding. As the electric locomotive left the station, Loretta spied a stripe-suited man walking swiftly in the couple's wake. When he reached up to pull down his fedora, maroon scars showed on his hands. Well, well, well, if it wasn't Sgt. Hardy.

Ruthie said, "How long are we staying in Philadelphia?"

"A few days," Loretta said vaguely.

There was no going back to their room at Mrs. Whitley's boarding house. As soon as Check-suit realized his mistake, he'd be back on Loretta's trail. Sgt. Hardy had only to telephone Mr. Kern's firm to obtain her home address. Loretta kept her hands away from the plaid pouch of uncut diamonds pinned inside her chemise. No need to check. It was the only cool spot on her body.

She wondered how long it would take her brother to sell some of the stones. Not too long, she hoped. It was time to rise.

JOHN M. FLOYD

An Edgar nominee, three-time Pushcart Prize nominee, four-time Derringer Award winner, the recipient of the Edward D. Hoch Memorial Golden Derringer Award for lifetime achievement, and the author of nine books, **John M. Floyd's** work has appeared in more than 300 different publications, including *Alfred Hitchcock Mystery Magazine*, *Ellery Queen Mystery Magazine*, *The Strand Magazine*, *The Saturday Evening Post*, three editions of *The Best American Mystery Stories*, and *Heartbreaks & Half-truths*, the second Superior Shores anthology. John is a member of Mystery Writers of America and the Short Mystery Fiction Society. Find him at www.johnmfloyd.com.

REUNIONS

JOHN M. FLOYD

Larry Taylor woke up somewhere over the Oklahoma panhandle, dreaming of a woman's voice. When he opened his eyes, a smiling and golden-haired flight attendant was leaning toward him over the passenger in the aisle seat. He thought he was still asleep—then he saw her service cart and put two and two together.

"A Manhattan, please," he answered.

Her Kaley Cuoco smile widened.

"That'll be five dollars. Sorry I woke you."

"It was worth it," he said, but if she caught the double meaning she gave no sign. Larry Taylor reached for his billfold and heard the man in the aisle seat order the same.

An hour ago, when the two men had exchanged nods while boarding, Larry pegged him as the typical male business traveler: fortyish, sport jacket, khakis, briefcase. On his lapel was a green-bordered stick-on name tag that said:

Hello! My Name Is

and underneath that, hand-printed in ink, the word ROGER.

But something wasn't right. The man in the sport coat had opened his wallet, closed it again, and was searching his pockets, looking ever more nervous. Meanwhile, Kaley had prepared both drinks and was reaching for napkins to put them on.

The problem was obvious. For whatever reason, Roger of the Leftover Name Tag was short on cash. Larry could remember a similar incident years ago in a roadside cafe, when he and Peggy were dating.

What Larry did next was totally out of character for him, and surprised him as much as anyone. And, although he didn't yet know it, it would later prove to be the worst decision of his life.

Larry Taylor, who had always believed in leaving well enough alone, said, on impulse, "Wait, Roger—it's my turn to buy." Ignoring the man's shocked expression, Larry handed the flight attendant a ten and settled back in his seat. He felt strangely pleased.

After she had moved on, Larry felt the man studying him. Finally, Roger leaned over and whispered, "You just saved me. My money's in my luggage, and I think the guy behind me's a friend of my Chief. This could've been embarrassing." He paused. "How'd you know my name?"

Larry glanced at his seatmate's left lapel. Roger followed his gaze, peeled off the name tag, and nodded. "Damn conferences. I can never remember to take these things off afterward." He stuffed it into his jacket pocket.

"Me either. The name's Larry." Smiling, the two shook hands over the empty seat between them. "What do you mean, your Chief?" Larry asked.

"I'm a sergeant in the Oklahoma City PD," Roger explained. "How about you?"

"Tax lawyer from Denver. I'm headed to Oke City on consultant work."

"Consultant work?"

"All perfectly legal, I promise," Larry said, nodding toward the bulge underneath Roger's jacket. "I'd hate to make you use that."

Roger grinned. "I'd hate to have to."

"I'm surprised they let you carry it on board."

A shrug. "I usually don't—too much paperwork. This time there was a handgun competition close to the conference site, and the Chief wanted me to enter. Had to bring my own piece."

"How'd you do?" Larry asked.

"Fifth place." Roger flexed the fingers of his right hand. "Carpal-tunnel."

"Too much arm-wrestling at the bar?"

"Too much paperwork."

Both of them laughed. Larry liked the man already. Talking to him was easy, and it seemed Roger felt the same way. So much so, in fact, that twenty minutes later Roger said something that sent a sobering shiver up Larry Taylor's backbone:

"Your wife ever worry about you, on these trips?"

Larry frowned. "Excuse me?"

"You said you travel a lot. Think your wife, back home, ever has any...doubts?"

"I hope not," Larry said, probably too quickly. "Does yours?"

"No, Sue knows she can trust me. I was thinking more of a buddy of mine. Both he and his wife are travelers, and this friend—Kevin's his name—well, he's afraid she's having an affair. No proof, nothing definite at all, just a hunch. But I feel for him."

Larry had no idea how to respond to that, and from the look on Roger's face, there was no need to. The man was apparently just thinking out loud, voicing a confidence to a newfound friend. Larry changed the subject, and thankfully it stayed changed until the noise of their descent stopped their conversation.

The two men remained together all the way through baggage claim, their talk now directed to safer issues like weather and sports and movies. But Larry still felt uneasy. He'd had a good reason for lying to Roger about his hometown and his occupation. Even though Larry had been here only once, and the chances of his being recognized by someone—anyone—who knew him back home in Boulder were remote indeed, he still had certain rules, and was grateful that no last names had been exchanged. Overcautious? Maybe so. But one never knows.

And this thing about Roger's friend's cheating wife—that subject was a little too close for comfort. Larry decided it was time to part company.

Once they'd picked up their luggage and passed beneath the To Ground Transportation sign, he turned and held out his hand. "Pleasure meeting you," he said.

Roger put down his bags and clasped Larry's hand with both of his. "Thanks again for what you did. Guess I'll just have to owe you that drink."

Larry had a sudden, terrible image of Roger trying to look him up this weekend to repay the favor. Overcautious or not, he wanted no chances of outside contact.

"Forget it," he said. "Expense account."

Roger smiled and nodded. "Where you headed from here?"

"A motel on north Portland," Larry said, remembering the precautions he'd taken last summer. "I'll just find a cab—"

"Cab, hell. That's on my way. I'll drop you off."

"Oh, but I couldn't—"

"I insist. Least I can do."

Larry cursed under his breath, but could think of no good reason to refuse. The motel was only an interim stop anyhow, and presented no risks. He wouldn't be checking in.

"Well, then, I'm much obliged," Larry said.

TEN MINUTES later they were out of the airport and rumbling north in a Jeep Wrangler that had seen better years. Its heater, for one thing, blew more cold air than warm. Larry could feel the chill in every fiber of his body.

Otherwise it was a pleasant drive. The city had received an early snowfall, a thousand-watt moon glowed in the sky, and from the passenger window the suburbs looked like a Currier and Ives print. After several minutes of silence, Larry's previous misgivings felt silly to him. He suddenly said, without thinking, "I hope things work out. With your friend and his wife, I mean."

Roger nodded, looking sad. "I hope so too. If it doesn't—and if I ever found out for sure she's cheating on him . . ."

The man's tone sent another little ripple up Larry's spine. He cleared his throat and said, "What would you do?"

"I don't know." Roger reached down to pat the bulge of the gun under his jacket. "If I met the guy, and if I had this at the time...I'm just not sure."

Larry wished he'd kept his mouth shut. He knew there was little chance that the person he had come here to see could in any way know Roger or Roger's wife Sue or Roger's friend (what was his name—Kevin?) or the friend's unfaithful wife, but the whole topic made him nervous. While butterflies frolicked in his stomach, the Jeep swung east off Meridian onto 23rd, north again on Portland, and pulled to a stop in front of the motel. The driveway was beginning to ice over.

"One more thing," Roger said, his breath smoking in the freezing air. "There's been some trouble lately, this side of town. Don't venture far off the beaten track."

"What kind of trouble?"

"Break-ins, mostly. Everybody's trigger-happy right now, even the police."

Larry pulled his overnight bag from the back seat and opened the passenger door. "So I shouldn't go for a midnight jog?"

"Not without a Kevlar vest."

"Maybe we should all carry guns," Larry said, smiling.

Roger smiled back. "A lot of folks do, here. Be careful."

"I will. You got much farther to drive?"

"I'll be home in half an hour, tops." He seemed to have a sudden thought and fished his conference name tag from his pocket. He smoothed it out on the dashboard and wrote something underneath the ROGER, then handed it to Larry. "That's my cell number. You run into any trouble, call me."

"I will," Larry said, surprised. "Thanks."

Roger stuck out his hand, and the two travelers shook a third and final time. As Larry watched the Jeep's taillights merge into traffic, he realized just how much—despite the doubts and fears he'd felt when their conversation ventured too close to home—he'd enjoyed Roger's company. He found himself wondering why the most pleasant people you meet are often only passing acquaintances, never to be seen again.

He glanced down at the wilted but still-sticky name tag, then folded it once and tucked it into his shirt pocket. He would, of course, never use the phone number, but Roger's giving it to him was a kind gesture.

With a sigh he shouldered the strap of his overnighter and checked his watch. Almost nine o'clock, Colorado time—ten here. Careful not to meet anyone's eye, he marched through the front entrance of the motel, straight past the registration desk, out the back doorway, and into the blackjack oaks behind the property. There he stopped and looked around.

So far so good. The moon on the snow was so bright he didn't even need a flashlight.

Larry pulled up the collar of his coat and trudged deeper into the trees. If memory served, he should continue east for fifty yards, then follow a drainage ditch to a hill overlooking a field.

It took five minutes. From the top of the hill the distant row of houses was exactly as he remembered it, though five months earlier the grass was high and green and no smoke rose from the chimneys. The houses themselves faced the other direction, their fenced backyards forming a wooden border on the far side of the field. Larry's gaze stopped on the second-to-last roof.

Keeping his eyes on that chimney, he crunched down the hill through the moonlit snow. His hands were numb and his feet soaked when he reached the correct fence and found its gate. And then he saw, off to his left, a man decked out in hunting orange emerge from one of the neighboring yards, a rifle or shotgun slung over his shoulder. By sheer good luck, the guy was facing the other way— Larry didn't want to be seen. He stepped through the unlocked gate and closed it behind him. Crouched like a thief (not a comforting thought, as he remembered Roger's warning about burglars and jumpy homeowners), he surveyed the scene before him.

The backyard was large and well-kept, streaked now with the moon shadows of half a dozen oaks. Yellow light bled from windows on both sides of the door, fifty feet away. As Larry watched, a woman walked past the open curtains. When he was satisfied she was alone, he hurried through the snow to the back door.

In a moment they were together, holding each other in the wind through the open doorway. After the first kisses, Dorinda pushed the door shut and drew away from him, her hands clasped behind his neck, her eyes fixed on his. Her face was radiant.

Dorinda, he thought, smiling. The only other Dorinda he'd ever heard of was a character in a Steven Spielberg movie, years ago. He couldn't remember the actress—Holly Hunter, maybe?—but Dorinda wasn't a name you forgot.

"Right on time," she said, sounding breathless. "Any trouble?"

"No. Just need to thaw out a little." He realized he was still holding his overnighter and stooped to set it on the floor. "I saw a hunter out back."

"A hunter?"

"I think so. They allow that, in the city limits?"

"We vote Republican here," she said. "We like our guns."

"So I'm told."

"Who told you that?"

"Guy I met on the plane." He shrugged out of his coat and dropped it onto his bag. Then he gathered her into his arms again, kissed her cheek, took in the sweet smell of her hair. "You feel good," he said.

She giggled. "What'd you tell your wife?"

"She thinks I'm in Tulsa on business. What'd you tell your husband?"

Dorinda pulled away far enough to look him in the face. "That I planned to spend the weekend curled up by the fire." She fluttered her eyelashes. "Did I lie?"

Larry grinned. "Sounds good to me." And for more reasons than one. He didn't want to risk running into Sergeant Roger again, somewhere out on the town. Despite its size and its apparent burglary problem, most of Oklahoma City was basically a big country town where everybody seemed to know each other. A casual chat between airline passengers was one thing—having to introduce a local cop to a married girlfriend would be something else again.

Holding her now at arm's length, he looked her up and down. Sweet, delicious Dorinda. Even more stunning now than she'd been on that very first day.

They'd met a year ago, at an art show in Denver. He'd asked her opinion of a painting, which led to a discussion over coffee and then to dinner and dancing. Since then they'd met secretly on three occasions—once more in Denver, once in Dallas, and once here at her house five months ago. They had never once revealed, or even mentioned, their spouses' names—it was something they'd agreed on, from the very first. It was always "your wife" or "your husband." Now a terrible thought occurred to Larry. What if Dorinda's husband was named Kevin?

No. The odds of that...it would be close to impossible.

Larry shivered. "How about a drink?"

Dorinda smiled, lights dancing in her eyes. "Later," she said. "We've got all weekend, remember?"

Their kiss was longer this time, and for the moment all other thoughts were pushed aside.

As LARRY and Dorinda embraced on the sofa at her place, Roger Farnsworth steered his Jeep into the garage of his home, a modest two-story on a tree-lined street. He switched off the engine and blew out a sigh. During the half-hour since he'd dropped Larry off, a tiredness had crept into his bones.

He left his luggage in the trunk, took the bottle of Chateau Margaux from the seat beside him, and entered the house through the kitchen door. In the darkness he shed his coat and unstrapped his shoulder-holster. The wine had been a bit of trouble—a trip all the way downtown just to buy it—but it was Sue's favorite.

Quietly he crossed the kitchen and peeked through the lighted doorway to the den.

What he saw made him smile. His wife was asleep on the couch. The couch's back faced the kitchen door, blocking his view; he could just see the top of her head at one end.

"Sue," he called softly.

No answer. Then he realized she wasn't asleep after all. Watching from the doorway, he heard her giggle something—probably to her folks in Houston, on her cell. He imagined what her reaction would be when he told her the ATF conference had adjourned two days early.

Grinning, with wine bottle in hand and his coat and gun belt draped over his arm, he called, louder this time:

"Dorinda Sue? I'm home."

LARRY TAYLOR, who was lying underneath her and nuzzling her earlobe when he heard the voice, stopped dead. Every muscle in his body froze.

But not his mind. His mind not only heard the voice—it recognized it.

Roger. Somehow—unbelievably, impossibly—it was Roger the Cop. The man who held marital fidelity in such high regard. Larry felt his stomach turn over. Sweet Mother Mary.

He forced his eyes to move and looked up into Dorinda's. (Dorinda Sue's, he realized now.) She stared back at him in wide-eyed shock.

And then an amazing thing happened.

"When you're done on the phone," the voice called, "I got a surprise for you."

Larry gulped air, felt his heart start beating again. The voice had moved farther away. The kitchen, maybe. He heard the rattle of utensils.

Warm, blessed relief flooded his body. He'd been spared. Or at least given a chance.

Larry's muscles unlocked, and he and Dorinda jackknifed off the couch and onto the carpet at the same time. They were still fully dressed, thank God—all Larry was missing were his wet shoes.

No time to search for them now. Without a single look back—though he could imagine her scrambling to her feet behind him, looking around, smoothing her hair and her clothes—he did a frantic paratrooper-crawl from the couch to the back door, snatched his overnight bag and coat from the spot where he'd dropped them, and eased through the door and into the frigid night. Once outside, Larry Taylor ran like he had never run before—across the backyard, past the oak trees and through the gate and out onto the snowy field. His head was roaring, his heart thundering, his stockinged feet freezing, his breath whistling through his teeth. But none of that mattered.

His only thought was run, run, RUN...

He almost made it.

ROGER FARNSWORTH UNCORKED the wine and paused, listening. "You hear that?" he called.

"What?" Sue said, from the kitchen doorway. He turned to face her. Her voice had sounded shaky, and her cheeks looked flushed. But at least she was off the phone.

"Sounded like a shotgun," he said.

"Somebody hunting rabbits, probably. In the snow." She stared at him as if she couldn't quite believe what she was seeing. "You're back early."

He smiled at her, crossed the room, and gave her a long kiss. She was trembling, he realized, and wore a sweater buttoned all the way to her chin. They should turn the heat up a bit.

"Are you okay?" he asked, studying her face.

"Just surprised to see you."

Then the landline rang. Still holding the wine bottle, Roger picked up the receiver.

DORINDA STOOD there with her heart in her throat, watching her husband talk on the phone. She saw, without really registering it, his folded sport coat and gun lying on the countertop beside the fridge. She was still trying to process all this.

Everything had gone wrong. Everything. Suddenly, incredibly, Roger was here. Larry was gone. Moments ago she had put a sweater on—she'd suddenly felt cold—and had wracked her mind for anything incriminating, anything Larry might've left behind. She'd finally thought of his shoes and stuffed them underneath the couch. Was that all? She couldn't remember.

Then she'd heard a shot. Was it really someone hunting? She decided not to think too much about that.

She found herself counting minutes, counting seconds. It seemed an eternity since Larry had fled the house.

Surely he was away and safe by now. Please, God, let him be away and safe.

Roger was frowning, saying into the phone, "Where are you?" He listened a moment, nodded, and added, "Stay there. I'm on my way." Dorinda watched him hang up and set the wine bottle down. It was her favorite, she noticed. That must've been the surprise he'd mentioned.

She'd almost given him a surprise, she thought, and in her terror she almost laughed aloud.

"You sure you're okay?"

"I'm fine," she said. "Who was that, on the phone?"

"Bill." He looked deep in thought. "From next door."

"Bill Myers?"

"He was calling from his cell phone. He's in the field out back." Roger turned, left the room, and came back with a heavy coat. He pulled it on over his shirt.

"Bill Myers never calls us," she said. She could hear her voice break. "What did he want?"

"He saw somebody run out our gate a few minutes ago. He

thinks the guy was in our house." He looked at her. "You haven't seen anything, have you? Heard anything?"

Dorinda Sue Farnsworth didn't have to fake her stunned expression. "Our *house*?"

Roger grabbed his pistol, shook it free from its holster, and stuffed it into a pocket of his coat. "The guy was running, he said, and carrying a bag."

"But...why's Bill think he was in our house?"

"Because he was barefooted."

Deep breaths, she thought. Take deep breaths...

"Did he—did Bill...shoot him?" she asked.

"No. Just scared him."

Thank you, Jesus. "But"—she stopped, cleared her throat —"why would he be barefooted?"

"Who knows?" Roger marched past her, past the couch, put his hand on the knob of the back door.

"Well, if he got away," she said, "...if he got away I guess we'll never know why. Right?"

"We'll know."

"How?"

"I'll ask him."

Her heart lurched in her chest. "What do you mean, ask him?"

"He didn't get away. Bill's holding him at gunpoint, out there in the snow."

Dorinda Sue felt dizzy. She put a hand on the counter to steady herself and unbuttoned the neck of her sweater so she could breathe. She almost didn't hear what he said next, as he pulled open the door.

"Maybe Larry was right," he murmured.

"Larry?"

"He said maybe all of us should carry guns."

"Who's"—she swallowed—"who's Larry?"

"Guy I met on the plane," Roger said. Then, as he was about to step out into the night, he seemed to notice something. He looked at her hard, a laser stare that made her back up a step.

"What is it?" she said.

He didn't answer. He stared at her for another half minute or so, his eyes focused on her, on her neck, or maybe her throat. Then their eyes met again, and without another word he turned and hurried outside.

She stood there a moment in the sudden silence, watching the closed door and breathing deeply, growing more nauseated with every passing second. Oh God oh God, she thought. Her world was falling apart, right here before her eyes.

Her mind whirled with possibilities. Would Larry confess, admit their affair? Would he invent some other story, in order to spare her? There was, after all, more than one gate to their backyard. He could say—well, he could say he'd gotten out of a cab at the wrong place, maybe, had lost his shoes in a drift, had thought someone was chasing him, had ducked in and across their yard, had then seen the hunter and been afraid of being shot by accident. He could say that. He could say anything but the truth. Right?

The more she considered that, the more convinced she became. Larry would never, ever do anything to hurt her—and if he were to admit their affair to Roger...

She swallowed, the sound loud in the quiet den. She knew Roger's attitudes on love and marriage, and she also knew his temper. He was a good man, and usually clear-headed, but if pushed too far, on a matter like this...

Who knew what he might do?

Trembling, her stomach churning, she made one last pass over the room and the couch and decided nothing was out of place. She'd done all she could.

Finally she stumbled to the bathroom, splashed cold water on her face, looked up into the mirror—

And saw what Roger had seen, just now.

Stuck to the collar of her blouse, covered until a moment ago by her sweater, was a folded, wrinkled, green-bordered name tag with the words

Hello! My N

visible on one side of the fold and a hand-lettered ROG below that. And the first digits of what looked like a phone number.

What the hell?

But she didn't have time to think about it. From outside, from somewhere behind the house, she heard the flat, sharp POP of a gunshot.

A single gunshot.

KATE FELLOWES

Kate Fellowes is the author of six mysteries, most recently *A Menacing Brew*. Her short stories and essays have appeared in several anthologies, as well as *Victoria, Woman's World, Brides, Romantic Homes,* and other periodicals. In 2020, she won the San Diego Public Library's Matchbook Short Story contest. A founding member of the Wisconsin Chapter of Sisters in Crime, her working life has revolved around words—editor of the student newspaper, reporter for the local press, cataloger in her hometown library. A graduate of Alverno College in Milwaukee, she shares her home with a variety of companion animals. Kate is a member of Sisters in Crime National, Wisconsin, and Guppy Chapters. Find her at http://katefellowes.wordpress.com.

A CURRENCY OF WISHES

KATE FELLOWES

Josh O'Leary shook his head.

"I don't want to hear this, Uncle Kenny," he said, scrubbing one hand over his face.

The older man, sitting across the booth from him, leaned forward. "Just hear me out," he said, his voice low. "I've got a foolproof plan."

"But your last foolproof plan got you ten years, didn't it?" Josh sat back, distancing himself from the ex-con. "I'm not going to jail. Ever."

"Hey, I was betrayed that time. My partner let me down. That won't happen this time. We're family."

The bell above the diner's door jingled, announcing another customer. Both men looked up.

The young woman who entered smiled at them as she walked to the counter, her summery skirt swaying just above her knees.

Kenny lifted his eyebrows in appreciation.

Josh noticed she smiled at everyone she passed. Even as Kenny made a remark—almost certainly vulgar—under his breath, Josh was blocking it out, listening instead to the lilt of her voice as she ordered.

Kenny, however, was back to the topic at hand. "So, no one's going to jail, see. Because it'll be just me and you. You know what they used to call me, right, Josh? Back in the day."

Josh knew, all right. He'd been hearing it since he was a boy.

"The Moonlight Marauder." They said it together, Kenny with pride, Josh with resignation.

Kenny slapped the tabletop with his palm. "Danny the Knife himself gave me that name and that's sayin' something. He said it was because all my ideas were...what?"

"As bright as the moon." Josh repeated the phrase he'd heard a hundred times from Uncle Kenny. The highlight of Kenny's life had been getting a clever nickname from a convicted felon. Josh shuddered at the thought.

"And we're both smart, right?" Kenny went on. "So, if you just listen, you'll understand how this will work. It's a perfect plan."

Josh shook his head. "No means no."

"In fact," Kenny barreled on, "we couldn't even try this if you weren't so smart. That's how you landed the internship at the museum, right? Being smart?"

"Well," Josh admitted, "yes."

"And what are you doing there? Tell me again."

Josh warmed to his subject, his studies. "I'm cataloging items for future exhibits. It's a small museum, so there's not a lot of money to spend on curators. They take on graduate students like me to help out. It's a great opportunity. I'll get valuable experience in my field."

"Which is?" Kenny had forgotten.

"History. American history with an emphasis on the Civil War era," Josh said. "The museum doesn't address that, exactly. It's more specialized—maritime history on the Great Lakes. But my research skills are applicable. And the methodology—"

"What are they paying you?" Kenny interrupted.

Just then, the young woman laughed at something the cook said, and Josh was struck by how pretty she was. "Thanks for this," she was saying, rattling her carry-out bag. "Have a great day."

She strolled past the booth where Josh and Kenny sat, leaving an enticing scent of onions, French fries, and a delicate perfume in her wake. *Lilacs? Lavender?* Something like that, Josh thought. And then Uncle Kenny broke in, ruining the moment. "What?"

"I asked what you were getting paid for your labors across the street."

"Oh, it's an unpaid internship. But it'll look great on my resume."

"When you graduate, to become a teacher?"

"Yes, two years."

Kenny pushed his coffee cup aside, leaning further over the table. "I hate to be the one to break it to you, but you'll never get rich that way."

"I don't need to be rich," Josh countered. "I want a career that will fulfill me, personally and professionally. I want to do something of value, in a field I enjoy."

"And live in my brother's basement your whole life? I like him fine, but I sure wouldn't want to live with him."

Josh sighed. "That's just temporary. Once I have a position—"

"Yeah, yeah, sure. Just listen, will you? You do this job with me and you can fulfill yourself all you want without starving. Will you listen?"

Josh glanced at the clock. "I've got to get back."

Kenny smiled, knowing he had him. "I'll talk fast."

"Do you make the same wish every day?" Mallory Vogel sidled up to the handsome young man standing at the edge of the fountain. He'd just flipped a coin into the water, apparently deep in thought.

"Excuse me?" Josh asked, turning to her.

Mallory recognized him from that day in the diner nearly a month ago, when he'd been with that older guy in the coveralls. She'd seen the young man several times since, from her office window, when she ate at her desk. He always came to the edge of the water, looked up into the spray as if admiring the sculpture's design, then, eyes closed, tossed in a coin. The bottom of the fountain was covered in coins now, at the height of summer, when there were plenty of visitors to the shops, the restaurants and, of course, the museum.

"Oh, um," he said, sitting down beside her on the wide rim of the fountain. "You know I can't answer that, or my wish won't come true." He smiled, revealing dimples in his cheeks, and Mallory's heart gave a happy skip. "I'm Josh, by the way."

"Mallory."

"Do you indulge?" He jerked a thumb at the fountain.

She laughed. "Half those coins are mine. I do my wishing in the morning on my way to work." She peered up at the office building across from the museum.

"There?" Josh asked, following her gaze.

"There," she said, pointing. "See that window on the third floor? Not the corner one, but two over."

Josh squinted up. "The one with a red blotch?"

"That's not a blotch. That's a geranium. It blooms there, on my windowsill, every summer."

"That's cool. My mom grows geraniums in the backyard."

"So did my mom. In fact, that's one of hers." Mallory smiled. "I'm so glad it still flowers. She'd be glad, too."

"I'll bet." Josh met her eyes in understanding. "So, what do you do in your office?"

"Insurance. Quite boring, actually. You?"

"I'm interning at the maritime museum for the year." The pride was evident in his tone. "It's fascinating work."

"I'd love to hear more about it, you know, sometime."

"Would you like to have lunch with me tomorrow?" Josh blushed, then, "I could tell you all about it."

"I'd like that very much."

THE PATTERN WAS SET. Lunch by the fountain every day at 12:30. Josh always seemed to get there first, sometimes stopping to chat with the maintenance man, who Mallory recognized as the guy from that day in the diner. She would wave to Josh from her window with the geranium and he'd wave back as the man drifted away. Then she'd scurry down the stairs, muttering under her breath, "Be cool, now. Don't wear your heart on your sleeve."

But Josh would always be there, taking her hands in his, squeezing tight. And she'd be lost in delight, listening to his stories, telling a few of her own, every day, all month long.

When they expanded to weekend dates, Mallory thought of the many coins she'd tossed in the fountain, wondering if her wishes were in the process of coming true.

One night, after a trip to the movies where they'd both laughed at the simplistic plot of the romcom, she and Josh went to dinner at a restaurant not far from the fountain. They'd settled into their usual bench, made romantic by moonlight, and exchanged more than one kiss. Josh touched her hair, brushing it back from her cheeks. *I could get used to this*, she thought with a sigh, *to life with this man in it.* When they rose, she slipped her arm around his waist quite naturally, enjoying the feel of his arm over her shoulders.

"Let's make a wish," she said, moving to the edge of the fountain. Her smile was wide as she held out her hand, waiting for Josh to deposit a coin in it. He closed her hand over his, so they were both holding the coin.

"At the same time," she said. "No telling."

"Maybe we'll make the same wish," Josh said, and Mallory hoped it would be true. They counted to three, together, then made their wishes, opening their clasped hands. The coin fell into the water, the moonlight dancing over the coins scattered on the tiled bottom.

Leaning over, her gaze on the coins, Mallory watched them shimmer. "There must be hundreds now," she said. "And so many different colors. Silver, copper, even gold. Look at that one." She pointed to a big golden circle, half-buried beneath the other coins.

Josh moved closer.

"It looks ancient, doesn't it?" Mallory asked, her eyes widening at the idea of treasure.

Sliding his arm around her shoulders again, Josh steered her away. "I doubt it. Folks throw all kinds of stuff in there. I've seen casino tokens and slugs. Even plastic coins from a kid's toy wallet."

"A kid's toy wallet," Mallory said, and laughed. Life was perfect.

Then, too soon, summer shifted to autumn. Her geranium stopped blooming, but still flourished. She wore a sweater to lunch by the fountain, where Josh would greet her with a kiss.

One morning, as Mallory crossed the square, a coin in her fingers ready for another wish, she paused in disappointment. The fountain wasn't flowing. The maintenance man stood in the moat, shoveling coins into a big plastic bucket. He bobbed his head at her greeting, then turned away, back to work.

ONE EVENING SEVERAL DAYS LATER, Mallory sat in front of her television, watching TV and eating lasagna she'd made from her mother's favorite recipe.

"It's a mystery," the reporter said. He was standing outside the maritime museum, telling a tale of stolen coins. "No one can be certain when the rare coins went missing," he continued. "An investigation is ongoing."

Mallory set her plate down with a thump, her appetite gone.

It's stupid to believe that wishes come true, she thought, pressing her lips together. She reached for her phone to call the police.

TRACY FALENWOLFE

Tracy Falenwolfe's stories have appeared in several magazines and collections, including *Black Cat Mystery Magazine*, *Flash Bang Mysteries*, *Crimson Streets*, *Spinetingler Magazine*, and *Heartbreaks & Half-truths*, the second Superior Shores anthology. She lives in Pennsylvania's Lehigh Valley with her husband and sons. Tracy is a member of Sisters in Crime, Mystery Writers of America, and the Short Mystery Fiction Society. Find her at www.tracyfalenwolfe.com.

CEREUS THINKING

TRACY FALENWOLFE

IT STARTED WITH A BARBIE DOLL. The kind that wore a frilly dress and a tiara that made her look like a theme park princess. I took it from a girl named Holly and hid it in the laundry room in dryer number four, which had been out of order for two years. For the rest of their stay at the campground, Holly's parents thought she'd dropped the doll off our fishing dock and had ridden the eight-year-old about how much money she'd tossed into the ocean. I didn't bother to point out Manatee Playground Campsite was on the Indian River, and not the ocean, since I knew Barbie wasn't in either body of water.

I'd been ten at the time and had lived in a 26-foot Winnebago with my grandparents, Don and June, at the campground they managed for as long as I could remember. Holly wasn't the first brat I'd ever met, but something about her struck a nerve with me. She bragged about the places she'd been and the places she'd go. She told me she was going to be a doctor; a pediatrician, she'd specified, and still I hadn't felt the need to take anything from her. Then she asked me where I lived when I wasn't on vacation but wouldn't believe me when I pointed to the Winnebago. That was when the urge struck.

Bratty little Holly what's-her-name may have gone home to Illinois or Iowa, or wherever she'd come from, but her souvenir from Florida stayed with me. Unfortunately, so did the way she made me feel—like I was less than her. Like she knew I'd always be less than her.

Everything changed for me that summer. I began noticing that everyone, even the snowbirds who stayed all winter, left the campground at some point. I realized the kids I hung out with weren't really my friends, because whether they stayed a week or a month, I was just a summer fling to them. Afterwards, they moved on, but I didn't.

I started asking about my parents. Where were they? Why didn't I know their names? When were they coming back? Gramma June just stroked my hair and sighed. "Ah, Gwen," she said. "They know where you are." It was the look in her eyes that told me the rest—that they didn't care, or didn't want me. Whichever it was, I knew they wouldn't be coming for me. Ever.

From then on, I noticed the material things everyone else had that I didn't, and when I saw something I liked I took it. I changed my game after Holly and her Barbie doll, though, and let the campers keep their souvenirs from Florida while I treated myself to souvenirs of the places they'd come from. I took a nice pair of gloves from one of the snowbirds who came all the way from Maine. They were leather on the outside and real fur on the inside, and they'd just been sitting there forgotten on the dashboard. I'd sealed them in plastic and buried them under the palm tree behind the bathhouse where they would stay until their rightful owner went back up North and they could be mine.

I knew I'd remember which tree it was because the trunk was wrapped with a cactus-type vine my grandparents had told me to cut down. I didn't, and the cactus turned out to be night-blooming cereus. It flowered once a year, and I was the only one who ever saw it. No one ever spent time behind the bathhouse because it smelled awful. My grandparents had started telling the campers the sulfur smell came from decaying grasses along the beach, but I knew it was because the septic system was failing, the same way I knew dryer number four would never be fixed, grass would never get planted, and no one who stayed at Manatee Playground would ever see a Manatee. I kept my mouth shut and enjoyed the cereus all by myself. Even that was bittersweet, though. Every time it bloomed, it marked another year in my prison.

By the time I was seventeen, I was practically running the campground on my own. It didn't take long for me to realize my grandparents didn't have any money because they ran Manatee Playground as if it were a charity. Some people paid, some didn't. The ninety-day maximum stay was overlooked when Don and June thought someone might have had nowhere else to go. Maybe they were kind-hearted, or maybe they were suckers. All I knew was that they didn't pay to maintain anything and that it was all going to rot away before they did.

I would have left that place with anyone, but no one had ever offered me a way out before the summer I turned eighteen.

I'd long since stopped mingling with the guests, but some of them were so irritating I knew their names on sight. Mr. Gilchrist was one of those guests.

He always referred to himself as *Mr.* Gilchrist. "Mr. Gilchrist. I have a reservation." Or after he tapped his fingers on the front desk annoyingly, "Yeah. Mr. Gilchrist. Sites one-forty-six and seven? Can we do anything about that annoying train?"

No, Mr. Dufus. If you'd have bothered to look on the map, you would have seen how close the train was to the sites you reserved.

He'd rubbed me the wrong way from the moment he rolled in. He'd reserved side-by-side sites, which wasn't unusual for families who wanted to park an RV and a truck and spread out a bit, but he showed up alone in a brand-new 30-foot Airstream and stayed locked inside of it when he wasn't badgering me about something.

His first name was Ford, and he was from Georgia. I knew that because I copied his driver's license when he checked in. I even asked him if he realized he'd reserved the two spots closest to U.S. 1. He was talking on his Bluetooth and waved his hand in the air as he turned his back to me in response. Whatever. The campground was right off the highway, so he'd have to be a fool to think he wouldn't hear the traffic. The train tracks ran parallel to the highway, and the train's whistle was earsplittingly loud. I was trying to explain that to him as he waved me off, so I stopped and didn't bother to tell him about the rocket launch that night.

We were in Brevard County, on the Space Coast. The Indian River was the only thing between Cape Canaveral and us. Our busiest time coincided with the scheduled rocket launches. We offered a great view—at five miles away from the Space Center, we were closer than any hotel.

My favorite place to watch was at the end of our fishing dock, which jutted 150 feet into the water. When I stood there and waited for the liftoff, I could look out over the river and imagine I was anywhere. If I turned back toward the campground, it looked like a desert island. I wasn't planning to join the spectators that night, though, because my cereus was ready to bloom.

While Mr. Gilchrist ignored me and yacked on his phone, I couldn't help but notice the keys he'd laid on the desk. Of the six or seven on the ring, two of them were fobs—one for the Airstream, and one with a BMW symbol on it. There was also a little squishy ball on the ring, hanging by two inches of gold chain. It looked like a globe, and I'd noticed him squeezing it like a stress ball when he'd checked in. As he talked with his back to me, as if I didn't exist, I unhooked the chain with one swift, stealthy motion and slipped the ball into my pocket.

He spun back toward me. "So, the train?"

"Ten, two and six," I said. "Like clockwork. I can move you to a site closer to the water if you like."

He rolled his eyes and clicked a button on his Bluetooth. Then he held up his finger to shush me and barked, "Gilchrist, here."

Whoever it was must have been more important than the train, because he scooped his keys off the desk and stuffed them into his pocket as he walked away. By the time he missed his squishy little globe, he would assume he'd dropped it somewhere.

Odd as he was, I probably paid less attention to Gilchrist than I normally would have that summer because I was preoccupied with someone else. Leroy Lafontaine was only a few years older than I was, but he seemed so worldly. He'd shown up on a Harley in the middle of the night about two weeks before Gilchrist arrived, and was especially nice to my grandparents. He was nice to me, too. He called me Miss Gwen and didn't treat me like I was inferior. Leroy was from Louisiana, and said he was just passing through. He had a backpack and a tent, and not much else. Well, he had one thing. I guess you could call it charm. I fell for him. Hard.

He told me he was staying for the launch, but would be leaving the next morning. I'd been hoping he'd stay for the summer. He was on my mind when everyone besides me gathered by the shoreline that night. The ten o'clock train whistle blew right around the time my cereus peaked. By morning, the flowers would wilt. I was admiring them when I heard a noise behind me. I turned, expecting to be annoyed with whatever guest had sought me out, but it was Leroy.

"You're going to miss the launch," he said.

I shrugged. "If you've seen one, you've seen them all."

"You ever thought about it?" His eyes twinkled in the moonlight.

"Thought about what?" The breeze off the water carried the scent of the cereus.

We both turned when we heard the rumble following the launch. It took about twenty seconds or so for the sound to reach us after actual liftoff, and when it did it was loud enough that you couldn't carry on a quiet conversation. Leroy looked up at the sky, but only for a second. Then he turned back. I think that's when I fell in love—when he chose to look at me rather than the thing he'd come to see.

When it was over, we heard the campers down by the water whistle and clap.

"That." Leroy hiked a thumb over his shoulder where the rocket had been. "Have you ever thought about blasting off? Getting out of here? Seeing the world?"

Only every minute of every day. The want was getting so bad it hurt. "Sometimes," I lied.

"All the time," he said quietly. "I saw the way you looked at that globe today. You know, the one you took off slick?"

The tips of my ears burned. "I don't know what you're talking about." I'd never been caught before. Not ever.

"Relax." He chuckled. "Who am I gonna tell?"

I chewed on the inside of my cheek. "I still don't know what you're talking about."

"The guy deserved it," Leroy said. "I didn't like the way he was talking to you about the train. And who wears loafers camping?"

I couldn't help but smile.

Leroy smiled too. "Ever been to Boston?"

"I've never been anywhere."

"Wanna go?"

"I can't leave. My grandparents need help with the campground," I said. I couldn't believe it, because inside my head I was screaming yes.

I thought Leroy was going to take me at my word, but instead he inched even closer. "What do *you* need?"

I don't know how much time passed, but Leroy didn't go away. The topmost cereus flower was already starting to wither. I started thinking how I only had a few hours left to enjoy it, and then I would wait an entire year for another glance. It dawned on me that my favorite flower, my secret pleasure, was exactly like the campers I'd grown to despise—here for a short time and then gone. For once, I wanted to be the one to leave.

At one-thirty in the morning, Leroy and I walked his Harley out of Manatee Playground. We were almost clear of the campground when Mr. Gilchrist stepped out from behind his Airstream. He paced around with his head down, kicking at the ground. I don't think he saw us at first. Then our eyes met. He didn't say anything, and neither did I. For a split second I wondered if he would tell my grandparents that I'd lit out with Leroy, but I'd already decided there'd be no turning back even if he did.

Leroy and I pushed the bike out of the campground, and I soon learned I'd misunderstood the plan. We weren't riding the Harley to Boston. It wouldn't make it all the way there, Leroy said, and he was running low on gas money anyway. So we were taking the train. The only problem was that the train was a freight train, not a passenger train, and it didn't stop. Not here anyway.

I had doubts. Still, the pull of being free of the campground propelled me forward. We pushed the bike across all four lanes of U.S. 1, and then down to the train tracks. I climbed on behind Leroy, clinging to a backpack crammed full of all my worldly possessions. He drove north alongside of the tracks for about ten miles before ditching the bike and leading me on foot to a rotting wooden platform. It was rickety and old, with vines growing up through the floorboards. He promised me the train slowed there, and that there would be a few empty cars with open doors that we could jump into.

When I heard the train coming, I almost passed out. I couldn't jump onto a moving train, especially not in the dark. But then I looked at Leroy, and in the glittery moonlight I noticed that he didn't look scared. He looked excited. Free. He looked like I wanted to feel.

As soon as the engine passed us, Leroy flicked on a flashlight I didn't know he had. "Ready?" he said.

My mouth was too dry to answer.

I was still looking at him when he yelled "jump!"

I did, and regretted it instantly. Because I jumped, but Leroy didn't.

I was alone in the train car, bumping along the tracks in the dark, and everything I owned was in a backpack that I didn't have anymore. What a fool. I clung to the inside wall of the car and looked out into the abyss. It was pitch black, and the train had sped up again. I couldn't jump back off. I was stuck. Trapped in the train car just as I'd been in the campground.

An hour passed, maybe more. I'd shooed a couple of geckos, and now I sat close to the open door because I couldn't see what else was in the car with me. I smelled fast food. I tried to imagine where I was, but I knew we were already out of my comfort zone. Even if I could see it, I wouldn't know what town I was looking at.

I didn't think I could get more scared until I heard a huge thump on the roof that echoed through the car. I pulled my knees into my chest and scooted back. Soon I heard another thump and felt something land next to me. It was my backpack. That was followed by another backpack, and then Leroy!

"Gwen?"

"I'm here," I said.

Leroy took a flashlight out of his back pocket and held it between us. "Are you okay?"

I started crying.

Leroy pulled me close and held me. "I'm sorry, Darlin'. I had to wait a few cars for another open door."

He was wet and smelled like sweat, but I didn't care. I told him to never leave me again, and he promised he wouldn't. We talked until the sun came up. He said he was headed to Boston to take a landscaping job, and that we could live with a friend of his until we found our own place. "It'll be a landscaping job come spring," he said. "For the winter I'll be shoveling snow."

I'd never seen snow, and I'd packed nothing but shorts and tanks and flip flops. Leroy told me not to worry about it yet. We changed trains in Georgia and Pennsylvania, and hitchhiked the rest of the way to Boston. It was the greatest adventure of my life, because I was with Leroy. I had one shaky moment when we were driving through New York with a sweet old man. Frank Sinatra's 'I've Got the World on a String' came on the radio and I was overwhelmed with guilt. Leroy squeezed my hand. "What's wrong, Darlin'?"

"My grandparents used to sing this song to each other," I said.

He put his arm around me and kept it there for the rest of the ride.

In Boston, we lived on the top floor of a triplex with Leroy's friend Steve, and Steve's wife Sherry—for a few weeks, anyway. When the landlord found out we were living there, Steve said we had to leave. It was cold by then. Sherry gave me some jeans and sweaters and a pair of boots, and wished me well.

Leroy and I stayed at a few other places, but never for very long.

His job seemed hard. Once he came home beaten bloody and told me we had to move that night, but wouldn't tell me why. By the time he started plowing snow, we'd moved twice more and were living alone together above a garage. We had no heat there and had to boil water on a hot plate for washing up. When I asked Leroy if we were allowed to be there, he told me as soon as he made some more money, we would find someplace better.

After his first full week of plowing snow, he came home with a pocketful of cash and asked me to marry him. I said yes. The last thing he said to me before he went out to plow the next night was that I'd made him the happiest man alive. I'm sure I was still smiling hours later.

He didn't come home the next morning, or the morning after that. After three days, I tracked down his boss, who told me Leroy had stopped showing up to work the night he asked me to marry him. When I stopped crying, I called Sherry. She gave me the number of a motel manager who was looking for a cleaning lady.

It was a terrible place to work. Marta, the other part-time maid there, gave me a rape whistle on my first day. "Wear it all the time," she said. "Never take it off."

After two weeks on the job, I came home to the room above the garage and found three guys there. They were about my age and strung out on something. When I told them to leave, they informed me that they lived there and I didn't. One of them threw my backpack at me. It was empty, but I took it and left.

Since starting my job at the Dewdrop Inn, I'd been keeping a close eye on the manager and had his routine down. I snuck a spare key while he was out in his car "negotiating" a room rate with a woman and let myself into room 302. Two days later I switched rooms. I lived at work for six weeks, and nobody was the wiser. I even had a TV for the first time. Every night I watched the news to see if my grandparents had reported me missing. I was disappointed, but not surprised, when I realized they hadn't.

I was adjusting to my new normal until one afternoon when I was changing the sheets in room 219 and the door banged open behind me. Ford Gilchrist barged into the room. He snorted. "I should have looked for you first."

I had no idea what he meant, but I knew enough to be scared. His lips were stretched so tight across his teeth they looked white. His face was red, and his fists were clenched. "Where is it?"

I blinked.

He charged at me and wrapped his hands around my neck. "Where is it, dammit? I'm not playing."

He squeezed so tight I couldn't breathe. I clawed at his hands and tried to knee him in the groin. He screamed in my face and shook me. "Tell me where it is, or you'll end up like your boyfriend."

"Leroy?" I squeaked.

Some of his spit landed on my face when he barked at me. "Where is the flash drive?"

I was starting to see stars.

He shook me again. "The globe! I know you took it. I saw it in your eyes the night you left the campground."

It all came back to me then. He wanted the squishy globe I'd taken off his keychain. "I don't have it," I croaked.

"You're lying." He let go of my neck and cracked me across the face. "I know you have it. There's no way your boyfriend could have taken all that abuse and not given it up if he had it."

As dire as my situation was, all I could think about was Leroy. "When?" I asked.

Gilchrist frowned. "When what?"

"When did you see Leroy?"

He slapped me again. "The only thing you should care about is that no one will ever see him again."

My knees buckled.

Gilchrist shook me like a ragdoll. "That's what happens when you don't cooperate. He sent me on a wild goose chase, and he paid with his life. Unless you want to be next, you'd better start talking."

Leroy was dead. I went numb. "It's in room 302."

Gilchrist let me up off the bed. He grabbed my hair and wrapped it around his hand. "Take me there," he said, getting behind me.

I opened the door and blew my rape whistle as long and loud as I could. Gilchrist almost ripped my hair out of my head. Two doors opened and then closed. I heard chains being engaged and deadbolts being thrown. No one was going to help me. Then Marta charged around the corner with her cleaning cart. I blew my whistle again and again. As Marta picked up speed, the hand in my hair loosened. I elbowed Gilchrist in the ribs and jumped out of the way as Marta rammed him with her cart.

Gilchrist went down, hitting his head on the ice machine. I looked at Marta. "Is he...?"

Marta was already patting him down. She pocketed his watch and ripped a gold chain from around his neck. Then she took his keys. She stood up and gave me his wallet. "Go," she said. "Don't come back."

Gilchrist moaned.

I took off. Gilchrist carried a lot of cash in his wallet—enough for a bus ticket back to Florida. I bought one, and left Boston with nothing besides the clothes on my back. Two and a half days later I got off the Greyhound in Titusville and took a cab back to Manatee Playground.

"Are you sure this is where you want to be?" the cabbie asked. "This late at night?" He told me the campground was closed because it had taken a beating during a recent hurricane, and as far as he knew there were no plans to reopen.

"I'm sure," I said.

He gave me a flashlight from his glovebox and left me standing where our welcome sign used to be. My wool sweater was too hot for the heat and humidity, but it was all I had. I wandered around the grounds, dumbfounded. The office building and the laundry room both showed water marks at least three feet off the ground. The bathhouse reeked of sewage. The pool was green and full of palm fronds.

My grandparents' Winnebago was gone. I wondered if they were okay. I could have stood there all night taking in the damage, but I'd come back for a reason—the squishy globe I'd taken from Ford Gilchrist was still at the campground. Somewhere.

I had a firm policy of never going near my souvenirs until after their previous owners had shoved off. When I'd left with Leroy, Gilchrist had still been a guest, so I'd left the globe behind. Whatever it was, Leroy had died because of it, and I was going to make sure Gilchrist paid. Somehow. But first I had to find it.

The easiest to reach of all my hiding places was in dryer number four. The laundry room was swarming with mosquitoes, but I braved it and was rewarded with a T-shirt I remembered swiping from one of the campers who'd come to watch the rocket launch. It said *Jersey Girls Don't Pump Their Own Gas*. Thankful, I switched it out with the heavy sweater. It smelled musty, but better than sweaty wool I'd been wearing for days.

My other favorite spot for keeping souvenirs was the fishing dock. I liked to wrap stuff in plastic, which I tied to a nylon rope and weighted down with a horseshoe from the horseshoe pit. I doubted whatever I'd stashed there would still be around after the hurricane, but I had to look. By some miracle, my stash was still there, but it wasn't the globe. It was an empire state building note pad. Water had gotten inside the plastic so mostly it was empire state building-shaped mush, but I remembered what it used to be.

I laid there on what was left of the dock for a minute with my hand in the water and the breeze washing over me. I'd forgotten what the river smelled like for all these months. Then I remembered another smell—my night blooming cereus. Of course. That's where I'd stashed Gilchrist's globe. I'd just finished burying it before the launch that night when Leroy had walked up behind me.

I picked my way over the branches and stumps, and rocks that hadn't been there before, and found my way to the bathhouse. My heart broke when I saw that the palm had been toppled, and my cereus had been uprooted, but the churned-up ground made it easier to find what I'd buried there. Gilchrist's squishy globe was lying right there at my feet.

I took it out of the plastic and squeezed it the way I'd seen him do. There was something hard inside. Resting on my heels, I twisted the globe and it came apart. The end of a flash drive was attached to one of the hemispheres. Whatever was on it had cost Leroy his life. It had cost me Leroy, and the happily-ever-after I knew we would have had. I twisted the hemispheres back together.

"Is that it?"

I fell on my ass at the sound of Gilchrist's voice. He had snuck up behind me. He must have followed me all the way back from Boston. I crab-walked backwards, away from him.

"I'm done playing," he said. "Hand it over." This time he was holding a gun.

"Okay," I said, knowing as soon as I did, I was dead.

I got to my feet. Gilchrist didn't see the rock I was clutching, which gave me the advantage. "Take it," I said, and lunged forward, rock in hand. I ignored the gun and aimed for his temple. I connected and took off running.

Gilchrist was hurt, but not down. I heard him gaining on me. I ran as fast as I could, darting right into traffic on U.S. 1. Somehow, I made it across in one piece. I heard horns blowing and tires screeching behind me, and hoped Gilchrist hadn't been as lucky, but he was on my tail again in seconds.

The train whistle blew in the distance. It was almost ten. I ran south, toward the train. Soon I saw the headlight chugging closer. I gained some ground on Gilchrist, thanks to pure adrenaline. When the train whistle blew again I turned around and faced Gilchrist. I held my hand out over the track. "Stop, or I'll drop it." I'd picked up a clod of dirt when I'd palmed the rock I'd hit him with, and I still had it.

He stopped dead. "Don't drop it." He piled his hands on top of his head. "Don't drop it."

I felt the ground shaking as the train drew near. I saw the headlight shining in Gilchrist's eyes. The engineer blew the whistle frantically. I heard the metal-on-metal screech when he applied the brakes, and I knew I couldn't wait any longer. I faced the train and hurled the dirt clod right into its path.

"No!" Gilchrist dove for it, thinking it was the flash drive. The train hit him while the clod was in midair. He had no chance.

The screeching from the train nearly deafened me. It took a long time for it to stop. Long enough for me to cross U.S. 1 again and go home. I was sitting on the end of the fishing dock when I heard the first siren.

I took the squishy globe out of my pocket and squeezed it while I looked out over the water and imagined I was somewhere else. Someplace I'd never been. I looked back toward the campground and imagined it was a deserted island. That I was alone in the middle of the ocean. I squeezed the globe one more time. Tomorrow I would find out what was on it, what was worth two lives, but for now, I sat on the dock and hummed a song my grandparents used to sing.

ROBERT WEIBEZAHL

Robert Weibezahl's stories have appeared in *CrimeSpree, Beat to a Pulp, Futures Mysterious Anthology Magazine, Mouth Full of Bullets, Kings River Life*, and the anthology, *Deadly by the Dozen*. He has been a Derringer Award finalist, and has also been twice nominated for both the Agatha and Macavity Awards in the nonfiction category. His two crime novels, *The Wicked and the Dead* and *The Dead Don't Forget*, feature screenwriter-sleuth Billy Winnetka. Robert is also an award-winning, internationally produced playwright, and a book critic whose monthly column appears in the national publication, *BookPage*. He is a member of International Thriller Writers, the Short Mystery Fiction Society, and the Dramatists Guild of America. Find him at https://robertweibezahl.wordpress.com.

JUST LIKE PEG ENTWISTLE

ROBERT WEIBEZAHL

GIRL LEAPS TO DEATH FROM SIGN
—*Los Angeles Times* headline, September 19, 1932

SUICIDE LAID TO FILM JINX
—*Los Angeles Times* headline, September 20, 1932

HOLLYWOODLAND SIGN SUICIDE IDENTIFIED AS ACTRESS

The body of the young woman found at the base of the Hollywoodland sign on Sunday morning has been identified as that of Peg Entwistle, an actress under contract to RKO. The identification was made by the woman's uncle, Harold Entwistle, of Beachwood Drive. Mr. Entwistle said that his niece had gone out on the night of the 16th, saying she was going to the drugstore. She never returned home. Police found the body after receiving an anonymous call from a hiker. A coat, handbag, and one shoe found by the hiker, and identified as belonging to the dead girl, were left on the steps of the Hollywood police station. A note signed by the victim was found in the handbag. The coroner ruled that Entwistle, who had her first role alongside Irene Dunne and

Myrna Loy in the film *The Thirteen Women*, released last Friday, committed suicide by jumping from one of the fifty-foot-high letters of the sign on Mount Lee.

—newspaper account, September 20, 1932

"I am afraid, I am a coward. I am sorry for everything. If I had done this a long time ago, it would have saved a lot of pain. P.E."

—handwritten note found in Peg Entwistle's purse

Found among the papers of R.E., a Los Angeles attorney, after his death on June 13, 2019:

These pages were extracted by me from the manuscript of the memoir of one of my clients before its publication. The client, a world-famous film actress, winner of two Academy Awards, left behind the manuscript for her third volume of autobiography, with instructions that it be published after her death. She died in 1989 and the book was published two years later. Before publication, I chose to remove the following pages, and have since altered some names with deference to any surviving family members. Upon my death, this testament can be made public. Perhaps it will clear up one of Los Angeles' most enduring myths.

SINCE THIS BOOK will not be published until after I am dead, I can finally tell the truth about a story that has long fed the lore of Hollywood's "dark side." It is a story I have been linked with over the years, though only peripherally, and only because of a comment I made when I was very young. When still just a girl, I saw a lovely actress named Peg Entwistle in Ibsen's *The Wild Duck*. From the moment I saw her stunning performance, I knew that I too had to be on the stage. After the play I told my mother that someday I was going to be an actress just like Peg Entwistle.

From the very moment I saw her on that stage, I felt that Peg and I were like twins. Sisters under the skin. She was much more beautiful than me, blonde, with liquid eyes that sparkled under the stage lights. Not that she needed stage lights—Peg was lighted from within, like all great actors. I was enraptured by her and dreamed I would one day be like her. I never imagined that my dream would come true so quickly, and that I would not only become a successful actress, but I would come to know the object of my inspiration.

It seems almost preposterous now, but the fates aligned in such a way that just a couple of years after that magical moment sitting in the theater, I was hired to replace another actress in the very same part, in the very same production of the Ibsen play where I had first seen Peg!

That was an experience of a lifetime in a life filled with remarkable experiences. Believe it or not, I got the measles just before opening and almost had to pull out of the production. But, in the end I went on. Yankee modesty prevents me from telling you what an early triumph that performance was for me, but you can see for yourself if you dig up the notices. It was my ticket to Broadway. And then, at the end of 1930, my mother and I boarded the Twentieth Century Limited, bound for Hollywood, armed with a three-month contract at Universal. It was there, in Los Angeles, that I would at last meet Peg Entwistle and our destinies would become inextricably entwined.

Much has been made about the fact that Peg committed suicide because she was despondent over her career. It is true, the life of a young actress in Hollywood was not an easy one back then. I suppose it still isn't. It didn't always matter how much talent you had, or how much ambition, or even how beautiful you were. Some people got the breaks, some people did not. I learned early that those "breaks" did not just come to you, you had to make them happen. Peg, dear thing, never learned that lesson. She was in many ways a proper English girl, politely waiting for good fortune to smile on her and her career. Even then, I had what we Americans call gumption.

Of course, before she came to Hollywood, Peg had had a very promising career on Broadway. Truth to tell, much more promising than mine. She had worked with Dottie Gish and Henry Travers and Sid Toler—who later played Charlie Chan—and out here in Los Angeles she had done a play with Billie Burke and Humphrey

Bogart. As it happens, it was through Bogey, at least indirectly, that we met. He had come out to Hollywood—Bogey, I mean—around the same time I had and eventually we both ended up working at Warners. Bogart and his wife, Mary—that was years before he married Betty Bacall, who would have been just a girl at the time—had a very tempestuous marriage, lots of drinking and caterwauling and the like. But they threw fabulous parties, and it was at just one such party that I met Peg.

I told her the instant I was introduced to her how I had seen her in *The Wild Duck* and that it was her performance that inspired my own acting career. She laughed in that self-deprecating British way, but I could tell that she was genuinely touched. I think Peg and I spent that entire party just talking, and I must say I felt as if I had found my long-lost sister. I think Peg felt the same way about me.

Of course, I had a real sister, whom I loved dearly. She was my baby sister, just nineteen months younger than me. When she was born, I have been told, I was terribly jealous of her, but that was only natural for a small child, the firstborn who was used to all the attention. I loved my sister, but she had some problems and over the years she suffered a number of breakdowns. In a way, it was because of her that things happened the way they did with Peg.

In 1932 I had been in Hollywood just a year and a half but had already made nine or ten pictures. That's how it was back then—the studios made you work for your money, moving you from one movie to the next. There was no room for the whining or the demands that are so prevalent among today's young stars. Some of the pictures were dreadful, of course, but I was starting to get better scripts and would soon be working with top directors like William Wellman, Mervyn LeRoy, and Michael Curtiz, who would later make *Casablanca* with Bogey and Ingrid Bergman. Peg, alas, was not faring as well. She had a huge success in the Los Angeles production of the play *The Mad Hopes*, but it did not go on to Broadway as she had anticipated. It did, however, lead to a screen test with RKO and that, in turn, led to a small role in the movie *Thirteen Women*. She was over the moon.

Around this time, my old beau, Ozzie, surfaced in Los Angeles. He had just finished college back east and had landed a job playing the trumpet for the Olympic Games that were being held in the city that summer. I had known Ozzie since our school days and he had pursued me relentlessly at one point back in Boston, but his blue-blood father did not approve of actresses and our ardor had cooled. Or so I thought. Suddenly he was back in my life, declaring his undying love for me. I admit it was flattering, but I had a career to think about and had no time for romance. I was working twelve-hour days at the studio, with six a.m. calls. Going out at night held no interest for me. So, I'll be perfectly frank and admit that I didn't really care at first when Ozzie started paying more attention to Peg than to me, taking her to jazz clubs in Hollywood and such. Then, since neither of them had any gainful employment, he started to take her on day trips up to Malibu, or out to the desert or the mountains beyond San Bernardino.

The only person who was upset by this arrangement was my mother, who felt that Ozzie was rightfully mine. I could see her point, and I do admit that I started to feel a little jealous of their budding romance, but none of it was as important to me as my career. My mother must have talked to Ozzie, though, and while I do not know what she said, he was soon paying attention to me once more. He swore to me that the time spent with Peg had been a trifling fling and that I was his one and only. I realized later that my mother had all but arranged our hasty marriage because she was worried about my reputation. I was still a virgin, you see, but the wolves and lotharios in the picture business were relentless in their pursuit of young actresses. Mother made no secret of the fact that she wanted me safely married, especially because she was about to leave California and go back east with my sister, who would be entering a sanitarium. I would no longer have a suitable chaperone.

So, I succumbed to Mother's pressure and Ozzie and I were married in August. I had convinced myself that I was in love with him. Peg was one of the guests at our small gathering. Just a month later she would be dead.

Of course, Ozzie and I never had a proper honeymoon. I was too busy for that. My new husband, on the other hand, was anything but busy, especially during the day, when musicians have little to occupy their time. So, I suppose I should not have been surprised to learn that he had not, in fact, put an end to his special relationship with Peg. Indeed, as I would discover, they were having a full-blown affair. We had been married less than a month when I learned the truth. It broke my heart.

So now, for the first time, I am free to recount the events of that fateful night—September 16, 1932. It was a Friday. I had been at the studio all day, and I arrived home exhausted. Ozzie and I were then living out at the beach, and after the long drive home from the studio I was looking forward to a relaxing weekend away from the rigors of my career. I was even hoping that Ozzie and I could use the time to rekindle our romance. So, I was quite surprised to discover that Ozzie was not at home when I got there. While it was not unusual for him to have a gig at one of the clubs on a Friday night, he had not mentioned such an engagement. I found no message from him.

I decided to take a bath and try to relax while awaiting his return. While I was in our bedroom undressing, I found a note, but it was not a note from Ozzie. It was on the floor near the nightstand beside our bed where, clearly, Ozzie had dropped it. All these years later, I can still recite its message by heart: "I am afraid, I am a coward. I am sorry for everything. If I had done this a long time ago, it would have saved a lot of pain. P.E."

I instantly recognized the handwriting as Peg's and the initials confirmed that the note was from her. I couldn't be certain what it meant, but I could sense the desperation, the drama, in those few lines. It definitely sounded as though Peg were contemplating something drastic, perhaps even suicide, and I immediately understood that Peg had sent it to Ozzie as a cry for help. When he had received it, he must have rushed to her side to prevent her from doing anything rash.

I knew that Peg was staying with her uncle, Harold Entwistle, a bit player who would later appear in two of my more forgettable movies. He lived up in Beechwood Canyon. I had the operator find the number and ring it, but there was no answer. I was beside myself with worry, and knew I had no choice but to drive back into town and find Peg myself. I threw on a skirt and blouse and rushed out of the house.

The low-hanging moon had been full just two nights before, and as I drove Sunset Boulevard its bright light illuminated the curves. I had plenty of time to think about Peg, whose film, *Thirteen Women,* had opened that very day to savage reviews. Rumor had it that RKO would not be picking up her option. Just two weeks earlier she had asked me to intervene on her behalf at Warner's. Now she might be suicidal, her film career over before it had begun.

Traffic was light and in just thirty minutes I was back in Hollywood, making my way up the narrow canyon road. I found no one home at Peg's uncle's house. Not sure what to do, I was driving back down the canyon when I spotted what looked like Ozzie's roadster parked along Beechwood Drive. Then I saw my husband lurking outside the drugstore in the little group of shops just before the bend in the road. I was startled by the sight of him, although I suppose I shouldn't have been. I parked my Packard and sat watching. Not long after, Peg came out of the drugstore. She looked distracted, lost in her own world, and seemed surprised to see Ozzie there waiting for her. At first she seemed hesitant to talk to Ozzie, who took her arm and held it firmly, as if to keep her from running away. After a minute or two more, she seemed to capitulate to whatever he had asked her to do, and the two walked across the road and got into his car. They drove back up the road, back toward Peg's uncle's home. I followed in my own car, keeping enough distance. Clouds had moved in, obscuring the moonlight, and it had grown quite dark. I kept my headlights off, relying only on the occasional streetlight and Ozzie's taillights as my guide.

I stopped about half a block from Harold Entwistle's little bungalow and, from a safe distance, watched my husband and my dear friend as they got out of the car and started up the street. They were now laughing and, I must say, Peg no longer seemed despondent. In fact, in the light reflected from the windows of the cottage, she looked absolutely radiant, not unlike the way she had looked the very first time I saw her on stage. Ozzie looked happy, too, and I knew at that moment what I had been pretending not to know since before my marriage. Peg and my husband were indeed in love.

Perhaps I should have quietly left the scene, resigned to the fact that my marriage was a sham. But anyone who knows me knows I have always been, and will always be, a fighter. I got out of my car and approached the pair, now standing on the sidewalk in front of Peg's house. As if to mock me, the moon came out from behind the clouds at that very moment, isolating the lovebirds like a spotlight. So absorbed were they in their rapturous embrace that neither heard me draw near. Finally, when I was perhaps six feet away, Peg seemed to sense my presence. She looked up, startled, and pulled quickly away from Ozzie.

What followed was an ugly scene, filled with recriminations. It could easily have been a scene from one of the more awful screen melodramas I had been forced to act in during my career. I barely remember what was said. The predictable questions, I suppose, of how they could betray me, of why they would betray me. Only later did I remember Peg's face, like a wounded bird, filled with what seemed to be genuine sorrow. At that moment I was too enraged to notice her remorse, enraged not so much at Peg, but at Ozzie, for entering into our marriage while still in love with someone else. Quite simply, for loving someone more than me. After a seeming eternity of accusations and tears, I stalked off, leaving them together on the sidewalk in front of the bungalow. In a fury, I returned to my car, fully intending to drive back to the beach, where I could nurse my emotional wounds with a couple of stiff drinks. The next day I would begin divorce proceedings. What would Mummy say when she heard? Only twenty-four and I had already become the ultimate cliché of a Hollywood actress.

I started to drive down the street. Once again the clouds had begun to move in, but as I neared the two who had betrayed me, through my tears I could just make out Ozzie standing there on the curb, looking at me through the windshield, an indefinable look on his face: Remorse? Relief? Pity? Rage overtook me. Quite impulsively, I turned the steering wheel and aimed my car directly at him. Ozzie managed to leap out of the path of my car. Poor Peg, who had been standing not far behind him, was not so fortunate. She did not even scream when the front fender of the Packard careened into her and threw her violently backward, although my own scream, within the echoing confines of the car, drowned out the thud that must have accompanied the impact against her flesh and bone. Then there was nothing but the purr of the idling motor against the silence of the night.

When I realized what I had done, I jumped from the car and ran to Peg, who lay on the lawn of her uncle's house. Her body was twisted, her face expressionless. But she was not dead. And then I was aware of Ozzie standing over me in the semi-darkness. I looked up at him and saw a face blank of emotion, or perhaps so aggrieved that an appropriate expression could not take form. I may have told him that it had been him I had been trying to kill, or I may have said that I hadn't meant to hit Peg, or I may have said nothing at all. One of us—me?—said that we needed to get Peg to the hospital right away, and between us we lifted her birdlike body and put her into the rumble seat of my car. But before we could even begin the drive down the hill, Peg was dead. Just like that, without uttering a word.

It was very dark out by then and, remarkably, it seemed no one had witnessed the scene. Ozzie and I got into the car. My rage still boiled, but it was tempered by a sense of panic. What would we do about poor Peg? I started to cry. My loving husband made no attempt to try to comfort me. He just started the engine and put the car in gear. He reversed the direction of the car and soon we were driving up into the canyon rather than back down to the city. I asked him where we were going, if he had lost his mind. He said nothing. I turned back and saw a car pull up in front of the Entwistle house, but then our car took a curve and I lost sight of the bungalow.

Ozzie drove up a narrow side road. The few houses soon gave

way to empty land, and then the road itself reached a dead end at the base of a small brush-covered incline. Ozzie stopped the car and shut off the engine. The only sound, the ordinary click of thousands of cicadas in the surrounding hills, seemed to rebuke me. Whenever the clouds would momentarily clear, the stars overhead—you could still see stars in Los Angeles then—provided a dim canopy of light. Ozzie pulled a half empty pack of Chesterfields from the pocket of his suit jacket and offered me one. I refused it. Under other circumstances, this might have been an overture to romance.

We sat in silence until Ozzie had finished his cigarette. Then he opened the door and got out of the car. I asked him where he was going. All he said was, "Come." Once out of the car I helped him lift Peg's body from the backseat. Silently we carried her up over the crest of the little hill and down into the arroyo beyond. We struggled along with the body for what seemed like miles, but must have been only a few hundred yards. We crested a hill and suddenly we were just above and behind the giant letters that spelled out HOLLYWOODLAND for all the world to see. Ozzie said, "Here," and together we got up enough momentum to fling Peg's body down the hill. Once again, the moon came out from behind the clouds and seemed to mock me. I looked down and saw where Peg's body had come to rest beneath the mammoth sign. Then, near-darkness returned.

Without a word, I followed Ozzie back to the car. We drove back to Beechwood Drive to retrieve his roadster. The car I had seen, presumably Harold Entwistle's, was parked in front of the bungalow. Now, only a single window was illuminated. Perhaps Harold had decided not to wait up for his niece. Ozzie and I each drove our own car back to our house at the beach. I remember nothing of that drive home.

They found poor Peg's body two days later, thanks to a phone call from an anonymous "hiker." That call, of course, came from me. Peg's uncle had reported her missing, but the police could not find her. The idea of her body lying there, abandoned in the hills was too much for me to bear. Peg had left her coat and purse in Ozzie's car, and one of her shoes had come off in mine when we had driven her body up the hill. I wrapped up the jacket, shoe, and purse and, late at night, laid them on the steps of the Hollywood Police Station. I had put the note I found in our bedroom in the purse. I called the station early the next morning and said I had been hiking near the Hollywoodland sign and had found the woman's shoe and jacket. A little further on, I told them, I had noticed a purse with the suicide note inside. I had looked down the mountain and seen a body.

I altered my voice, of course, and did not tell the police my name.

The coroner found that Peg had sustained multiple fractures of the pelvis from her fall. The fact that she was found below the sign, where a workman had conveniently left a ladder propped up against the letter "H," seemed to indicate that she had climbed to the top and jumped. The enigmatic note in her purse hastened the suicide verdict.

I have always wondered if Peg had truly intended to commit suicide that night, if she had sent that note to Ozzie as a true cry for help, or just to lure him back to her. If he had prevented her from acting on her baser impulses, then the unfortunate turn of events was perhaps preordained. But I never asked Ozzie why he had rushed to Peg that night. In fact, we never spoke of the incident again. We stayed together for six years, then divorced, our marriage a victim of the classic Hollywood syndrome. Ozzie could never cop to being what would now be called a Hollywood husband, with a wife making ten times more than he did. He visibly cringed whenever someone called him by my last name.

The legend grew that Peg had killed herself because she was too fragile to withstand Hollywood's brutal indifference. Her uncle told the press that the day after her body was found, Peg received notification in the mail that she had been cast in a play. I do not know if that is true or just a bit of Hollywood myth-making. I do know that the next time I met with Jack Warner at the studio I told him that just before Peg's death I had offered to get her a screen test. "Oh, Hon," he said, the look of money in his eyes. "For you, I would have gladly ordered one." Strange to think what might have been, that Peg might have come to work at Warners and we might have done a picture or two together. Maybe we could have played the sisters on screen that I always felt we were meant to be in real life.

The next few films I made for Warners were rather tepidly received....

MICHAEL A. CLARK

A singer, songwriter, and storyteller, **Michael A. Clark's** stories have been published in *Liquid Imagination*, *Mystery Weekly Magazine*, *Galaxy's Edge*, *Tales from the Moonlit Path*, *Cosmic Horror Monthly*, and Gypsum Sound Tales' anthologies *Colp* and *Thuggish Itch*, as well as the benefit anthology *Burning Love and Bleeding Hearts*. Michael lives in Charlotte, North Carolina, and works in industrial automation and CNC machining, while spending as much time as he can outdoors. Find him at www.reverbnation.com/michaelaclark.

SCAVENGER HUNT

MICHAEL A. CLARK

I KILLED the outboard motor as we approached the dark lagoon, moonlight shining over our ebbing wake. Slid my paddle into the dark water as the other two did the same. The pungent stench of brackish tides rolled over us in the soft breeze as we made for shore. A heron took wing, startled by our quiet journey, and I heard a turtle gently slip into the water from its half-sunken tree trunk perch.

It was a good night to hunt for a lost atomic bomb.

The mosquitos could have been worse, and the air held the first tinges of fall. Quietly we pushed forward, deeper into the coastal swamp, far (hopefully) from prying eyes.

Jeb hunkered in the bow of our small skiff. A camouflage vest covered his round back, and the small craft nosed down under his hulking weight. Andy sat between us, slim arms paddling with economical effort. The boat would have handled better if the big guy were back by the motor. But Jeb claimed he knew these inlets like the back of his hand and could navigate better at the bow. The boat bumped against a floating whiskey bottle, and Andy cleared his throat as a water moccasin swam lazily across a plank of soft light laid down by the autumn moon.

The B-47 carrying the missing A-bomb had collided with an F-

86 fighter while on nighttime simulated war maneuvers in February of 1958. The MK-15 thermonuclear weapon had fallen from 15,000 feet, landing somewhere in this swampy intercoastal wilderness. You'd have thought the Air Force would have made more of an effort to recover such a dangerous and expensive piece of government property. But after several teams of investigators combed the wetlands for a month or two, the Feds basically gave up looking. An official notice released to the wire services stated that the missing bomb was considered "absent from the nuclear inventory," and anyway, the thing didn't have its plutonium fuse inserted and posed no immediate danger.

People forgot about it ever happening.

I imagined my parents, teenagers groping around in the back seat of my dad's Plymouth back then. Funny how your mind wanders at times.

We moved deeper into the Wassaw Sound, the faint glow of Savannah far off to the south. No one had spoken for half an hour.

Andy smoothly pulled his paddle into the craft, and I heard a soft zip as he opened the worn green duffle bag he'd brought aboard when we'd put into the darkening waters an hour before. Andy hadn't allowed either of us to help him with it. He grunted as he reached into the open duffle, extracting a device pocked with dials and sockets.

Jeb glanced over his egg-sloped shoulder. "Will that thing work?"

"Yep," Andy said, sticking a cable from an old Delco car battery into one of its orifices. He methodically flipped toggle switches and turned knobs on the dormant instrument. "Genuine U.S. government surplus," he said. "State of the art radiation detector. Got it off e-Bay."

"State of the art when Buddy Holly died?" I asked.

"It'll work," said Andy. "Come on. We've got buried treasure to find."

The Geiger counter sparked to life, and Andy gave a satisfied grunt as he pointed the instrument's blunt nose over the starboard rail of the boat. The plan was to follow the fading radioactive emissions from the weapon's explosive core with the Geiger counter and mark the spot, then return later to raise the bomb from its miry grave and sell it to the highest bidder.

My plan was to make sure they either didn't find the bomb, or at least couldn't excavate it for sale. Jeb and I put our paddles back in the water, slowly urging the boat forward.

Andy tracked the vintage Geiger counter's business end to and fro over the dark water, hunched in concentration. A random "click" sounded every few seconds, and he'd narrow his sweep. "Swing around right over here," he said.

"That's probably just some normal background radiation," I said.

Andy's ball cap turned my way.

"What're you talking about?" Jeb rumbled from the skiff's bow.

"I mean, everything's radioactive...a little bit." The frogs who'd been croaking along the shoreline chose that moment to be quiet. "That thing'll pick up radiation from just about anything." I leaned into my paddle. "Didn't you read the instruction manual?"

Andy turned back to his tool. "Didn't come with one. If you know so much about it, why don't *you* give it a try?"

"I... just remember what I saw in old monster movies." I licked my lips. "They always had a Geiger counter around, and the head scientist would say something like 'There's radiation in everything.'"

"Like that movie where the giant grasshoppers climbed all over Chicago?" Jeb asked. "Or the big spider came out of the desert? Or the giant Gila Monster?"

"Yeah," I said. Andy was slowly weaving his budget radiation detector over the boat's side again.

"I used to love those," Jeb said. "Ever see the one that had the giant praying mantis? It flew around and smashed all these planes and stuff."

"Yeah, I remember that one," I said, glad to change the subject from my knowledge of physics. "Anybody want a beer?"

"Hell, yeah," Jeb said, and I reached into the mottled cooler between my legs for a Busch. Andy shook his head once, as he stared intently at the collection of dials on the Geiger counter. I handed a can forward into Jeb's paw, and got one for myself. One beer couldn't hurt, right?

The FBI had been trolling white supremacist websites for keywords relating to nuclear weapons. A hit on a site out of Clover, South Carolina, had me being assigned to track a group seeking a nuclear warhead to sell to disreputable third parties. Why I got the job, I don't know. My FBI career had been trending stagnant, and I was lying awake at night wondering if the next round of budget cuts might cost me my job.

"There was this one movie with the giant scorpions," Jeb said. "And this other one that had these huge rock crystals that'd grow up and fall down on buildings. They used SALT to stop those!"

Andy snorted, but it was more of a body movement then a sound. Did he really think that ancient Geiger counter might turn up the missing bomb? I kept stroking the swamp water with my paddle, as the night sounds rose behind us.

"SALT," Jeb said. "That KILLS monsters!"

"Yeah," I said. "Electricity does it, too."

A few more clicks came from the Geiger counter.

"And the giant ANTS one," Jeb continued, as he took a swig from the can I'd just handed him. "I remember Daniel Boone and Matt Dillon were in that one."

Big Jeb was right, in a way. Fess Parker and James Arness had been in *Them*, a '50s sci-fi movie featuring pathetic shaggy ants that invaded LA's sewers.

Andy pointed the Geiger counter like a bird dog spotting a pheasant in a cornfield, and it clicked again.

"Those were the best," Jeb said. "Then they got all stupid, with big bunny rabbits and blobs and stuff." He shook his fire hydrant skull sadly. "Just plain stupid. Like those crappy Japanese monster movies."

"You don't like *Godzilla*?" I asked. "Or *Rodan*?" The stars above were clear and bright, polished by the storm that had blown through here two days ago. I took a sip of my beer.

"Move over this way," Andy said. He motioned with the bill of his ball cap at a wide expanse of dark water that ended at a shoreline dense with fallen trees and thick rushes. Jeb and I complied. Something broke surface with a solitary splash.

"Nah, those Jap monsters were just guys in rubber suits kicking over toy buildings and shit," Jeb said. "Not real monsters, like the old movies."

I was about to ask him what was so "real" about Hollywood ants made from old carpet and coat hangers, when the Geiger counter reeled off a machinegun burst of staccato clicks. Andy fixed it on one spot of the black pond, then slowly pulled the detector's probe from side to side. The clicks ebbed and flowed as the Geiger counter came back to the original hot spot.

"You think that's more of your 'background radiation?'" Andy asked.

"I don't know," I said. Something started gnawing at my gut.

Jeb shifted his bulk. "Should we go closer or circle around, or what?"

"Looks like we got a hot spot right over there, about twenty yards away," Andy said. He sounded confident, as if he'd trained intently for this mission. I'd figured him for a wingnut rube who got his kicks stockpiling rations for the coming apocalypse and holding turkey shoots for autographed copies of G. Gordon Liddy books.

"We're not going to get...radiated, right?" Jeb asked.

Andy shifted his weight, rocking the boat a little. "Nope. I got rad dosimeters here, to monitor us. We won't get much from this thing."

Andy was more on the ball then I'd expected. Not such a rube, after all.

We eased forward in a gentle circle, barely breaking a wake. Savannah was only a few miles away, but it might as well have been in China. The Geiger counter clicks mingled with the swamp sounds of the unseen life around us. A stray cloud wandered over the brilliant moon, lunar shadow dampening the shine on the water's surface.

"How deep's the water here?" I asked.

"I dunno," Jeb said.

"Thought you knew this area like the back of your hand?"

"Not in the dark!"

Andy shook his head. The Geiger counter clicked like a cue ball off a combo bank shot.

"Well, do you even know where in the hell we're *at*, exactly?" I asked.

"We put in at the end of Cobb Road, by the big white oak that got struck by lightning. Savannah's uh, that way. South. So, we've been heading sorta north for the past hour or so."

"It's been fifty-seven minutes," Andy said. "Pull back a little more to the right. It's down there. Close." The Geiger counter snapped off a barrage.

Something had been bothering me for a while. Aside from being on a rowboat in a swamp with two armed, white supremacists, that is. The FBI field office out of Savannah had sewn a transponder into the lining of the camo vest I wore. Due to department cutbacks, I hadn't been given a government-issue handgun for the mission. What was my escape plan?

"You guys ever see *Creature from the Black Lagoon?*" Jeb asked, nudging the boat's nose around with his paddle. "You kinda feel sorry for the monster, you know? He's just hanging out in this big swamp, and these people come in and mess with him."

"Yeah, they did," I said.

"I'm going to drop a marker, right about...here," Andy said. He placed the Geiger counter on the floor of the skiff and pulled something out of his gear bag.

These hicks weren't supposed to *find* anything. I was riding along to see who they'd call after their swampy snipe hunt failed. The Bureau could follow the trail from there.

"Yeah," Jeb said. "And then The Creature wastes a couple of them, but you know kinda subtle like? Not all gory and intestines like they do in movies these days. He just grabs them, and they're gone." He drained his can of Busch.

Jeb's film reviews weren't calming my nerves.

Andy cast a weighted line attached to a small bulbous float over the side.

"What's that?" I asked. I hadn't questioned them about all the gear they'd brought along. The only thing they asked *me* to bring was the beer.

"A marker." Andy played out the line until it stopped, then unscrewed the top of the float exposing something small and electronic inside.

"How's it work?"

Andy turned toward me. "It sends out a signal encoded with GPS coordinates that only a special frequency receiver can pick up." His sunburned face was just recognizable under the moon shadow of his ball cap. "You know the kind." He clapped the float cover around the transmitter shut.

"Huh?"

"Like the kind you got on you, somewhere," Jeb said. "Mr. Federal Agent Man."

"Now wait a minute," I said. "That's not funny. Not even joking."

"Who's joking?" Andy asked. A frog croaked in the darkness.

"If I *was* a government man, then why the hell would you bring me out here looking for this damn bomb?"

Jeb turned his bulk around in the boat's bow to face me. "En-trap-ment."

Andy nodded. "Those socialists in Washington want to smoke out freedom-fighting entrepreneurs like us."

"You thought we was just wingnut rubes or something?" Jeb asked, now balancing a sawed-off shotgun on the damp paddle bridging his lap. The shorn metal of the weapon's muzzle was the same color as the tiny waves cresting our boat.

It is amazing how quiet the world can be, just before your heart stops beating.

SUSAN DALY

Susan Daly writes short crime fiction for fun, fame, and fortune. Well, for fun, anyway. And to take a stand for social justice. Her stories have appeared in a variety of anthologies, including *Mystery Most Theatrical* and *The Best Laid Plans* and *Heartbreaks & Half-truths*, the first and second books in the Superior Shores anthology series. 'A Death at the Parsonage' won the 2017 Arthur Ellis Award for best short story from Crime Writers of Canada. She lives in Toronto, a short social distance from her remarkable grandkids. Susan is a member of Crime Writers of Canada and Sisters in Crime National, Toronto, and Guppy Branches. Find her at www. susandaly.com.

MY NIGHT WITH THE DUKE OF EDINBURGH

SUSAN DALY

I SHIFTED my body for the third time. Even in a black leotard and tights, behind the magnificent Haida totem pole in the center of the marble stairwell, I still wasn't convinced I was invisible to the guard.

Across the darkened grand entrance hall of the Royal Ontario Museum, Ted was hidden by the other totem pole. A shaft of moonlight slanted down from the high east window of the atrium, hitting the floor almost at midpoint between us.

We waited, timing the guard's second round.

How HAD it come to this? Three weeks ago, we'd all been sitting around the living room of Donovan's comfortable off-campus apartment, enjoying his excellent rye and discussing life and politics and, as ever, the Leafs' chances for the upcoming season.

We really should have known better. As modern history majors in our final year at the University of Toronto, we knew about cause and effect and how international incidents could rise up out of the most innocuous actions.

Not that kidnapping Princess Elizabeth's husband could be considered innocuous.

In the early autumn of 1951, there wasn't a soul in Canada unaware of the upcoming Royal Tour. Princess Elizabeth, the lovely young daughter of King George VI and Queen Elizabeth, would be arriving in Canada for a month-long visit. She and her husband— her fairy-tale prince—would travel from one end of the country to the other, as far west as Vancouver Island and then out to the eastern tip, to our newest province, Newfoundland, before sailing home aboard the Empress of Scotland.

"I expect you're all starry-eyed at the prospect, Cathy," Donovan teased. "No doubt you'll stand by the side of the road among the cheering hordes, as though waiting for the Santa Claus Parade. Waiting hours in the glaring sun or miserable rain, just for a fleeting glimpse of the future queen and her golden sun god of a husband."

"Oh, I promised to go with my sisters," I said with a martyr's air. "They're all excited about it." I took refuge in my glass of Northern Spirit Rye. Granted, I was two months short of twenty-one, but our little group had no use for such arbitrary, state-imposed nonsense. A person could either hold their liquor, or they couldn't.

"Come on, Donovan," Ted said. "Hardly comparable to the Santa Claus Parade."

"True," Donovan conceded. "After all, Santa Claus is real."

I tuned myself out of the discussion that followed, nursing my drink. Twelve years ago my family—three generations of us—had gone to Riverdale Park to enjoy the historic sight of the King and Queen themselves, the first time a reigning monarch had come to Canada. I'd returned home, enchanted with having seen them. In person! *In my own city.* My sisters and I had talked of little else for weeks before and after. Grandma swore the Queen had looked directly at us and smiled.

Now, I was damned if I was going to miss this chance to see their daughter when she dazzled her way through Toronto.

I was equally damned if I was going to admit any of this to my fellow students at Victoria College. This year, I had somehow fallen in with the most desirable sub-subset of intellectuals, and I wanted to keep it that way. A clique, furthermore, that revolved around the star that was Donovan Grant.

While Ted and Peggy and Gordie and I were the products of Toronto collegiates and small-town Ontario high schools, Donovan, newly transferred from McGill University, seemed somehow more highly evolved. He was everything we weren't. Bohemian to our bourgeois. Cosmopolitan to our suburban.

"So, if I'm to understand what you're saying..." Gordie's verbosity poked its way into my consciousness, "...the adoration of the masses heaped upon these peripatetic figureheads is more than harmless amusement, that it can actually be detrimental to Canada's growth as a nation?"

Wow. What had I missed?

Donovan's slight nod indicated Gordie had summed it up nicely. "Indeed. The financial cost of supporting the monarchy aside, the cost to our autonomy as a sovereign nation is even greater."

"And you're suggesting the overthrow of the monarchy is our only hope?" I wasn't sure if Ted was for or against the idea. "Like Cromwell's republic?"

"Which didn't actually endure," Peggy pointed out. "You need to look closer to home for a lasting example." She glanced in a more-or-less southerly direction.

"A re-enactment of the American Revolution on Canadian soil?" Gordie said. "Hardly going to improve our graduating marks. In fact, it could conceivably get us executed for treason."

Before Peggy could offer the statistics of how many Canadians had been executed for treason, I needed some clarification.

"Wait a minute," I said. "Are we talking about *applied* historical science here? Applied by us as a graduating class project?"

Donovan leaned forward to refresh my drink. "Not quite, Cathy. A symbolic act against the monarchy would be quite sufficient, I think, for the purposes of presenting the anti-Royalist sentiment among the students at U of T."

While not exactly wholehearted about participating, I had no wish to forfeit my place among the members of this charmed circle, with their promising vision of a modern Canada at the midpoint of the twentieth century.

"A banner saying *Lizzie Go Home*?" I offered.

I swear I heard Peggy's eyes roll at my suggestion.

"Perhaps something a *little* more original, Cathy. Something that will make the Monarchists sit up and take notice."

"But avoiding anything felonious," Gordie added.

The Northern Spirit flowed freely, along with ideas.

THE MOONLIGHT INCHED across the marble floor toward Ted's totem pole. Ten minutes since the guard's last appearance. No sound of his return yet.

NOTHING HAD BEEN DECIDED that night in Donovan's apartment, and by the time we headed back to our respective residences, I was ready to believe it would come to nothing. But the following week when we got together again, the others were still gung-ho, and Peggy accused me of being half-hearted, having contributed nothing. (The others had come up with lots of suggestions, ranging from impractical to idiotic, so I was hardly delinquent.) To keep my end up, I mentioned an article I'd seen in *The Telegram*.

"I read there are going to be wax figures of the royal couple, on loan from Madame Tussaud's, on display at the Royal Ontario Museum for the duration of the Royal Tour." For what it was worth.

"Ahh..." Peggy began rummaging through yesterday's papers. "Here it is. They've been shipped from London and are being installed today. Perfect."

We crowded around to read the article, complete with a picture of the waxworks, each dressed in formal splendor. Princess Elizabeth in swaths of tulle and jewels and the Duke very impressive in evening wear, like they were off to some swanky party.

"Large as life and twice as natural," Donovan murmured. "Certainly there are possibilities."

"Really?" I hadn't been serious, but if Donovan thought we were on the right track...

The ideas buzzed around us. Commit an indignity, perhaps? Put them in a compromising position, place cigarettes between their fingers, switch their heads.

But Donovan merely said, "Perhaps a tad sophomoric?"

"Donovan's right." Peggy's voice held a laying-down-the-law tone. "Those are nothing but student pranks, the kind of games first-year meds play with their skeletons. We want to do something impressive that will display our disdain for the monarchy."

Like what?

"I think we should kidnap the Princess."

As it turned out, Her Royal Highness's princess finery was deemed too cumbersome for us to manage, whereas the Duke, in his svelte evening wear, was more conducive to being wrapped in a blanket and spirited away.

Sure. Piece of cake.

Gordie worked out how we'd get into the museum. He'd read it in a true-crime book. You don't break in after hours. You go during the day and hide until closing time. When the coast is clear, you get into position. Then, you wait.

Right. Another piece of cake.

Ted and Peggy and I did some cautious casing of the ROM. *Very* cautious, since we didn't want the staff to notice the same people kept returning to the future scene of the crime.

Okay, not *crime*. A political statement. Standing up for the idea of a progressive, independent nation, not a satellite of an antiquated monarchy.

And after all, it was just a wax dummy. Our plan was to spirit him into place at a public event, bearing a sign saying, "*No Figureheads Ruling Canada.*"

But then, out of the blue, it all hovered on the verge of cancellation. Not our plot. The entire Royal Visit. King George's health was worse than his loyal subjects had been allowed to believe. The massive logistics of plotting the Royal Tour down to the finest minutia went into a holding pattern, and Canada—the entire Commonwealth—held its breath.

Much as I didn't want the King to be *very* ill, or worse, to die, I knew that either of these events would mean the Princess would stay home by her father's bedside—or take up her duties as Queen. The waxworks would be shipped back to England and I could, with honor, avoid taking part in this whole plot.

But the King underwent lung surgery, and he appeared to benefit by it. The world exhaled, and the Royal Tour was on again. Every state dinner and prairie whistle-stop, every flower presentation by a Brownie and Native dance demonstration: they were all pushed back exactly one week.

Along with our plot to kidnap the Duke. Except with a slight change of cast. Yesterday, Donovan had announced his mother would be visiting Toronto, so he'd be tied up entertaining her. And during the week's delay, Peggy had taken a fall in a field hockey game and broken her ankle.

Which is why, on the very day the royal couple arrived in Toronto, I found myself hiding behind a totem pole at the Royal Ontario Museum, twenty paces from where the facsimile Princess and Duke stood on a cordoned-off dais, left of center in the entrance hall.

If I peeked out from my hiding place, I could see them, calm and regal, as though ready to greet visitors. Hordes of school children on a day trip, a visiting palaeontology professor, an American honeymooning couple fresh from the wonders of Niagara Falls.

The guard made his next appearance exactly when expected. Good. His full round took precisely twenty minutes. When he went off down the stairs for the third time, Ted and I went into action.

We stepped onto the dais, and I found myself at eye level with the well-dressed chest of this gorgeous man. I looked up, way up, to his waxen face.

Okay, it sounds crazy, but lifelike recreations of actual people can be creepily off-putting. I froze.

"What's wrong?" Ted whispered.

"He's looking at me."

Ted made a sound of disgust. "Get a grip, Cathy. He's just a dummy."

Uh-huh. Then why had Ted said "he"?

I got a grip. With a little awkwardness—he was heavy as a human—we eased him down to horizontal, wrapped him in the blanket we'd brought, and between us, we carried him off the dais.

I glanced over to see what Elizabeth was making of all this. The look she gave me was frigid with disapproval. Well, who could blame her?

"It's okay," I assured her in a whisper. "We'll take good care of him."

"Are you nuts?" Ted's voice was almost a squeak. "Let's get out of here."

To my amazement, it all went according to plan. We'd scoped out an escape route to the back passageway where an unobtrusive door led to the loading area out back. Hours earlier, just before closing time, Gordie had propped the door ajar with an old hockey stick.

Now, bang on schedule, Gordie waited outside with his third-hand Hillman Minx.

The Minx is not a big car. Certainly, we now realised, not big enough to accommodate a tall man in the trunk. Originally, we'd planned to use Peggy's father's station wagon. But it was with her and her broken ankle back in Bobcaygeon.

"We'll have to put him in the back seat," I said. We'd already discovered that the Duke had articulated limbs. Bless Madame Tussaud's for that.

We unwrapped him (we could hardly drive around with a mummy in the back seat) and arranged him in a more-or-less natural pose. I got in beside him.

"You two make a lovely couple," Ted observed.

We drove off through the moonlit night, with my arm tucked through the Duke's to keep him steady every time we turned a corner.

THE NEXT STUMBLING block was where to stash him, since the back of the station wagon was now out. So was Donovan's apartment; his mother might have asked questions.

We decided on Gordie and Ted's room in their residence. Gordie went in to see if the coast was clear. It wasn't. A party was going on on their floor, and guys were everywhere.

"Cathy's residence," Ted declared. "Girls don't have wild parties."

"Not a chance." I could imagine the danger. "It's after nine, so no guys are allowed in the residence. And if you think I'm dragging him up to the third floor by myself—"

"No, it's perfect," Gordie said. "Your room is right at the end of the corridor, by the staircase up from the side entrance. We can get him into your room and slip out again, and no one's the wiser."

"How do you know where my room is?"

"Uh..." Ted and Gordie exchanged glances.

I got it. Peggy. My roommate.

"Okay," I said with a sigh. "And we do *too* have wild parties." But not tonight, I hoped. Because by this time I just wanted to get it all done and crawl into my bed.

It was easier than I'd expected. We parked the car near the side entrance, where it was hidden by a row of cedars. The boys positioned themselves on either side of the Duke, his arms around their respective necks, and they really did look like a couple of frat boys escorting a drunken friend home from a party.

I waited just inside the door to let them in, then ran up the stairs. When the coast was clear, the three guys slipped into my room.

"Where do you want him?" Gordie asked, as if they were delivering a chesterfield.

I looked around. "In the chair, I guess." Probably lying down on Peggy's bed would have been better, but something about that idea unsettled me.

Within a few minutes, His Royal Highness, Philip Mountbatten, Duke of Edinburgh, was settled into my desk chair (fortunately with arms), sitting there in stately disdain.

"Okay, goodnight," I told the boys. "We'll talk tomorrow."

"Wait!" Ted cried. "We still have to—"

"Call me in the morning. You guys are leaving now, before anyone finds you."

They protested, but I escorted them down the stairs and practically kicked them out the door.

Back in my room, I regretted not having put my new roommate to bed, after all. He could have lain hidden under the bedspread. Now, I had to get undressed under his imperious gaze.

I got into bed, reminding myself my visitor was an insentient dummy, and that the real Duke of Edinburgh was sound asleep in the royal railway carriage, his arms around his princess. My last waking thought was, *Do they sleep together....?*

THE POUNDING on my door came all too early. I cracked my eyes open and nearly had a heart attack at the sight of a large, imposing man sitting across the room staring at me.

Right. The Duke.

"Who is it?" I called out in a voice far too loud for 6:30, while dragging my body out of bed.

"It's me. Alison," came the would-be whisper. "Open up. I can't stand out here yelling."

I opened the door a crack, blocking any possible view inside my room. "What is it?"

"There's a message for you." The bank of phones stood near Alison's room down the hall, and while she complained of being everyone's social secretary, I think she liked being in the know. "Some guy named Ted wants you to call him right away."

She pushed on the door to hand me a slip of paper, but I stood firm. This seemed to make her suspicious.

"Have you got a man in there?" She tried to look around me.

"Of *course* not."

"Because I know Peggy's away, and I thought I heard voices last night..."

Oh damn. As I hesitated, she managed to peer past me.

"You *do*—"

"Shut up!" I opened the door enough to drag her in and then shut it behind her.

Alison's mouth fell open at the sight of Princess Elizabeth's husband, sitting there in my desk chair, a look of —amusement?— on his handsome face.

Her expression held a mixture of shock and admiration.

I couldn't resist. "Alison, you must promise *never* to breathe a word of this to anyone. If anyone found out—if *Elizabeth* found out. Or the King..."

She shook her head emphatically and turned back to my visitor. I swear—she practically curtseyed.

"Oh no, of course not. Sir, your Highness—I mean, your, your Grace—"

I had to put her out of her misery.

"It's all right, Alison. He's just a waxwork." I stepped over and put my hand on my new boyfriend's knee. When he didn't react, Alison's mortification turned to fury.

It took me a good ten minutes to calm her down and explain it all, though granted, it sounded pretty foolish in the telling. Meanwhile, she kept stealing glances over at the Duke, perhaps not completely convinced of his inauthenticity.

I finally got her to leave, having sworn her to secrecy (for real this time) with an implied threat to reveal her naïveté about my having a tryst with the Duke of Edinburgh. Then, I got dressed and went down the hall to call Ted.

He wanted us all to meet in the Junior Common Room as soon as possible. At that hour on a Saturday, we'd have it to ourselves.

When I got back to my room, Alison was waiting at the door, looking even more distraught than before.

"Oh my gosh, Cathy. You are in big, *big* trouble."

I GOT to the JCR just before 8:00, to find Ted and Gordie, along with Peggy, who'd just arrived on the night train from Peterborough. Still no Donovan.

"Okay, let's move on to today's agenda," Gordie said as I closed the door.

"Never mind that. We have a problem. Put on the CBC news."

Peggy and Ted looked uneasy as Gordie switched on the radio. It took a long minute to warm up. After the lead stories involving the Royal Visit, the war in Korea, the Leafs' season opener tonight against Chicago, the announcer reached our event.

"And finally, in Toronto, His Royal Highness, the Duke of Edinburgh has gone missing. No, not the real one, but the wax figure at the Royal Ontario Museum. The effigy, along with that of Princess Elizabeth, is on loan from Madame Tussaud's in London as part of the celebration of the Royal Tour of Canada. It was last seen Friday night when the museum closed, and was discovered missing this morning."

"They didn't notice until morning?" Gordie said with glee. "Some guards!"

"Just listen," I snapped.

*"A spokesman for the museum says the thieves must be highly professional and well organized—*I noticed Ted smirk at this—*to have pulled off such a daring theft.*

"Madame Tussaud's creates images of members of the royal family only with special permission, and doesn't actually own the figures, all of which are possessions of the Crown. As such, in order to secure the loan of these waxworks, both the Canadian government and the Royal Ontario Museum had to post bonds to guarantee the safety of the figures. The Duke's figure has a value of 4,000 pounds, or over 12,000 dollars."

"Oh shit..." Gordie murmured. "For a wax dummy?"

"It's just a prank," Ted said, protesting to the room in general.

"I thought we agreed that's what it *wasn't*." Peggy said. "The whole idea was to make a political statement. Remember? *No figureheads.*"

Matters got worse with the nine o'clock news. It included an interview with Toronto's Chief Constable about security for the Royal visit.

"We're fully prepared for this sort of thing. Police at all levels across Canada have been issued with the identities of known anarchists, crackpots, and Reds in every city on the itinerary."

"So you think this theft might be part of a Communist plot?"

"Let's say we're not ruling it out. But rest assured, due to the seriousness of the theft, the RCMP may have to be called in."

The newscast ended and I switched off the radio. We all stood silent for a few seconds, then Gordie murmured, "The Mounties?"

"We need to return him..." Ted sounded far from confident.

"That's out of the question," Gordie said. "We wouldn't get within a hundred feet of the museum now."

"We'll leave him somewhere else," Peggy decreed. "A public place, but private enough we won't be seen."

Phone booth? Not enough room. Bus station? Too busy.

At length, we hit upon Allan Gardens. A public park with lots of tree cover. Not too far from here, but far enough to be unconnected with U of T.

THAT SATURDAY NIGHT IN TORONTO, the streets were relatively quiet following the tumultuous celebrations of the big day. Hundreds of thousands of royal watchers had gone home exhausted and happy, excitedly reliving their long-awaited once-in-a-lifetime moment.

Isn't he dreamy? She's so lovely! She looked right at me and smiled.

The diehards who hadn't yet got enough were down on Front Street waiting outside the Royal York Hotel, where a gala banquet was being held, while others were camped out by the York Street railway siding, where the royal carriage was parked for the duration of the visit.

Meanwhile, tonight was the season opener for the Toronto Maple Leafs. They were playing Chicago, and Maple Leaf Gardens would be jam packed, as always. Those without tickets would be home glued to their radios listening to the play-by-play from Foster Hewitt.

We would have the streets more or less to ourselves at ten p.m.

At nine, we began removing the Duke from my room. I recruited Alison's help to keep lookout at the far end of the hall. She didn't realize I was making her a conspirator to ensure keeping her mouth shut later on.

Peggy, still on the injured list, had a sedentary but crucial role to play. She was waiting in a late-night coffee shop at the corner of Gerrard and Sherbourne, kitty-corner from Allan Gardens.

We got my unwelcome guest back into Gordie's Hillman, and in a repeat of last night's arrangement, I got in beside him. This time, I tied a silk scarf over my hair, and put a tweed cap on Philip, to make him look a little less regal, more sporty.

It was a matter of some twelve blocks. We kept to the side streets until our final turn onto Gerrard, a few blocks from our destination.

And there was a police car. With a policeman. He signaled us to pull over.

"Oh shit," the guys murmured in unison.

Gordie rolled down the window, and I could hear his innocent, co-operative tones.

"Evening, constable. Anything wrong?"

"No sir. Just want to caution you one of your headlights is out."

"Oh. Yes, thank you. That's very helpful." I swear Gordie was ready to add, "my good man."

I suppose our collective nervousness was filling the air, because the policeman didn't move away, but leaned in closer and raised his flashlight. Before the beam could reach the back seat, I pulled my new sweetheart toward me in an embrace and planted a long, passionate kiss on his unresponsive lips.

"Uh, miss, are you all right?"

Did he think the Duke was attacking me?

Gordie jumped in. "Oh, she's fine. She and Phil just got engaged, so they're a bit lovey-dovey right now."

"We're just heading home from their big announcement party," Ted added. "He wants to introduce Cathy to his mother."

Shut up, Ted. I came up for air, and, keeping my fiancé turned away from the policeman, I smiled and tried to look starry-eyed. "I'm fine. Thank you for asking."

My would-be protector nodded. "Congratulations, Miss. Sir. And you, sir, be sure and get that light repaired on Monday."

"I will."

The constable stepped away. Gordie put the car in gear, and we drove on.

AFTER PARKING the car out of range of the streetlights, with the nearly full moon hidden behind a cloud, we carried the Duke through the darkened park to the statue of Robbie Burns, a few yards from the Sherbourne Street sidewalk. We arranged him on the broad base of the plinth, leaning back against the column. For good measure, Gordie put an empty bottle of Northern Spirit Rye on the step beside him.

Just as we stepped back to admire our handiwork, the moon emerged from behind the clouds. Bathed in the cool blue light, the Duke cut a rakish, romantic figure.

Satisfied, we returned to the car. The boys got in, ready for our getaway, while I dashed across the street to the coffee shop.

I gave Peggy a nod. She got up and maneuvered herself into the phone booth, crutches and all. I stood guard in the doorway, though no one was paying any attention; they were all captivated by the hockey game on the radio. Peggy called the police number and for some reason put on a plummy but not-terribly-convincing English accent.

"Yes, hello.... I wish to report a drunken reprobate hanging about Allan Gardens.... I was walking my dog along Sherbourne and saw this *man* sitting by the statue of Robert Burns. Just lolling there, desecrating the memory of the greatest poet that— no, certainly not! Well...he was dressed like a gentleman. In fact, I rather thought he looked like the Duke of Edinburgh, but I daresay — Oh, let's just say I'm a concerned citizen. Goodnight."

WE ALL NEEDED a drink after that, so we went round to Donovan's apartment to see if he was back from showing his mother a good time in the big city. It was late enough that she should be asleep, and we could tell Donovan how it had all panned out.

Just as we drove up to the apartment block, so did a taxi. The driver held the door open for a lady and gentleman, dressed no less elegantly than the royal waxworks. I took a second look. *Donovan—* in a tuxedo? The lady had to be his mother, in a formal dress, fur stole and—were those diamonds?

As the taxi drove off, we piled out of the Hillman and greeted the stylish couple. Donovan didn't look thrilled to see us, but made the introductions. Mrs. "Walter" Grant was delighted to meet us, her eyes filled with stars, glad to have someone to share her excitement with.

They had just come from the gala dinner at the Royal York Hotel. With the Princess and the Duke and nine hundred high-end invitees.

At last, I broke the stunned silence.

"How lovely for you, Mrs. Grant. Donovan never told us, uh..."

"Yes, Donnie was thrilled to step in as my escort tonight. His father, Justice Grant, hasn't been well lately."

"Uh, the Supreme Court Justice?" Gordie hazarded.

Mrs. Grant nodded and went on about Donnie's elegant bow and correct manners. "And Princess Elizabeth even chatted with him for a few moments."

Donovan mumbled something about getting his mother out of the night air. She bid us goodnight, and we watched them disappear into the building.

"I hope he was polite," I said.

WE TUNED in the news the next morning. The Princess and the Duke were leaving for Niagara Falls at noon, following one last public outing at Riverdale Park; the Leafs had blown the game against Chicago 3-1; and the missing waxwork of the Duke of Edinburgh had been restored unharmed to its rightful place at the ROM. No mention was made of his moonlight carousing in Allan Gardens or the anonymous phone call to the police. Whether the theft was still deemed the work of anarchists and Reds was not mentioned.

At last, I went off to keep my date with my sisters and 100,000 other royalty lovers, all held at bay by stalwart Boy Scouts and valiant Girl Guides, as the motorcade circled Riverdale Park. Listening to the resounding cheers of the rapturous crowds, it was clear to me that not one of these people, myself included, would give a damn if we'd actually made some kind of anti-monarchist statement using our friend the Duke.

And as for Donovan—Donnie—had we really allowed ourselves to be so bedazzled by all that pseudo-anarchist rhetoric, hiding his high-class background and his ease with royalty, that we'd risked possible expulsion and loss of our various scholarships?

As I said, we should have known better.

When the car swung past us, bearing the stars of the commonwealth in all their glory, my youngest sister grabbed my arm.

"Did you see that? She looked right at me! She smiled at me!"

"Wonderful!" I said. But I knew better.

The Princess had looked right at *me*.

She was *not* smiling.

KM ROCKWOOD

KM Rockwood draws on a varied background for her stories, including blue collar jobs in steel fabrication and glass making, and supervising inmate work crews in a large state prison. Now retired from working as a special education teacher in correctional facilities, inner city schools, and alternative schools, she spends her time writing and caring for her family and pets. Published works include the Jesse Damon Crime Novel series and numerous short stories. KM's stories also appear in *The Best Laid Plans* and *Heartbreaks & Half-truths*, the first and second books in the Superior Shores anthology series. KM is a member of Sisters in Crime National, Chesapeake, and Guppy Chapters, and the Short Mystery Fiction Society. Find her at www.kmrockwood.com.

DEAD ON THE BEACH

KM ROCKWOOD

OLIVER WAS MY BIG BROTHER. He wasn't supposed to die like that.

I knew Oliver was no saint. But when our parents were killed in a car crash, he pulled himself together to make sure that his little sister didn't end up in some group foster home. He got a legitimate job and rented a reasonable apartment, giving me the chance to finish high school. I worked hard at both academics and athletics, honing my pitching skills into a softball scholarship to college. I found a job with a future at an investment bank and never looked back.

But Oliver drifted and returned to his world of petty crimes and drugs and get-rich-quick schemes.

That was seven years ago. We kept in touch sporadically. Recently, in one of his semi-coherent phone calls, he told me he was getting older and that it was time to rethink his life. He moved to Cape Cod from Bridgeport, swearing he was putting the drugs behind him once and for all, and picked up a job renovating summer rentals.

Now he was dead. The autopsy results weren't in yet, but according to the police report, someone found him in the light of a full moon, face down in mere inches of frigid bay water at high tide on a freezing December night. With a gash on the back of his head.

I'd come to pick up his ashes from the funeral home. Then I went to gather his pathetic possessions from a cottage he shared with a roommate named Harvey. The cottage was part of a tourist complex where Oliver and Harvey worked fixing roofs and painting exteriors battered by the salt winds off the bay.

Harvey wasn't home, but the property manager let me in.

The inside of the cottage smelled of must and salt marsh. The fire in the wood burning stove was banked and did nothing to dispel the damp chill. I shivered, not entirely because of the cold.

The manager stood by as I gathered Oliver's scant possessions— a sleeping bag, a trash bag full of worn clothes—I felt a huge lump in my throat and was having trouble forming words.

But I had to know how this had happened.

"What..." My voice was so weak I could hardly hear myself. I cleared my throat and tried again. "What was Oliver doing out on the beach on a cold night like that anyhow?"

The manager raised his eyebrows. "Turtle patrol."

"Turtle patrol?"

"Yep. This time of year, the turtles migrate south for the winter. Some of them get caught in the bay and trapped. It gets colder and colder, and if they can't find their way out to the open ocean, they get cold-stunned. Then they can't move, and they get washed up on the beach at high tide."

"What does the turtle patrol do about it?"

"They go out on the beach and look for stranded turtles. They cover 'em with seaweed to keep the wind off and mark the spot. Then they report in and a team goes to pick them up and takes them to a rehab."

"And that's what Oliver was doing? Saving turtles?"

"Yep. He went out about once a week."

"Was this a job or something?"

"No. It's all volunteer."

My heart warmed just a tad. Oliver had selflessly volunteered to save turtles. That was the Oliver I wanted to remember.

But it led to his death. I felt my heart go cold again.

"What happened?"

The manager shrugged. When a rickety car pulled up outside, he said, "That's Harvey. He can help if you need it," and left.

Harvey came in. "Get all of Oliver's stuff?" He looked longingly at the flat screen TV in the dingy living room.

"Is the TV Oliver's?" I asked. I was having trouble using the past tense when I talked about Oliver.

"Yep."

"You can keep it if you want it. I have a TV, and that would be hard to transport."

Harvey brightened. "Thanks. Need any help getting stuff to your car?"

"Not much to carry, thanks." I hesitated, but if anybody knew anything, it was likely to be Harvey. "Do you know what happened to Oliver? The manager said he was on turtle patrol."

"Yeah. Oliver did that. Seems like he got hit in the head somehow. Must've fell face down in the water. And drowned. Bum luck."

I shivered. "How'd he get hit in the head?"

"Who knows. But a real wind was blowing that night. He was found not far from a lobster shack. You know, where they sell lobster rolls. The sign was gone from its mounting. Maybe it blew off and hit him from behind or something."

"Who found him?"

"Somebody from the turtle patrol. They pulled him out of the water and called 911, but it was too late to do anything."

Hoping they could tell me something, I decided to go talk to the people who coordinated the turtle patrol. I thought it was pretty crass that they hadn't contacted me. After all, Oliver died doing work for them. Volunteer work.

Righteous indignation crowding out some of my grief, I headed toward the wildlife sanctuary in Wellfleet that coordinated the turtle patrols. Several people were leaving as I pulled up.

"We're just closing up. Can I help you?" one woman asked as I got out of my car.

I felt myself tearing up. "I'd like to know about Oliver Swendall. He was my brother."

"Oliver Swendall?" The woman looked at those behind her. "Was he the one who..." Her voice trailed off.

I squared my shoulders. "Drowned?"

"Yes. I'm so sorry for your loss. How can we help you?"

"He was on the beach late at night. Full moon. High tide." I stared at her.

"So I understand."

"On turtle patrol." I spit out the words.

The woman blinked. "Turtle patrol? Really?"

"Don't you keep records of the volunteers you have out there on the beaches?"

"Yes. Of course, yes. But I'm pretty sure we don't have any records of Oliver Swendall going out for us. Or volunteering."

"He was out there."

The woman turned to someone behind her. "Reggie? You coordinate that section near Barnstable. That's where the man was found. Do you know anything about Oliver Swendall volunteering for turtle patrol?"

A man stepped forward. "No. That night, I was on patrol. As a matter of fact, I was the one who found the body and called 911. I'd seen him—or somebody who looked like him, it's hard to tell in the dark—a few times before, but I never talked to him. We certainly never had him on turtle patrol."

I felt like I'd been hit in the gut. "But then what was he doing out on the beach?"

"Good question." The man pulled his jacket closer around him. "Sometimes people walk along the beach at night. They like the solitude. Like I said, I never talked to him."

If Oliver wasn't on turtle patrol, what was he doing out there? Walking on the beach at night for solitude didn't sound like Oliver.

"Was it always at high tide you saw him?"

"Yeah, but high tide was the only time I was out. That's when the turtles wash up. He could have been out there other times."

"Was it always the same man you saw?"

"Like I said before, I don't know for sure. Might not even have been a man. Could have been a woman, the way we have to bundle up to stay warm out there."

There were probably a thousand other things I wanted to know, but I felt tears welling up at the thought of Oliver alone on the windswept beach, staring out into the dark bay. I thanked them and went to my car in the parking lot.

I sat in the driver's seat and watched as the others left.

The late afternoon sun slanted over the marshes. *The beach*, I thought. I wanted to see the beach where Oliver had drowned. I pulled out the report I'd gotten from the police. It was very brief, written in the static language that such reports often are, but it told me which beach and included a sketch of the exact location where his body had been found.

I pulled out a map of the area. It wasn't a far drive. If I hurried, I could get there before dark.

The lobster shack was at the edge of the small parking lot, boarded up for the season. Blowing sand skittered across low dunes. A single lamppost stood where a gap in the dunes looked out over the restless gray water.

A cold wind whipped across the sand from the bay, reaching icy fingers down the neck of my jacket at I got out of my car. The rank smell of ebb tide tickled my nose.

Maybe the sand and the sea would be magnificent on a sunny afternoon, despite the cold. But why would anyone come out in the darkness on a windy night, even in the light of a full moon?

Clutching the police report with its map, I headed toward the lamppost and the beach.

A movement near the lobster shack caught my eye.

Someone was pulling on one of the boarded-up doors.

I stopped, unsure whether I should proceed. Who was this person? Were they trying to break in?

The person turned to face me. It was a middle-aged woman. "Hi, there!" she called. "Just come to check on everything. A lot of wind and rain lately."

She was just checking on her business premises. Breathing a sigh of relief, and chiding myself for being such a scaredy-cat, I went up to her. Perhaps she could tell me something about the area.

Walking around to the side of the building facing the beach, she grabbed one of the shutters and gave it a tug. It held. "Spring tide tonight." She gave another shutter a tug. "No telling how far the spray will reach." She walked to the edge of the concrete patio in front of the shack. "Or how high the water will rise."

"Spring tide?" I looked down at the churning water, still far down the beach. "It's the middle of winter."

The woman laughed. "Spring tides come all year round. They're the especially high tides that come when the sun and the moon are in line with each other. Around the full moon."

She stepped back and examined the lobster shack. "Would you believe that, when I was a girl, this shack used to be back behind dunes? Now it's at the edge of the beach. Talk about erosion."

I looked at the sign bracket over the building's porch by the front steps. Had there been a sign there that had blown off, hitting poor Oliver in the head? And knocking him face down in the water?

"Is that where your sign blew off the other night?" I nodded at the empty bracket.

"Oh, no," she said. "We take it down any time there was any indication of a strong wind. And we don't leave it up in the winter at all. When the shack's closed, it's stored in the pantry."

No sign? Then it couldn't be what hit Oliver and knocked him unconscious.

I glanced around. A pile of driftwood lay just above the high tide line. A length of two-by-four leaned against a notice by the end of the parking lot, warning of sharks. "I guess if the wind were strong enough, it could pick up all kinds of things and blow them around."

"Oh, yes. The wind can be very powerful. Last week, the wind was so strong one morning it knocked over an entire picnic table and moved it a few feet. We decided to put them all in storage."

"Wasn't it pretty strong one night last week, too?"

The woman shook her head. "No, I don't think so. My son fishes, and he keeps a close eye on the weather watches and warnings. No point in taking stupid chances and going out if there's a weather watch."

"But somebody told me there was one night when the wind really picked up just about high tide, when they do the turtle patrol."

"Somebody's wrong. It's been pretty calm at night. That one storm that blew the picnic table started just before dawn and was over by noon."

Confused, I looked away from her and squinted at the moon. I could probably stop by the local public library and check the newspaper weather reports for the last week or so. But why would Harvey tell me it was windy if it wasn't?

And if it wasn't windy, and the lobster shack sign was put away, what had hit Oliver in the back of the head?

I was no closer to figuring out what had happened to Oliver. In fact, I seemed to have backtracked on any reasonable explanation that I'd been forming. I went back to my car and pulled out the police report to read it again. Its stilted language was heavy on facts, including the visible wound in the back of Oliver's head, but offered no opinions or speculations.

Would going out on the beach tonight at high tide give me any insights? I didn't see how it would, but then, I didn't see anything else that might be helpful, either. Maybe I would see what Oliver had found so appealing about it.

After a quick supper, I found a hardware store to buy a flashlight. The store was one of those that sell combinations of everyday necessities and souvenir merchandise which abound on Cape Cod.

As I waited in line to pay for my new flashlight, complete with batteries and bright LED lights, I noticed a display of snow globes. Among them was one of a solitary figure standing on the shore, gazing out toward a tiny sailboat painted on the horizon. To me, the figure looked haunted and sad. Was he perhaps looking for meaning in a lonely world? It reminded me of Oliver.

I grabbed the snow globe and put it down on the counter with the flashlight. As these tourist-attracting things tend to be, it was outrageously expensive, but I bought it anyway.

When I got outside, I pulled it out of the bag and stared at it.

It was heavy and sturdy, made of glass, but the figure inside was cheap plastic, the sailboat a crude painting, and when I shook it the globe rained glitter instead of imitation snow.

A waste of money. I stuck it into my pocket, grabbed the flashlight, and climbed into my car. High tide tonight was soon after dusk, not late the way it had been the night Oliver was found.

I pulled into the parking lot beyond the lobster shack. I could hear the water in the bay swirling and gargling. The wind wasn't particularly vicious, but the numbing cold crept through my boots and gloves.

In the rapidly gathering gloom, I walked up to the lobster shack and turned on the flashlight. I could see that the water had risen to lick at the concrete patio surrounding it. I turned the flashlight off and tried to clear my mind.

Standing on the patio, I stared out into the darkness. The sharp tang of salt water made me sneeze. A shimmering path of light led out over the water, fading when clouds scuttled over the full moon, only to reappear as the clouds continued their flight across the sky.

A few additional lights blinked on the surface of the water. Odd. I peered toward the source. A boat, perhaps? The blinking had some kind of rhythm, almost like a code. It stopped.

Flicking on the flashlight, I shone it in that direction and swept it back and forth a few times over the surface of the water, but it was much too far for me to see anything.

The blinking started up again. I was concentrating so hard I didn't hear anyone coming up behind me.

"What are you up to?"

I spun around. "Harvey! What are you doing here?"

"I might ask you the same thing, but I'm pretty sure I know the answer." Harvey stood a few yards away from me, one hand in his pocket and the other behind his back.

"What do you mean?"

"Apparently Oliver told you about his little operation. And when the next shipment was due in. Not to mention how to signal the suppliers that it was okay to deliver."

"What are you talking about?" I glanced around nervously, suddenly aware of how isolated this beach was at night.

Harvey laughed. "Oliver thought they were so clever. Get deliveries at night by drone from a boat and bringing them to Provincetown the next morning. Great market there. Even if somebody's watching for him at the two bridges onto the Cape, Oliver could get his cocaine through. Not that it did him any good."

"Oliver used cocaine?" Somehow, that didn't surprise me.

"Sure did." The moonlight shining on Harvey's face distorted his grin into a grimace. "I told him and told him he needed to deliver first, then he could use. But as soon as the shipment arrived, it'd be going right up his nose."

I stepped back. "Well, I'll be going now—"

"Not so fast." Harvey pulled a piece of two-by-four from behind his back. "Won't that be sad? Oliver's little sister dies the same way he did. How could she manage that? But she does."

He raised the piece of lumber and leaned forward.

I looked around, desperate. The water was at my back. Dunes rose on either side. The only way out was past Harvey. I'd never make it. The flashlight wasn't much of a weapon, but it was the best I had. I gripped it and steadied myself. At least I'd go down fighting.

As I shifted to take a battle stance, a hard lump banged against my hip.

Of course. The snow globe. I switched the flashlight to my other hand and shined it in Harvey's eyes as I reached into my pocket. My hand closed on the globe.

Yanking it out of my pocket, I used my best softball pitcher's grip and let fly with a fastball. Right at Harvey's head.

It connected. His expression went from startled to slack as the globe connected. He sank to the ground, dropping the two-by-four.

I stepped forward and grabbed the two-by-four, in case he was just momentarily stunned, but he lay there unmoving.

A buzzing sound approached from behind me. I whipped around, raising the two-by-four.

A drone. It zipped up next to me and hovered.

Without thinking, I smashed it. Its buzz skipped into an uneven lurch, wobbled a few yards further and tumbled to the ground. A slight scent of machine oil rose from it. It hiccupped a few times and lay still.

"What's going on here?" Reggie, from the turtle patrol, stepped around the corner of the lobster shack. "I saw the lights from down the beach and..."

He stared at Harvey, lying still on the sand.

Shivering, I said, "I'm not completely sure, but we need to call 911."

I wasn't happy about it, but I was pretty sure I'd figured out what had happened to my big brother. May he rest in peace.

SUSAN JANE WRIGHT

Susan Jane Wright was a lawyer and executive in the energy sector before she became a writer. Her nonfiction has appeared in *Alberta Views* and other newspapers. A regular guest on TV, radio talk shows, and podcasts, she received a PIA Public Interest Award and the Canadian Law Blog Award for her legal blog, *Susan on the Soapbox*. A career highlight was interviewing Beverley McLachlin, former Chief Justice of the Supreme Court, for Wordfest. *Madeline in the Moonlight* is her first fiction publication credit. Her novel, *Cat with a Bone*, was shortlisted for the 2021 Crime Writers of Canada Awards of Excellence for Best Unpublished Manuscript. She lives in Calgary, Alberta, with her husband and two daughters. Find her at https://susanjanewright.ca/ .

MADELINE IN THE MOONLIGHT

SUSAN JANE WRIGHT

SOMETHING HIT the floor and shattered into a thousand tiny pieces. I stepped out of the shower, slipped into Mom's cotton bathrobe and flung the bathroom door wide open. "Dammit Moriarty," I yelled at the cat, "I knew it was a mistake bringing you here."

A man was standing in the kitchen, his face turned away from me. Moriarty meowed loudly and rubbed his head on the man's shoe. The man wiggled his foot to shake him off.

"What do you think you're doing?" For some reason I decided the circumstances—half-naked thirty something woman confronting an intruder in her recently deceased mother's house—called for bravado. I squared my shoulders and thrust out my elbows, trying to look as big as possible. He turned his head and I recognized him.

"Jeez, Peter you scared the life out of me. What are you doing here?" Peter was Mom's baby brother. She'd practically raised him after their parents were killed, though they'd lost touch as adults. Peter became a globe-trotting concert violinist and Mom, a successful artist. Quite an achievement for two orphans raised by assorted relatives in the dust and tumbleweeds of a small prairie town.

"How did you get in here?" I asked.

Peter stared at me blankly for a moment. He was wearing the same elegant suit he had worn to the memorial service earlier today. For some reason he made me uncomfortable, and I tightened the belt of Mom's bathrobe around my waist.

"I just wanted to see how you girls were holding up," he said.

"We're still in shock. It was all so sudden." I glanced at the obituary notice lying next to a stack of papers on Mom's cluttered desk. The obit had been unbelievably difficult to write and I'm a lawyer, words are the tools of my trade. My sister Claire said Mom was not the kind of woman one would describe as sweet, gentle, or kind to all living creatures. Sure, she was loving, but she was also impulsive, unorthodox, and had a hair trigger temper. And she certainly did not expect to be welcomed into God's loving arms, assuming she believed in Him in the first place. Then there was the tricky bit around Mom's estranged brother, Peter, and the fact that neither Claire nor I had any idea who our fathers were. We decided the best course of action was to keep it brief. The obit barely ran to five lines. I was concerned no one would show up but the hall was packed. The memorial service lasted twice as long as we expected because so many mourners insisted on describing how privileged they felt to have been a part of Mom's amazing life. When the service was over, they clustered around the cocktail tables guzzling wine and devouring appetizers until the food ran out. It was exactly the kind of bang-up wake Mom would have enjoyed.

When it was finally over Claire and I returned to Mom's house, exhausted. Claire changed and went for a walk down by the beach while I had a steaming hot shower...and now found myself standing damp in the hallway staring down Mom's brother.

The patio door slid open and the chirp of songbirds broke the uncomfortable silence. Claire was back. Moriarty leapt off the sofa and made figure eights around her legs.

"The door is off its runner again," Claire muttered as she stooped to pick up Moriarty. I said Peter had dropped in to check on us. Perhaps she could put the kettle on while I got dressed? She stared at him for a moment before proceeding to the galley kitchen to assemble the teapot, mugs, and cookies.

"Oh, and your cat broke something," I glared at Moriarty who was purring loudly, the image of feline innocence. It would take hours to find the bits of whatever it was that crashed to the floor and disappeared under the mismatched furniture, giant pottery jugs, wire sculptures, and assorted handwoven rugs.

Years ago, Mom purchased two brightly colored beach huts— she called them beach boxes—and towed them to this heavily forested lot on the outskirts of the village. Her idea was to push the beach boxes together and convert them into a cozy home and studio. The bulldozer guys were under strict instructions to rip out only the trees that absolutely had to go. The bulldozers spent a week piling evergreens and dogwoods into an untidy pile in the backyard. Despite complaints from the neighbours, who thought the unsightly mess would destroy their property values, the heap became a permanent fixture.

The following summer, when the temperature soared to the high 30s and the humidity was at 80 percent, Mom invited the neighbors' kids over to explore the Fairy Forest, the tangle of tree trunks, wildflowers, vines, and moss that was slowly commandeering the back half of her lot. She sprayed the kids with the garden hose at random intervals to make their adventure even more exciting as they crept deeper and deeper into the leafy grotto. When they finally emerged, covered in pine needles, she fed them pixie pillows and nectar (marshmallows and lemonade) before sending them on their way. All summer long children shrieked in Mom's backyard and eventually their parents stopped complaining about the artist who lived at the end of the lane.

Last week, that's where her neighbor found her, barely alive under a bower of broken branches, ferns, and dripping salal leaves. She was groggy and confused with a blue-gray bruise on her cheek and three broken ribs. Her small body had stopped shivering hours ago. The medics rushed her to the local hospital, where she was treated for hypothermia, but she died four days later.

I flew in from Edmonton to Victoria the minute we got word. Claire met me at the airport, and we tore up the Island highway trying to convince ourselves everything would be all right. We sat by her bedside, day after day, talking quietly and holding her hand until it was all over.

I pushed the memory out of my mind as I pulled on my jeans and T-shirt. When I returned to the kitchen, I found Peter and Claire sitting at opposite ends of the cedar plank that serves as a kitchen island. Claire was pouring honey from a sticky plastic bottle into her mug. She stirred it thoughtfully with an Ogopogo spoon. Peter's eyes flicked around the tiny kitchen.

Claire broke the silence. "Mom said you visited her in the hospital."

Peter stopped, a cookie halfway to his lips. "Yeah, she didn't know who I was."

"The nurses said you upset her, and they made you leave."

"Yeah, well, like I said, she didn't recognize me. She flew off the handle and Nurse Ratchet threw me out."

"The nurses said you argued with her." Claire was watching Peter carefully.

"That's ridiculous." Peter glanced over his shoulder into the living room. "She didn't have to live like this, you know." He waved one arm in the general direction of the sofa, a green velvet lump wedged between two dark rattan end tables. "Was she trying to make a statement? 'Look at me, I'm a starving artist.'" He sniffed and took a sip of his tea.

That was unfair. Mom was eccentric, but she wasn't a slob.

But Claire would not drop it. My little sister can be really stubborn sometimes. "Why are you here, Peter?"

"Well, there's the matter of her estate."

"What? You've got to be kidding." Now it was my turn to get annoyed. "Other than this property, and some unsold paintings in her studio, there's nothing of value."

A splotch of color appeared on Peter's neck. "Nevertheless, we were family, all we had was each other, I'm entitled to my share."

"She had us," I said, anger rising. "We're her family. You disappeared thirty years ago." Peter swung around in his chair to face me. The blotch on his neck had spread to his cheeks. He was starting to light up like a Christmas tree.

"I'm on the road from March to December, you know that. Flying all over this godforsaken planet from Lisbon to Sydney and back again. Eighty to ninety performances a year. I have no time to see anyone."

And yet you find time to live the good life in your fancy condo in Toronto and your cabin at Whistler.

Claire raised an eyebrow warning me off. I'm not as stubborn as she is, I let it go.

Peter pushed back his chair and stood up. "I have to get going. Meeting some friends for drinks, then driving back down to Victoria tonight."

I looked out the patio doors. The afternoon sun was tangled in the tall evergreens surrounding the house. It would be dark soon. I walked Peter to the door, which took all of three seconds, while Claire disappeared down the hall without saying goodbye.

"Make sure you latch it securely," she called out to me after Peter had left.

I had to jiggle the patio door in its frame before the locking mechanism would catch. "Claire, did you lock up before you went out this afternoon? I can't figure out how he got in here."

She spooned wet cat food and kibble into Moriarty's dish. His purrbox went into overdrive. I stoked his grey and white head. "You're easy to please, aren't you? That's why you're so fat."

"He's not fat." Claire said, indignantly. "He's just big-boned."

"He shouldn't be here," I said.

"Moriarty?"

"No, not Moriarty, Peter." I slipped back onto the chair at the island and poured myself a second cup of tea. "Why is he here and what was he doing at the hospital? How did he even know Mom was ill?"

"Who knows. Maybe he's got Mom on google alert or something." Claire set Moriarty's dish down on the floor and the cat took a delicate bite of the something only a cat would like.

"Why would he care what Mom is doing after all these years? He certainly had no time for her before."

Claire looked at me thoughtfully. She may be two years younger than me but she's much more practical. Probably a good trait for a doctor. I've always been the inquisitive one, maybe that's why I went into law. Then I smiled. Mom may have been unconventional, but she'd been extremely proud of her girls with traditional careers.

I suggested a walk to the village and pizza for dinner. Claire liked the idea and we rummaged around in Mom's studio searching for a flashlight, knowing we'd need it for the walk home, grabbed our jackets off the coat rack, and, after fiddling with the key for a minute, managed to lock the patio door. We crunched down the gravel lane and turned onto the tarmac leading down the hill to the main road. The village, a cluster of odd little buildings, a gas station, a grocery store, a pub, and a pizza shop, lay at the intersection of the road and the highway.

The screen door of the pizza shop snapped shut behind us as we entered. The regulars lifted their heads to check us out. We settled at a two-top near the window and debated for a few minutes whether to split one large pizza or order two small ones. After we placed our order—two small ones—Claire leaned closer to me and said, "I keep thinking how tiny she looked in that hospital bed."

Claire was right. Mom was small to begin with; under the thin white sheet she'd looked as frail as a bird. "Remember when she opened her eyes and recognized us?" We'd been by Mom's bedside for a couple of hours when she suddenly clutched the sheet and said, 'Oh good, you made it.' Notwithstanding her matter-of-fact tone, her breathing was labored. We begged her not to talk, but she shook her head, black curls bouncing on the white pillowcase, saying there wasn't much time. She gripped our hands and made us promise to take care of each other, "You're sisters," she said, "you're all each other has." Then she coughed and said, "Take care of the Schnabel and it will take care of you. Promise me." *Schnabel? Like the artist?* I glanced at Claire. From the look on her face, she had no idea what Mom was talking about either, but we made the promise anyway. That seemed to ease Mom's mind because she relaxed and closed her eyes. A few minutes later her eyes popped open again; she glanced from me to Claire and said, "Peter is a shifty one, watch him." She pressed her lips together but did not say another word. Her breathing became more irregular and around 10:30 it stopped.

"Claire, is she asleep?" I asked quietly.

Claire eyes brimmed with tears. "No Sylvie, she's not." We continued to murmur to each other and stroke Mom's hands until it was time to say good-bye.

I was jolted out of the memory when our server reappeared and set two small pizzas down in front of us. I waited while he topped up our wine glasses before speaking again. "Do you want to start sorting through her stuff tomorrow? The sooner we get that done and put the property on the market, the sooner we'll get back to normal."

"Normal?" Claire sighed. "I'm not sure what normal looks like anymore now that Mom is gone."

It was inky black outside by the time we finished dinner. I couldn't bear to live in a place as small and isolated as the village, but I had to admit the stars in the moonless sky twinkled much brighter here than in the city.

"Are you ready to trek up the big hill?" Claire asked.

"You bet," I said. "Race you."

"You're kidding."

"Yes, I'm kidding." I chuckled as I pulled the flashlight out of my backpack and we reminisced as we followed its wobbly beam up the hill. Both of us were panting slightly when we reached the gravel lane leading to Mom's house. Light spilled out of the windows painting the tangled garden yellow and black.

"Claire, did you leave—"

"Someone's in the house." Claire broke into a sprint. "Moriarty. If he gets out I'll never find him." She flew down the gravel path, sliding on the tiny stones that shifted under her feet, and tore open the patio door.

"Claire, wait!" I yelled. *She's worried about that bloody cat when there's an intruder in the house?*

Claire glanced around the living room, frantically calling his name. There was movement at the end of the hall. Not Moriarty. A dark shape disappeared into the bedroom. The door slammed shut.

By the time I pushed it open he was gone. The night air whistled through the open window where the screen had been twisted out of shape.

I found Claire in the kitchen. Her arms were wrapped around Moriarty who blinked sleepily at us. She was crying. I hugged them both until Moriarty squeezed out of her arms and dropped indignantly to the floor.

That's when I looked into the living room.

"Claire," I said slowly, "look." She wiped her eyes with her sleeve.

Mom was an abstract landscape artist—her canvases swam with cool blues, blacks, grays, and greens—but her love of art was eclectic, with many different painting styles represented on her walls. Her house may be a chaotic jumble of furniture and dried flowers, but the art on her walls was hung with a level of precision that would rival the Louvre.

Claire inhaled sharply. Some paintings tilted this way and that like bits of glass in a broken kaleidoscope, others were stacked in willy-nilly piles on the floor. She went directly to the painting across from the wood stove and straightened it. "Look at this mess," she said. "Mom would have a fit."

"It's that wretched Peter," I said, "it's got to be."

It took us over an hour to rehang and realign the paintings, a process made more difficult by Moriarty playing gotcha with our shoes.

"What was Peter looking for," I muttered, "a wall safe? This is a beach box house, not his condo in Toronto."

"Clearly he's looking for something." Claire said. She paused. "You don't think...?"

"The Schnabel?" I stepped back and looked at the paintings facing me. "Mom could never afford a Schnabel." Claire agreed. She made a pot of tea and we sat in the living room staring at the walls.

I said, "I don't know about you, but I'm too wired to sleep now."

"Me too. Let's start sorting out Mom's stuff."

"Yeah, well I was thinking of watching TV or something, but okay, we may as well do something productive."

I said I'd tackle the studio while Claire started on Mom's bedroom. The studio side of the beach box is the mirror image of the living quarters but without the clutter. Spare white walls and a steeply sloped skylit roof flooded the studio with luminous light in the daytime. Large patio doors opened out onto a cobblestone terrace and the Fairy Forest. A half-finished painting lay on a large square table—an abstract rendering of a small red-roofed building tucked into a grove of fluffy green and gray trees. Mom had just started working on the clouds. A dozen paintings were propped against the walls. In a corner sat a battered blue steamer truck. The brass latch was broken.

I knelt before the trunk and opened the lid. Inside were a stack of photo albums and two boxes. The chocolate box contained some brightly coloured buttons, a small ring, some gritty shells, and a miniature Coca Cola bottle attached to a key chain. A large, flat box held our report cards and yellowing newspaper clippings describing our achievements (Claire took second prize in the Science Fair when she was in grade 6). I smiled when I found an inexpensive picture frame holding the origami bird I made for Mom when she turned thirty. Claire's lumpy clay dragon, I think it was a pencil holder, was wrapped in newspaper next to it.

"You're supposed to be working, not wandering down memory lane." Claire was standing behind me, a bulging green garbage bag in her arms.

"Look at this stuff, Claire." I sat back on my heels while she rummaged in the trunk. She produced a large plastic folder containing menus and beer mats from French cafes and Italian bars.

"This must be from her first trip to Europe, she won that scholarship when she was eighteen." Mom would become very animated when she described where she went and who she met on her two-month adventure in Paris and Rome.

"What's this?" I slipped a framed poster out of a wrinkled paper bag. It was a map of ancient Rome. Claire said it looked like a souvenir poster, a bit kitschy for Mom's taste. I agreed and wondered why she kept it all these years.

The twisted hanging wire on the back scratched my wrist as I slid the poster back into the paper bag and I noticed a slight bulge in the brown backing paper. Something was sandwiched between the poster and the backing paper glued to the picture frame. I asked Claire to pass me the box cutters lying on the paint splattered table.

"Why?" she asked.

"There's something in here." I made a small slit in the backing paper and ripped it off. Lying inside the frame was a thin rectangular package wrapped in acid free paper. I put the package on the floor between us and slowly unwrapped it.

"It's another poster." Claire said.

"No, it's not."

It was a pen and ink sketch touched with gouache. A portrait of a woman with glossy black hair, dark eyes, and thinly arched brows. Moonlight traced the contours of her pale face and the pearly gray folds of her dress.

"Oh my god Claire, it's Mom."

Claire took the drawing from me and peered at the scribbled signature on the back. *R Schnabel, June 1982.*

With trembling hands, she lay the drawing down on the acid free paper. Just then Moriarty galloped into the studio heading straight for us; he loves to sprawl on discarded newspapers. Claire caught him by the collar before he could fling his furry body down on top of the drawing and carried him out to the bedroom. He yowled in protest when she stuffed him into his carrying crate.

I pulled out my phone and googled Schnabel's name and the year. Images of a painting titled *Madeline in the Moonlight* floated across my screen. I clicked another link. Art critics said the painting was an enigma. The pale young woman in the deep blue dress was a fine example of Schnabel's work during his brooding period, but he painted it much later in his career, after he had become famous producing the radiant paintings that defined his golden period. Schnabel refused to explain this anomaly or identify his model, Madeline. The furor over the model's identity intensified when

Schnabel committed suicide a few months after the painting was sold to a wealthy collector in Switzerland.

I related all this to Claire when she returned to the studio. She stared at the image on my phone. Even reduced to pixels on a glass screen the painting was breathtaking.

"He's captured her essence very well," she said quietly.

"It's stunning, isn't it?"

She gripped my arm. "Sylvie. This is it. This is what Peter is looking for. It's probably worth a small fortune."

"Right, but it's Mom's fortune, not his."

Claire shook her head at me. "You know for a lawyer you can be pretty dense sometimes. The drawing is part of Mom's estate, it belongs to us."

Take care of the Schnabel and it will take care of you.

The following morning, we woke early, made a couple of phone calls, set up a couple of meetings, and packed everything we needed into Claire's car. We were heading to Victoria.

I called Peter when we reached the highway and asked him to join us for lunch at a little café in Oak Bay. Claire was flying down the Malahat in her usual reckless fashion, so we had plenty of time to get there.

"It's all set," I said after I hung up. "He's agreed to meet us at 1:30 at Blighty's...assuming you don't kill us on the highway first."

Claire just smiled.

We spotted Peter at the back of the restaurant when we arrived. He was sitting in a dark booth in the corner, methodically folding and unfolding a large white napkin.

"Promise me you won't hit him," I whispered to Claire as we approached Peter's booth.

"Depends on how he reacts to our news."

We eased onto the bench opposite Peter and made small talk until the server took our orders and disappeared. Then I began.

"Peter," I said, "we want to talk to you about Mom's estate."

His eyes danced. "It should be a two-way split, half for me as her brother and half for you two as her kids."

Claire choked on her water. I nudged her under the table and continued. "No, that's not how it's going to work. We met with our lawyer this morning. He confirmed that all of Mom's estate comes to us."

Peter clenched his jaw, his eyes darted from me to Claire and back again.

Claire said, "And you should also know...we found it."

The color drained from his face. "Found what?"

"The Schnabel drawing. It was in the steamer trunk and now it's in our lawyer's safe."

Peter reached for his cup. Coffee slopped over the rim and splashed onto the table. He cursed and dabbed at it with a crumpled napkin.

The server returned with our food. Peter sat back in his seat, drumming his fingers on the table while the server positioned the plates in front of us. When the server left Peter said, "No. The Schnabel is mine. She told me as much."

"Oh, really," I said. "When?"

He looked over my shoulder into the street before responding. "When she came back from Europe, the first time. She said the drawing was my souvenir. I said I didn't want it. What did I know, I was just a kid. But I need it now."

Claire snorted, "I don't believe you."

"No, really." He focused on Claire. "You don't understand how tough it is out there. All these young kids coming up through the ranks, grabbing bookings and taking concert slots that by rights should be mine."

I raised my eyebrows and said, "Oh, please, Peter, you've had a long run. You've earned more than enough money to set yourself up for a comfortable retirement."

Claire cut me off. "That's not what I meant when I said I don't believe you. I was talking about Mom. She would never give you the Schnabel. She knew you, Peter. Even as a kid you were nothing but flash. You'd just sell it and buy yourself a trinket, a Rolex or something."

We all glanced at his wrist. He was wearing a Rolex.

He adjusted his shirt sleeve. "So what? That's what you're going to do with it, sell it." He stared steadily at us, daring us to deny it.

"As a matter of fact, we met with Mom's agent this morning," I said. "We dropped off the rest of her paintings and told him about the Schnabel. He's scheduling a media event in a couple of weeks where we will reveal the identity of Schnabel's *Madeline* and announce we're going to lend the drawing to museums around the world."

Color was rising in Peter's face. His eyes looked glassy. I was beginning to worry about his blood pressure. Claire, however, took no notice of his appearance. She glanced at him slyly. "Mom's agent says the publicity will significantly increase the value of Mom's work."

He opened his mouth, but it was my turn to speak. "Come on, Peter, you know what happened. You lived the high life, you blew through all your money, and then you remembered the drawing. You showed up at Mom's place and demanded she hand over the Schnabel. She refused and you two had a vicious argument, you chased her into the garden where you hit her or she fell, it doesn't matter which, because she broke her ribs and you left her there to die."

"That is absolutely not true."

Claire scoffed. "Don't try to deny it, Peter. The neighbor heard you screaming at Mom in the garden."

"What that old scarecrow next door? Who's going to believe..." He stopped, realizing he'd just made what we lawyers call an admission.

We were almost there. He just needed a little nudge.

He shoved his plate into the center of the table. "Stupid woman," he muttered. "She was sitting on a gold mine and she refused to share it."

"Is that why you hit her and left her there all night?" I asked quietly.

"I barely touched her," he said, indignant. "I just wanted to teach her a lesson. When I came back the next day, the ambulance was there."

"And you were so overcome with remorse that you went to the hospital, and instead of apologizing, you flew into a rage. No wonder the nurses threw you out."

Peter's face hardened. "You won't get away with this. I'll sue."

I stared at him. "Just try it, Peter. We talked to the neighbor, we talked to the nurses, and we've got everything you just said on tape." Claire pulled her phone out of her pocket and set it on the table. "If you think your career will survive this kind of scandal, then be my guest."

Peter slammed his fist on the table. The other diners looked at us as the sound of rattling plates, glasses, and cutlery echoed across the room.

"Good-bye, Peter," I said. He stood up abruptly, banging the table with his thighs, then flapped into his overcoat and stalked out the door.

"Well, that was quite a spectacle," Claire said as she tapped the red record button on her phone.

I looked down at my plate, my pasta was stone cold. "I don't know about you, Claire, but I'm ready for dessert."

She laughed and signaled the server who was disappointed we had not touched our meals but brightened immediately when we asked for the dessert menu.

We smiled as we raised our mugs in a toast. True, there wasn't enough evidence to convict Peter of causing Mom's death, but still we were satisfied. Mom would not be vindicated in the courts, but she would receive the recognition she deserved in the art world. We could live with that.

"Claire, you've got a dreamy look in your eye, what are you thinking about?"

She looked up at me and grinned. "I was thinking about Mom and Schnabel. I wonder if they were lovers. Maybe...maybe he's my dad."

I laughed so hard I dropped my ice cream spoon into my coffee.

BUZZ DIXON

Buzz Dixon writes oddball movies, games, comics, TV shows, and novels, putting words in the mouths of Superman, Batman, Conan, The Terminator, Optimus Prime, The Teenage Mutant Ninja Turtles, Mork & Mindy, Scrooge McDuck, Bugs Bunny, Yosemite Sam, plus more G.I. Joes and My Little Ponies than you can shake a stick at. His short fiction appears in *Mike Shayne's Mystery Magazine*, *The Pan Book of Horror Stories*, *National Lampoon*, *Analog*, and numerous "best of" and original anthologies, including *Heartbreaks & Half-truths*, the second Superior Shores anthology. Find him at www. BuzzDixon.com.

NOT A CRUEL MAN

BUZZ DIXON

FEELING GOOD AFTER HE FINISHED, he set the bloody sledgehammer down headfirst on the white shag carpet.

What remained of the producer emitted a long, low, melodiously flatulent tone as his sphincter relaxed. One pale gray eye, incongruously still intact, peered lifelessly from the bloody bone and brain hamburger of the producer's face.

He stepped up to the plush upholstered bar in the producer's living room, reaching around behind it for the bottle of Johnnie Walker Black Label kept there.

Pouring himself a good stiff shot, he mentally ran through the checklist of things he needed to do that evening, as the producer's rapidly cooling corpse seeped all sorts of bodily fluids into the thick shag. The sledgehammer's handle stood upright by the body. Splatter from the hammer speckled the gleaming white walls and the large-framed prints of wide-eyed Keane kids.

He knew blood splatter covered him, as well, but he'd anticipated that: he wore a black ski mask, a dark blue jumpsuit, black leather gloves, and high-topped sneakers.

Carefully avoiding the ever-widening pools of liquid oozing

from either end of the body, he grabbed the sledgehammer and headed to the den.

Upstairs a radio softly played Peter, Paul and Mary's new hit, *I Dig Rock and Roll Music*. The producer made—*had* made—cheap, syndicated, pop music shows for low budget radio and TV stations. "Hook the kids and hook 'em good," the late producer enjoyed saying, and cheap junk worked just as well as the high-priced, quality stuff.

A large print of Picasso's *The Old Guitarist* hid the den's wall safe. He swung it aside and, using the combination the agent provided, opened it.

Inside the safe lay a small plastic bag of cocaine, a slightly larger bag of marijuana, some expensive, if tacky, jewelry, several stacks of high-denomination bills, and the Polaroids.

Quickly flipping through the hundreds of Polaroids, he sorted them by age and sex to find the ones the agent wanted him to recover.

The agent represented a sparkling young singer who'd just landed a starring role in a Disney movie. The producer's modus operandi was to find young, struggling talent, seduce them, dig them deeper and deeper into his own peculiar kinks, document that progression with Polaroids, then leech off their careers.

A lot of what the producer liked would result in serious jail time for all involved. In the case of the agent's client, she'd never again be regarded as a sweet and wholesome, much less virginal.

He found one, then two, then three-four-five-six Polaroids of the young singer and slipped them into his pocket. He dropped the rest into one of the large heavy duty Bullock's shopping bags he brought, along with the dope and the money.

The tacky jewelry he locked back in the safe: too easy to trace. He smashed the safe dial with the sledgehammer, then bashed the face of the safe a few times to make it look like a burglar failed to break it open.

With any luck, the cops would call this a simple burglary gone wrong and not look any further.

To complete his ruse, he ransacked the desk in the den. It

contained nothing but files and papers, and a .357 revolver. That he put into the second bag, the bag of items he'd need to dispose of once he finished his job. Leaving the gun might signal to the cops that the break-in was more than a robbery gone wrong.

The agent was paying him handsomely for his evening's work; he counted the drugs and money as a bonus.

The other Polaroids? Well, that depended.

The agent wanted the six of her client. Whether to destroy them or keep them as insurance or leverage was her business, not his.

But the rest? He'd look through them at leisure, see if he could recognize any exploitable faces. Maybe he would destroy them to break the chain of evidence, maybe he'd keep them as a side hustle.

He'd make that decision later.

Climbing the curving gilded staircase, he perfunctorily ransacked the two guest bedrooms and hall bath before going on to the master bedroom.

The door to the producer's walk-in closet stood just inside the threshold of the master bedroom. He flicked on the light in the closet. It seemed bigger than his first apartment.

In order to fake a petty burglary, he raided the producer's jewelry box—cheaper than the items in the safe but no less tacky. He threw those contents, as well as a couple of Rolex watches, into the bag of evidence to be discarded, then looked for the producer's car keys.

His escape hinged on stealing the producer's brand new, bright red, Mustang convertible. The previous day, while the producer strutted about the set, he'd driven up and hidden the sledgehammer on the property. That morning he'd parked his car in the lot of a deli owned by a guy who owed him a favor, then took a bus to Laurel Canyon, carrying his ski mask, jumpsuit, and gloves in one of the Bullock's bags.

He'd walked up the side road leading to the producer's house, past the happy and stoned young people laughing and singing at the Laurel Canyon Country Store. As far as they knew, he was just another happy hippie making his way deep into the musical heartland of Los Angeles.

Once out of sight of the main road, he'd ducked into the underbrush and snaked up to the rear of the producer's property to stretch out for a long nap in the shade.

The moon rode high in the night sky when he woke up. He craved a cigarette— tobacco or grass— but didn't want to ruin his night vision.

And waited.

As expected, his target did not return until midnight, so he felt fully rested for the crime. He watched the lights come on in the producer's bedroom, then donned his burglary outfit and retrieved his hidden sledgehammer.

He broke a window on the side of the house just loudly enough to lure the producer downstairs. The producer obliged by coming to his rendezvous with death wearing nothing but an open robe. He dispatched the producer with ruthless efficiency, then began staging the fake burglary.

He smiled to himself: *Did faking a burglary to cover a murder actually make it a burglary?*

Unable to locate the Mustang's keys in the closet, he turned on the main light in the master bedroom.

A skinny, naked, teenage boy, tied spread-eagle and face down on the bed, whimpered behind the necktie, which had been shoved in his mouth as a gag. He grimaced. The boy was, at most, sixteen. The producer had never been particular about where he got his jollies, so long as his jollies were gotten.

The producer's wallet and car keys lay on the nightstand by the bed along with a small stack of recently snapped Polaroids. The boy's clothes lay in a pile on the floor. The producer carried only a couple of hundred in his wallet, but a couple of hundred was a couple of hundred and unlike the gun, watches, and tacky jewelry, couldn't be traced.

Once he pocketed the cash, he checked the Polaroids. Not the most outrageous he'd seen that evening, but nothing to send home to mother, either. Tossing them into the keeper bag with the others, he looked at the boy, wondering what to do.

The producer almost never brought anyone home on a

weeknight but "almost never" didn't mean "never ever." It was a complication. He couldn't run the risk of the kid talking, but he could also see the boy shaking with fear, the tears streaming out of his tightly closed eyes as he lay in his own urine and feces.

Flicking open his switchblade, he knelt on the boy's back and pressed the sharp point against the kid's throat. "You want to live, you do exactly what I say. Understand?"

The boy nodded, eyes open wide, terrified.

Cutting the neckties binding the kid's ankles and wrists but not the gag around his mouth, he picked up the boy's clothes and dropped them in his discard bag.

The boy stood cowering before him, trying to cover himself. He pulled his necktie gag loose and tossed it aside.

A large unlit candelabra sat on the producer's dresser, obviously meant for romantic evenings, and, just as obviously, the producer had not seen this evening as romantic.

"Light it," he told the boy.

The boy blinked in surprise but quickly did as told, using an ornate table lighter on the dresser.

"Good. Now go downstairs. Slowly. Stop when I tell you."

The boy, still whimpering but too terrified to bolt for freedom, crept down the stairs. He paused at the bottom when he saw the lifeless producer.

"Into the kitchen," he told the boy.

Once in the kitchen, he gestured to the gas range. "Turn it on. Blow out the pilot light so it doesn't ignite."

Again, the boy looked puzzled but did as told. Gas hissed from the unlit burners into the kitchen.

"Through that door. Into the garage."

Once in the garage, he ordered the boy to open the garage door and forget any thoughts of running.

The boy appeared too terrified to think about anything, and dutifully opened the garage door. The moonlight outside lit the garage with a pale, blue light.

Fishing the kid's clothes out of the second bag, he tossed them at the boy's feet. "Get dressed."

The boy quickly pulled his clothes on.

Dropping his two shopping bags in the Mustang's rear seat, he started the car. "Get in."

The boy hesitated for a moment, until a single glare cowed him and he climbed in.

As they roared off, he pulled his ski mask up off his face to make it a cap. Los Angeles accepted a lot of eccentricities, but a ski mask at night might attract attention.

The boy studiously looked away. "Please, mister, don't hurt me."

"Shut up."

The boy shut up.

They drove up Laurel Canyon to Mulholland. The warm Southern California night blew past them, but the boy still shivered.

"Where do you want me to drop you off?"

The boy blinked and looked in his direction. "Drop me off?"

"Yeah."

"Hollywood...?" the boy said tentatively.

"Hollywood it is."

They'd been racing along Mulholland in silence for several moments, zigzagging at a breakneck speed on the wild and winding road as if chasing the distant moon, when the boy finally asked. "You're just gonna let me go?"

"Yeah. Why? What should I do with you?"

The boy said, "I thought...I'm a witness...?"

"The house is going to fill with gas. When it reaches the candles upstairs, it will ignite and blow the house off the face of the earth, along with any evidence either you or I were there."

The boy digested this, then said, "Thank you."

"Don't thank me."

"You could have left me to die."

"Yeah, I could have."

More silence, then, "What now?"

"I'm going to drop you off on the outskirts of Hollywood. No matter what you hear, what you learn, you keep your mouth shut. Understand?"

The boy nodded.

"Got any family?"

The boy gave a wistful sigh, launching into Hollywood sob story #143: Cruel parents, abusive home, nobody understood him, ran away, came to Hollywood to seek fame and fortune in the Summer of Love.

They raced along Mulholland to Cahuenga, over the Hollywood Freeway, through the ever-narrowing neighborhood streets on the other side, then up Mt. Lee Drive to the rear of the Hollywood sign.

The boy wrapped up his story along the way, how he'd gotten work as a background dancer on one of the producer's shows, how the producer asked if he wanted to make a little money on the side, how one thing led to another, and eventually to getting tied naked to the producer's bed.

The moonlight created deep, dark shadows behind the Hollywood sign. He turned the headlights off but kept the motor running as the boy finished talking. The million and one glimmering lights of Los Angeles spread out below them as far as the ocean.

"I'm dropping you off here because I need to put some distance between us before the sun comes up," he told the boy. "You got any money?"

"Just a couple of bucks. You can have it—please!"

"I'm not robbing you." He reached into the second bag in the back seat and pulled out the producer's two Rolex watches. "Here. Pawn these. You should get a couple of hundred for them. Take the money and go home, you follow? Go home."

The boy blinked in amazement, then smiled. "Thanks."

"Don't thank me. Just get out and go home."

The boy opened the door and scampered out, away from the car and into the moonlight.

He drew the producer's .357 from the bag and with unerring accuracy shot the boy perfectly in the base of his skull, killing him instantly and painlessly. Tossing the gun as far away in the opposite direction as possible, he sped down the narrow road, across Hollywood Boulevard, then on to a side street near the deli where he parked his car.

He dumped the tacky jewelry onto the floor of the backseat,

then pulled off his ski cap, gloves, jumpsuit, and sneakers, tossing them into the second bag.

Leaving the key in the ignition, he walked over to the deli. Recording artists and session players, coming off long late-night gigs in the nearby recording studios, took no notice of yet another barefoot person walking the streets of Los Angeles in the wee morning hours.

With any luck some idiot would steal the producer's car and get caught with it and the tacky jewelry in the back seat. By then he would have disposed of his bloody clothes and stashed the money and dope and other Polaroids.

Tourists would doubtlessly find the dead boy shortly after sunup. Once police linked the watches and the gun to the dead producer, they'd assume the kid participated in a burglary gone bad, only to be double crossed by his partners.

They'd focus all their attention into locating the boy's associates, shaking them down for whatever info they could about his non-existent partners in crime.

Meanwhile, he would deliver the singer's Polaroids to her agent, and enjoy the money and dope he took from the producer.

Tough luck for the boy, but those were the breaks.

At least he didn't leave him to die alone and trapped in a house filling up with gas.

Instead, the boy felt happy and full of hope when he plugged him.

And why not?

After all, he was not a cruel man.

C.W. BLACKWELL

C.W. Blackwell was born and raised in Northern California, where he still lives with his wife and two sons. He has been a gas station attendant, a rock musician, and a crime analyst. His passion is to blend poetic narratives and pulp dialogue to create evocative genre fiction. His recent work has appeared in *Pulp Modern*, *ADR Books*, *Shotgun Honey*, *Gutter Books*, and *Rock and a Hard Place Magazine*. C.W. is a member of the Short Mystery Fiction Society. Find him at https://twitter.com/CW_Blackwell.

12 MILES TO TAYLORSVILLE

C.W. BLACKWELL

THE CLATTER OF LIQUOR BOTTLES.

Moonlight sparking in the broken glass.

Angie Kritt shook the stale booze from her fingers, slipped her vape pen from her apron pocket. She took a big drag and blew down the stars. On a normal night, she'd have already taken out the recycling, counted the till, mopped the floors. Maybe she'd be a mile down the road already—heater blazing, radio loud. But the timber company had just cut a stack of bonus checks and it made the guys thirstier than drunks at a monastery. Sure, she could use the tips—and the boys felt generous tonight, no doubt about it. Maybe even a little reckless. But all she wanted was to hit the twelve miles of lonely, ice-crusted road back to her single-wide in Taylorsville, where she'd crank up the space heater, turn on the TV, and roll a jay with the Lemon Haze she bought at the dispensary in Chico earlier that week.

She wasn't long in the alley, and when she went back inside some of the men were ready to settle up. Soon, they'd zag up the mountain in their beat-up four-wheel-drive pickups, back to the logging camp where they'd wake in the morning as cat-skinners, fallers, and knot bumpers, trying to make their nut one felled pine at a time.

"What time you *get off*, sweetheart?" asked one of the men as he fumbled with the cash in his wallet. Most of his buddies had already tottered into the parking lot, some peeing on the side of the tavern in big splashy arcs.

"None of your business when and how I *get off*," Angie said. It wasn't the first time she'd said it, wouldn't be the last. She nodded to the group outside. "Better not miss your ride."

The man looked her up and down, a strange watery stare like a toad's gaze. He took a ten-spot from the stack and stuffed it in his pants, rocking to his back foot as if by some fault of gravity. "Not leaving a tip," he said.

She swiped the stack of bills on the table and walked off. "Buddy, all the Lord gave you was the tip."

"Excuse me?"

"I said *have a nice night*."

After a torrent of diesel exhaust and icy mud, the work crew cut onto the road and rocketed up the mountain, debris peppering the facade of the old tavern. Angie looked over the mess they'd left behind and hung her shoulders. Her cozy trailer never felt so far away.

Another trip to the recycling, another drag from the vape.

She marveled at how starlight could feel so cold.

Then: something out of place.

Soles clapping on the asphalt. Someone running down the road.

A scream. *And another.*

Angie went through the back door and peered across the tavern. A woman stood in the lot, cupping her hands over the front window. Early thirties, blonde. *Panicked.* When she pulled away, a bloody print stained the glass. She pleaded for help and yanked at the front door, deadbolt rattling in the jamb.

One-thirty in the damn morning.

How much longer the night would get, Angie couldn't guess.

⸺⛬⸺

Her name was Meena, and she'd nearly leapt into Angie's arms as soon as the door was opened. Other than a busted lip and a torn coat, Angie couldn't determine the source of the blood.

"Please hide me," she pleaded. "Stockroom, bathroom, anywhere. Do you have a gun?"

Angie locked the door and they moved away from the window. "No guns. There's a baseball bat behind the bar. A few old knives in the kitchen. Let me call the Sheriff—"

"No. Please don't."

"I'm not a fan of law enforcement either, but whoever's chasing you—"

"A cop is chasing me. A bad cop. A dirty cop."

Headlights passed over the road and the strobe of blue and white take-down lights popped into the lot. The screech of tires locking up.

A car door opened and shut, icy footsteps.

Meena ran to the kitchen and closed the door behind her. "Please don't tell him."

There wasn't any time to discuss it. By the time Meena disappeared behind the doorway, the cop's dark form had filled the windows. He took notice of the bloody print on the glass, pulled a baton from his duty belt and rapped on the aluminum doorjamb. He caught Angie's gaze through the window and pointed to the door handle. Tall, broad-shouldered. Heavy beard. The old cliché of high school sports as a pipeline to law enforcement rang true here.

Angie unlocked the door, slipped her phone from her pocket. It didn't always get reception this far up the mountain, but threats of a livestream might do the trick in a pinch.

"Plumas County Sheriff's Office," said the cop. "You alone?" The voice didn't match the stature. It sounded boyish, undeveloped. He looked around the tavern with his thumb resting on the butt of his pistol. The patch on his blood-spattered uniform read: TOEFFLER.

"Yes, sir," Angie said. "Just closing up for the night."

"There's fresh blood on the window."

"A fight. The logging crew tied one on tonight."

"I didn't hear it on the radio."

"I didn't call it in."

"Why not?"

"Long as they keep it outside, I'm okay with it. Something I can help you with, officer?"

"Deputy."

"Okay. Something I can help you with, *deputy?*"

"I'm looking for a woman. About so-high, blonde. She foot-bailed when I tried to cuff her."

"Foot-bailed?"

"She ran. What is your name?"

"My name is Angie. I swear I haven't—"

"Angie what?"

"Angie Kritt."

"Before you swear anything, you need to know that impeding an investigation is a crime." He pulled at the collar of his uniform. It looked too tight, buttons tilting under the strain. "I know the woman is here. If you lie to me, I'll arrest you, cuff you, and book you at the county jail. And that's before we talk about harboring a wanted felon. *Aiding and abetting.* See how quickly the charges rack up? Do you understand, Angie Kritt?"

She nodded. "Funny, I've never seen you before. You know Deputy Higgins? We call him Huggy. Sometimes Huggy-Bear."

Toeffler gave a hard stare. "I work South County. The Forty-Nine corridor."

"So, what happened to Huggy?"

Something clattered in the kitchen. A metal spatula, maybe.

"One last time, *who's back there?*"

Angie tossed a glance at the kitchen and shrugged. "You know, I've never seen a cop with so much facial hair. You guys are usually so clean-shaven."

Toeffler combed his beard with his fingernails, eyes hard on the kitchen door. "Open it."

"Don't you need a warrant?"

"There's blood on the window. I don't need a warrant."

"Is that true?"

Toeffler took the pistol from his duty belt and pointed it at the floor, both hands laced on the grip. "Get behind the bar," he said, moving toward the kitchen door.

Angie did as he said, watching him inch forward. He announced himself and gave an order for Meena to come out. He tried the doorknob. Locked. He tapped the door with the toe of his boot. He kicked a little harder. Then he lifted his boot off the floor and heel-kicked above the knob, shattering the jamb and sending the door crashing off its hinges. It looked like he was about to raise his weapon when a jet of powder whitened the doorway in a ceaseless flood of extinguisher spray.

Toeffler stumbled back and fired.

More powder spray.

He now looked like a flocked Christmas tree.

Meena came out screaming with both hands on the fire extinguisher.

Another shot.

A spark cast from the extinguisher and the whole thing jolted in Meena's hands. With Toeffler blinded, she swung the butt-end of the canister at his head. It connected, and he went down hard. Angie couldn't tell if he'd been knocked off his feet or if he'd slipped in the powder spray. Meena gave another wild swing, and all was silent.

"I could have used your help," Meena said, patting down the cop.

"I hid you," said Angie. "That's all you asked me to do. What are you looking for?"

"Keys. I'm looking for his car keys."

"Why?"

"He took something from me."

"Maybe they're in the car. You hurt?"

Meena checked herself. "Looks like I'm still in one piece. You?"

"Far as I can tell."

"How about a drink?"

Angie laughed, sort of a sarcastic little snort. "How about we get the hell outta here before he wakes up?"

As if on cue, Toeffler groaned and pawed at the air. By the time he'd unholstered his taser, they'd already made the parking lot.

TURNED out Meena worked for a legal weed grow down in Santa Cruz County, but went on the lam when they caught her skimming bud for a side hustle. The hammer came down hard, and the boss tipped off Deputy Toeffler that she'd probably come back to Plumas County for the holidays.

"So, he stopped you for a warrant?" Angie said, one hand on the wheel and the other clutching her vape pen. A big white moon blinked in the pine canopy. With four bald tires and a busted headlight, she had to be careful around the turns, and it seemed to cause Meena some concern.

"That's just it," said Meena. "I don't have any warrants. My boss never pressed charges. He just wants me dead. Could you speed up a little?"

"He paid Toeffler to kill you?"

"You shouldn't be so surprised. These mountain deputies get salty after a decade on the job. Then they start working the angles. They take a bribe here and there. Look the other way when someone else does it. Next thing you know, you've got a little blonde woman on her knees up some logging road, pleading for her life —*just a little faster, if you can.*"

A flurry of snow appeared in the single beam of the headlamp.

"I thought it was suspicious that he had a beard," said Angie. "His uniform didn't even fit. I thought he was a fake cop."

"It's entirely possible."

"But where would he get the car and the uniform?"

"My boss is richer than God. He could buy his own police agency if he wanted, cars and uniforms included."

Lights appeared in the rearview, flashing blue and white.

Meena saw it too. "Speak of the devil," she said.

A curve loomed ahead, just in range of the sallow beam of the headlight. Angie hugged the corner of the road and put her foot into the pedal, tires squealing. She usually took the turn easy, but tonight wasn't usual. The rear tires broke completely loose before catching again, and the pickup launched down the next straightaway.

Halfway to Taylorsville.

Six miles to go.

Angie wasn't sure what would happen when they got to town, but at least it would be in the public eye. There would be witnesses, cell phone video. Whatever hit job Toeffler had signed up for would need to be explained, justified. Maybe he'd even pull off the highway at the last minute like the headless horseman unable to cross some magical boundary.

The lights closed in. *Sirens blaring.*

A loudspeaker: *PULL OVER.*

"Don't do what he says," Meena said. "He'll kill us both."

"What if he tries to run us off the road?"

"He won't do that." She unpocketed a pistol from inside her jacket, still covered in extinguisher powder. "I have his Glock. It was just lying on the floor."

Angie watched her in the glow of the dashboard lights. For the first time, she realized how high the stakes had become. Sure, there was something dangerously exhilarating about the whole thing. But now she wished she'd never unlocked that front door.

The truck shuddered and the wheel jerked in her hands.

A solid knock from behind.

Headlights bright in the rearview.

"Looks like he's going to take his chances," Angie said.

Another jolt. Tires chirping. The police cruiser was right on top of them.

Angie had the pedal to the floor, knuckles tight on the wheel, both axles shuddering. She knew the straightaway wouldn't go on forever, that another curve lay just ahead—this one sharper than the last, followed by yet another. How long now? Five miles—*maybe four?*

The cruiser swerved and accelerated, pulling alongside them in the oncoming lane. Toeffler's dark form sat poised behind the wheel.

"Roll down your window," Meena said. She lifted the gun, racked the slide. "Before he sends us into a tree."

"Please don't shoot that thing in my face."

"No choice."

Angie cranked the window, frigid air pouring into the cab of the truck. When the cruiser came up even, Meena fired two rounds into the windshield. Toeffler pitched into their lane and the rear axle broke loose again.

The truck wheels shook like the castors of an old shopping cart.

Angie couldn't hold on anymore.

One more sideswipe and the axle broke loose for good. The truck pitched sideways, and Angie stood on the brakes, but the cruiser kept coming, kept barreling onward. Both vehicles spun into the shoulder and off the roadway, a cataclysm of glass and sheet metal. Spinning, rolling, into the pines.

The truck settled at a forty-five-degree angle, high-centered on a young fir tree.

Smoke everywhere.

Angie unfastened her seatbelt, checked herself all over.

Meena stirred, groaning. She searched the floorboards for the Glock, and when she found it, she pulled the handle and kicked the door open.

"You all right?" Meena asked.

"I think so." Angie checked again. Her neck hurt, but nothing felt broken.

"He's out there. You better stay close."

The truck was so slanted, it took a minute or two to climb out. Smoke billowed from the engine compartment and the suspension steamed in the frigid night air. It was all so suddenly quiet. They edged through the pines toward the road. A flashing light up ahead, pulsing in the unsettled dust. The police cruiser lay upside down on the shoulder with the blinker signaling some phantom left turn. Meena inched forward, Angie close behind.

"He's in the driver's seat," Meena whispered.

Angie looked. She saw Toeffler's uniformed arm hanging out the window, laying in the frozen mud. Still as can be. "Is he dead?"

Meena didn't answer. She knelt at the window a moment and reached inside, the cop's arm limply jostling as she worked to get something free. When she stood again, she held a key ring, spun it once in her hands. She went to the back of the cruiser and worked the trunk lock until the trunk dropped open and all of the contents spilled into the dirt. Flares, space blankets, rubber waders—and a canvas duffle. She unzipped the duffle and lifted a bundle of cash to the flashing blinker light. She pawed through the bag a second time and inspected another bundle, thumbing through the bills. "Looks like it's all here."

"Jesus," Angie said. "Is that the bribe money?"

"Not exactly." She returned to the driver window and ripped out the radio handset and threw it across the road. "I told you I had a side-hustle. It just takes a while to get all this cash into a bank account, if you know what I mean. It ain't easy."

"You know, I could use a little help getting my truck fixed up."

"Your truck?"

"The one smoking like a BBQ out in the pines."

"I wouldn't worry about your truck."

"Why not?"

Meena tossed a pair of handcuffs at Angie's feet. Maybe she'd taken them from the cop. "Sorry, girlie. I'm going to need every bit of this money for my big escape. Gonna ask you to cuff yourself to Johnny Law, here. Need your phone, too."

Angie took a step back. "Are you kidding me?"

"Nope. I don't have much of a sense of humor."

"What if I say no?"

"This nine-millimeter will change your mind, I'm sure of it."

Angie pressed her hand to her forehead. "I can't believe you've been playing me this whole time. I helped you."

"Don't beat yourself up. I just wanted a ride into town, that's all." Meena raised the pistol one-handedly, closed one eye as if lining up the shot.

"I'll freeze out here."

"You might get lucky. Someone is bound to pass by."

"And if they don't?"

"Not my problem."

Angie plucked the handcuffs out of the dirt. They felt ice-cold and smelled faintly of bearing grease. "Okay, let's talk this through. There's got to be something we can work out."

Meena shook her head and wagged the pistol. "There's nothing to work out, girlie. I already decided not to kill you as long as you did what I said. You return the favor by giving me your phone and cuffing yourself to the dead cop. See, that's what you get out of this. You get to watch me walk away with three-hundred grand slung over my shoulder without a steaming bullet hole in your forehead."

Angie slipped her phone out of her back pocket and held it out.

"Fine," she said. "Take it."

Meena had begun to reach for the phone when a clacking sound erupted from the open window of the cruiser. She fired an errant round at the sky, muzzle flash brightening the roadway. Then she stiffened and toppled to the ground, gun smoking. From her thigh hung a pair of black wires that led back to Toeffler's hand.

He squeezed again.

TAK TAK TAK TAK

This time Meena's body flexed and arched like a dying fish.

When Toeffler let up, the pistol fell to the ground. Angie picked it up.

"Call dispatch," Toeffler said. He sounded weak. "I need help. I'm really hurt."

Angie looked the pistol over, then kicked the duffle with the toe of her left foot. She worked the zipper halfway down and peered inside. All hundreds. Three-hundred grand easy. Maybe more. She looked sideways into the driver door. Toeffler hung twisted and upside down, blood dripping from his chin and wetting his unkempt beard. Glass sparkled in the bloody whiskers.

"You a crooked cop, Toeffler?"

He shook his head no. "She has a felony warrant. Call. Please."

"Still not sure whether to believe you. What's with the beard?"

"What?"

"The beard. Cops don't have beards."

His voice came as a quiet murmur. "'Movember.' We grow it out for charity."

Angie looked Meena over. Groaning, muscles spasming.

"I'm a bystander, you know," she said. "I never met this woman before."

"I know. She took you hostage. That's what the report will say."

"She stole my truck too."

"Fine."

"And the money?"

It took him a while to reply. "Just leave me a stack or two."

"Ah, there it is. It's true what they say. Everyone has a price."

She reached into Meena's pocket, found her phone, and pressed the woman's thumb into the sensor. It blinked on. Two bars, forty percent charged. She dialed 911 and waited till a woman's voice came on, then rested the phone on the ground, tucking the Glock into the back of her pants. She pulled a couple stacks of bills from the duffle and handed them to Toeffler. He took them and passed the cash to his other hand.

"Don't go," he said, his voice barely a whisper.

"You'll be fine. Just keep working that taser, sparky."

Angie flung the duffle over her shoulder, looked up and down the road. Nothing but pine trees and moonlight in either direction. She knew of a fire road just a few yards past the bend that she could follow into town. Her neck felt stiff, and she thought maybe she'd cracked a rib, but with only two miles to Taylorsville she knew she'd make it in one piece. Maybe she'd feel better with the covers pulled up, TV loud, heater cranked high. The sweet plume of Lemon Haze dancing at the end of her fingertips. And if that didn't do the trick, maybe she'd stack the cash in her kitchenette and imagine all the places she could live that didn't start with a "T" and end with an "E."

Maybe someplace warm.

Someplace where they paid decent tips and had affordable single-wides.

She thought Palm Springs had a nice ring to it.

K.L. ABRAHAMSON

K.L. Abrahamson is a well-traveled writer who has explored cultures and countries around the world in her fiction. She is the author of literary, romantic and fantasy fiction, including the highly regarded Cartographer fantasy series and three mystery series. She lives on the west coast of British Columbia, Canada, with eagles, bears, and orcas for neighbors. When she isn't writing, she can be found with a camera and backpack in fabulous locations around the world. K.L. is a member of Sisters in Crime National and Canada West Chapter, and the Oregon Writer's Network. Find her at www. karenlabrahamson.com.

CHICKEN COOPS AND BREAD PUDDING

K.L. ABRAHAMSON

OLD MAN HARPER's undulating fields were fallow with the fall's last cut of hay, but around the edges the grass stood tall and brittle like the hair around an old man's ears. The grass rustled and, beyond the ragged snake fence, the lodgepole pine creaked in the chill wind and lifted up onto the dark sides of the mountains. The clouds streaming over the moon said that the first snows were on their way. It was late for them this year. Late enough and still warm enough that I snuck out regularly to visit my friends, though I wore my old navy ski jacket zipped up to my chin underneath my dad's red flannel work shirt.

My cheeks and ears tingled in the cold and the air smelled of frost and pine. Across the field the lights of the Harper house gleamed warmly golden. All a lie, really, because Old Man Harper was a perv who liked to prey on teenage girls like me. At least that was what my best friends Katy and Ron told me. It was all over school, too. And Katy, Ron, and I had made it our mission to do something about it by making trouble for Old Man Harper. He was new in town. Maybe we could encourage him to move again. After Ron put sugar in Harper's ATV engine and Katy left the barn door open so Harper's pigs got loose, tonight was my turn to leave a mark. The trouble was, I'd never done anything like this before. My mom and dad always described me as "Grace-Rose, our good girl." I was out to prove them wrong tonight and hopefully not ruin my chances for a university scholarship in the process. But Old Man Harper needed to be taught a lesson.

Out beyond the house a lone truck rattled out from the Harper place and onto the main road that was the only access to our farming community of Big Lake and the unlikely-named town of Likely. I watched the taillights heading west toward Williams Lake, the rattle gradually dying away in the night. A coyote chorus came from behind me down near the creek. The truck had probably disturbed their hunting as it crossed over the bridge. I shivered and it wasn't just because of the cold. If Old Man Harper had gone to town that made my task a lot easier and the chances of getting caught a whole lot less.

Shoving my hands in the red flannel shirt pocket, I set off across the field, trying not to stumble in the stubble of cut grass. It didn't take long to cross. At the rear of the Harper place a simple barbed wire fence separated the house and outbuildings from the field. I ducked between the wires and headed for the chicken coop, carefully opening the wire pen and stepping inside. The hens were roosting inside the small wooden shed and I went inside, into the scent of straw and chicken poop, blindly feeling for the hens and sliding my hands under them seeking eggs. I found five and figured that was enough to make a mess of Harper's front door.

Leaving the coop behind, I set off around the house and stopped dead in my tracks. Harper's battered blue pickup stood beside his five-ton, Fitzhenry Breads delivery truck, just outside the dilapidated picket fence that marked the house's front yard. Harper was still home.

I almost dropped the eggs and ran, but I'd promised I'd do my part in the Harper campaign.

Cautiously, I stepped through the open front gate and crossed the brittle lawn. Lights streamed from the windows of the house's lower floor, but there was no sound. No television. No radio. No music. Nothing.

The house wouldn't be so silent if anyone was home. At my house there was always noise, whether my mom was playing piano or my dad whistling. I even hummed while I was reading.

What was Harper doing?

I looked down at the eggs in my hands and up at the door.

I'd only agreed to do something so Harper knew of our displeasure, but I'd go up a ton in Katy and Ron's estimation if I could report another Harper perversion. I could peek in a window, before throwing the eggs and running.

Still holding the eggs, I approached the house. The first window glowed brightly past the chipped clapboard wall. I slid up to the edge of the window and, holding my breath, darted my head up to take a quick look.

No one there. It had been a living room, I thought, though it didn't look anything like the comfortable living room we had at home. This had a lounge chair and a television. I chanced another, longer, look. Yup. Television, chair, and couple of empty beer bottles and newspapers on the floor.

Tramping the brown, unmown lawn, I crossed to the corner of the house and eyed the windows. There was a small set of stairs leading up to what was likely the kitchen door. Creeping along the side of the house, being careful not to trip on anything, I made it to the next window.

This was such a stupid thing to do. It I got caught there was no way Harper wouldn't call the police. I'd get arrested and be convicted and would never get into college with a criminal record, let alone get into the RCMP, which was all I'd ever wanted. But Katy and Ron said they knew a girl Harper had molested, but she was afraid to call the police or even tell her parents. We had to do something to protect our friends. I should stick to my plan to throw the eggs and run for it. That was the way to keep out of trouble.

Instead, I stood up and looked inside.

It was the kitchen as I'd expected. Worn tan-colored linoleum floor, cupboards painted dingy yellow, and the kitchen sink on the other side of the window from me, the faucet dripping. I'd found Old Man Harper, too.

He was seated at his kitchen table, but instead of eating a meal or reading a newspaper, Old Man Harper slumped face-down in a bowl, his head twisted oddly.

I stumbled back from the window, the eggs escaping my fingers. They smashed on the cold ground as I scrambled back into the shadows.

It didn't make sense.

No one sat with their face in a bowl.

I stepped gingerly over the eggs and once more peered in the window.

Harper hadn't moved.

That was when the cold settled into the pit of my stomach. Old Man Harper was dead.

I spun around to run, tripped on my own feet and fell. I staggered through the gate and slammed hard into the cab of the delivery truck before turning to hightail it back through the barbed wire fence and across the field. My house was a distant glow around the edge of Big Lake. The trail along the water seemed full of tripping roots and branches that tore at the flannel shirt and my hair. I pounded the last few feet, ran up the stairs to the porch that overlooked the lake, then slammed in the front door and up the stairs to my room. Inside, I huddled on my bed with my knees hugged to my chest.

"Grace-Rose?" My mom's concerned voice came through the closed door.

"Here, Mom," I said, trying to sound normal, though I thought I might be sick.

I toed off my boots just as she opened the door. She wore her pink fleece housecoat, and her long, dark hair framed her face. She frowned. "Were you out?"

I couldn't very well lie when she must have heard me come in. I looked down at myself. There were bits of bark on the shirt and a small tear where I'd likely caught it on a branch.

"I went out. I'd planned to meet up with Katy and Ron, but I got spooked in the woods. I heard the coyotes too close. Sorry. I wore Dad's shirt. I think I likely got it dirty."

"I told your father to call Fish and Wildlife. Those darn animals are getting too familiar. Someone's going to get bit." She eyed me, but when your daughter has been a good girl for the full fifteen years she's been alive, how can you imagine she's just seen a dead body? "Well, get ready for bed. It's a school day tomorrow."

She pulled the door closed and I heard her soft footfall pad away. I pulled out my phone and texted Katy.

Problem. Went to OMH house. Dead.

I hit send and waited for a reply. The phone burred in my hand.

"Hello?"

"Dead?" Katy's voice was a whisper. "What are you talking about?"

I told her what happened, what I saw.

"Are you sure? Maybe he's soaking a zit or something."

"Katy, I know when something's not normal. He wasn't soaking a zit. His face was in the bowl and he wasn't moving. His hands were dangling down beside him, and his nose was in whatever was in the bowl."

"I'm calling Ron. Meet you there in twenty minutes."

"Katy, come on! If he's dead, we don't want to be there. We don't want to be accused of killing him. At least I don't."

"So, you're just going to leave him there to stink up his house? No one ever visits Harper. It'll be weeks before he's found. Besides, maybe he's just hurt? Did you think of that?"

"I thought you didn't like him. And now suddenly you're worried about him..."

"Get real. Now I'm calling Ron. Meet us there or not."

She hung up. Katy Baxter, my best friend, hung up on me.

I stared at the phone. Do what she said? Or listen to Mom? She hadn't exactly said I couldn't go out again...

I climbed off the bed and listened at the door, then eased it open. Except for a light glowing under Mom and Dad's bedroom door, the house was dark. Tiptoeing, and carrying my boots, I gently shut my door behind me and went down the stairs. At the back door I took one last look at the darkened house, with its scent of roast beef and Yorkshire pudding from dinner, and wondered what Mom would say about me now. I silently opened the back door and stepped out onto the porch, pulling the door closed with a soft click.

It was colder now than it had been when I came in. My breath was frosty, and the clouds placed a spooky silver halo around the moon. I retraced my steps along the lakeshore path and then hurried across the moonlit fields. The pines looked skeletal. The grasses rattled as if something lurked there. The Harper place was still lit up, but now shadows flitted across the windows. Had the killer returned?

I started to turn away when a powerful spotlight pinned me in the field.

"Police! Stop right there!" a male voice ordered.

My first instinct was to run. I stumbled a step, but then my "good girl" kicked in and I stopped and turned. A silhouetted figure stepped up to the fence. "Come here."

Obediently, I approached but stayed cautiously out of reach in case he wasn't who he said he was. Closer in, I could make him out. Youngish, good-looking face under the vizor of an RCMP uniform cap. A typical dark, heavy jacket with the buffalo-head shoulder flashes and a name plate on his breast that said LaCroix. His dark eyes looked me over.

"What are you doing out here?"

"Meeting friends." The truth seemed best at this point.

LaCroix glanced over his shoulder. "We got another one." He yanked up the top line of the barbed wire. "Come through."

Crap. He wasn't going to let me go. He was going to arrest me for murder. He was going to call my mom and destroy all my parents' illusions about their good girl.

Obediently, I climbed through the fence and stood looking up at him.

"Name?" he asked.

Lie? But a false name escaped me. I sighed. "Grace-Rose Heatherington."

He frowned. "The doctor's kid?"

"Yeah." Busted and double busted. Mom and Dad were going to kill me.

He caught me by the upper arm and steered me around the house. In the front yard stood two cop cars. Beside them stood another police officer—this one older and less friendly-looking, judging by the frown on his face. His name plate said Brooker. With him were two forlorn-looking slighter figures. Katy and Ron.

LaCroix pulled me to a stop. "Anyone here know each other?"

Katy and Ron didn't say a word, but I nodded. "They're the friends I was meeting."

"Interesting. And can you enlighten us as to why you were meeting at a house with a dead man in it?"

Katy and Ron's gazes, and LaCroix and the mean-looking cop's glare, all turned on me.

"We—we meet out here sometimes," I said, wondering why now of all times I went for the lie. But it wasn't a total lie. We did meet out here.

"Uh-huh. Were any of you here earlier?" LaCroix's gaze flicked like a whip between Katy and Ron and me.

I couldn't do it. I just couldn't. I sighed and looked down at my shoes. "I was. I—I came over to egg Harper's house. He's a creepy guy and I didn't want him staying around here. I looked in his kitchen window and saw him and got the heck out of here. I—I dropped the eggs."

"Smart. So why are you here now?" The implication being that coming back wasn't so smart. Boy was he right.

"Because Katy said we needed to check whether he was really dead. He might need a doctor." I toed my shoes into the soft soil.

"Is that true?" he asked Katy.

She scowled at me as if I'd thrown her under the bus or something, but finally nodded.

"So, you brought a friend," he asked with a nod at Ron.

Katy nodded again.

"And you were all going to have a little party at the dead man's expense. Maybe traipse all over the crime scene while you were at it?"

I stayed silent. I could tell a lecture when I heard it.

"Well, Grace-Rose Heatherington, you're coming with me.

Brooker, if you've got their information, how about you drive our looky-loos home. I've got some more questions for this one."

And like that I was all alone with LaCroix. "But I've told you all I know. Everything I did. I didn't go into the house at all."

My objections apparently meant nothing as he dragged me toward the house and up the three steps to the kitchen door. He opened the rear door and held me at the open entrance. "Is that what you saw through the window?"

There was that horrible image again. Old yellow kitchen cupboards, worn tiles, and—like a horrible centerpiece to the room, the kitchen table. Old Man Harper still slumped as I'd seen him, but from this angle the image was worse. I was closer and from up at the same level, I could see his face half-turned toward the door. His damp brown-gray hair was a frame for his face. Skin pasty. Eyes half-open.

As if he was looking at me.

Shivering, I tried to turn away, but LaCroix wouldn't let me.

"Let me go!"

"Why? Isn't that why you came back? Isn't that why you brought your friends?"

"No. I didn't want to come."

"Then why are you here?" His grip was tight on my arm.

"Because...because Katy said I should come. What if Mr. Harper had been alive and hurt? How would I feel if I left him there to die?"

"So, she guilted you into it?" LaCroix's gaze drilled into me.

"Yeah." I was *so* not the good girl Mom and Dad thought.

"Think he's alive, now?"

I shook my head and glanced back at the door. "What's wrong with his face?"

His skin was covered with ugly lumps of white.

"From the bowl. Bread pudding, I think," LaCroix said.

When he said it, I could smell the cinnamon and raisins, the heated and now souring, milk.

"But why...?"

LaCroix tugged me back down the stairs to the yard as a black van pulled up beside Old Man Harper's delivery truck. "Why would you come and egg his house?"

"Because he was strange. Because whenever I saw him, he looked at me and my friends strange."

"Strange?"

"I don't know. Like a dirty old man. Always watching and licking his lips. Weird."

"And so you and your friends egged his house. Anyone else think like you three?"

"Everyone. Absolutely everyone at school knows he molests girls. Whenever Harper comes to deliver bread, we make sure we're not around."

"Maybe one of you killed him."

It took a moment to sink in. "No. No way. I couldn't kill anyone."

The three people in the black van piled out, pulled on blue paper suits and hefted boxes of equipment. They nodded at LaCroix.

"Kitchen. The rear door's open," he said.

They dutifully trucked around the house and LaCroix looked back at me. "Time to get you home, I think."

"How did you even know to come here?" I asked.

LaCroix glanced at me. "I was out on rural patrol and noticed all the lights. Thought I'd pop in and make sure everything was all right."

He ushered me to a police car, opened the rear door, then waited for me to climb in. My stomach was flip-flopping. I'd never been in the back of a police car before, but I knew what it meant. I was a suspect. I could only imagine my parents' reaction.

I wrung my hands between my knees as LaCroix climbed in and started the car. My house was dark when he pulled into the yard.

"You—you can just let me out here…" I hoped. Maybe I could get inside and to bed without Mom and Dad ever knowing.

Not to be.

THE NEXT DAY I rode the bus to school along with Katy and Ron. Katy wasn't speaking to me because my parents had called hers and she was in trouble. At first I was hurt, but then I decided not talking to her was fine by me. It was Katy who'd dared me to go egg Harper's house in the first place. If I hadn't gone, I would never have found him.

Ron tried to make peace between us, but it wasn't working. I was content to ride the bumping bus and stare out the window and think about how my life was over. I was grounded. I was likely a suspect and would be charged with murder. Mom and Dad weren't angry—they were disappointed and that was worst of all.

I couldn't get the image of Old Man Harper's face out of my head. That pasty skin and the solid glare of his eyes. Worst of all were the weird white lumps of bread dried all over his face as if he was wearing a mask. Why would someone kill him like that? Drowned in bread pudding didn't seem a typical way to be murdered.

Last night, after Officer LaCroix questioned me further, I'd heard him talking with my dad about Harper. Dad did medical exams when he wasn't dealing with live patients. Harper was relatively new to the area and not well known. When he'd first moved in, he'd dropped over to our house to introduce himself and had brought a loaf of bread and three packages of cake donuts as a gift for Mom. I'd thought it was weird; usually it was neighbors bringing gifts to the newcomer. I'd heard that he'd done the same things to other families in the area. Dad had heard the 'pervert' stories, too, but told LaCroix he didn't think they were true. Dad had said he thought that Harper was simply lonely and trying to make friends.

I wasn't so sure.

But why would someone kill him? For really doing what he was rumored to have done? Had he really molested someone?

"You guys told me you knew someone Harper molested. Who was it?" I asked Ron. He was a nice guy, good looking, too, with dark hair that kept falling in his baby blue eyes. Unfortunately, he was more like a brother to me, given his dad and mine had shared a medical practice for the past eighteen years.

"Why?" Beyond Ron, I could see Katy was listening.

"If he molested someone, they could have been out to get him. Or someone in their family might have been." I swallowed. "Reason I'm asking is last night? I saw someone leaving Harper's house."

"What?" Katy said, her attention now openly on me. "What are you talking about?" She'd dropped her voice.

"Last night when I arrived at Harper's house someone was leaving. I saw a truck leave and head toward town."

"Did you tell the police?"

"They never asked. That cop was all about what I'd seen in the house and whether I'd gone inside. Frankly, I was scared. I totally forgot until just now."

"What did the truck look like?" Ron asked.

"I don't know. It was dark. It was a truck. Dark colored, I think." I thought for a moment. "It had a rattle?"

"Lots of trucks around here do, what with the gravel roads and all," Ron said.

I nodded. "But it had to be someone who Harper would invite into his house in the evening," I said.

"A girl?" Katy offered and looked around the bus. There were twenty-three of us kids bussed into Williams Lake for school. Most of them were younger, but there were eight of us in high school. Five of us were girls.

"If whoever killed him drove into town, doesn't that suggest he or she lives there?" I asked.

"Or somewhere close," Ron suggested.

"Who was the girl Harper molested?" I asked, because that was our most likely suspect.

Katy and Ron looked at each other and then Katy looked away.

"I don't know her name. I just heard it had happened," she said.

"You need to find out who it was. Where they live."

Katy nodded.

"But they might not have done anything and we're causing them trouble," Ron said.

"Maybe." I turned back to the window as we turned onto the highway. The glimmer of Williams Lake lay beyond the fallow golden fields of Williams Lake Indian Reserve. Maybe I should call the police and tell them what I knew and suspected, but since I was a probably a suspect, who'd believe me? First, I needed more information.

Behind me Katy and Ron whispered theories at each other.

AT SCHOOL we all agreed to ask around for the name of the girl Harper molested. News of a murder travels fast in a small town like Williams Lake. News of the murder of a man none of the kids liked traveled through the school faster and with more embellishments than a high school rodeo queen on her barrel racer. By the time mid-morning break rolled around I barely recognized the stories being told. To escape all the questions *I* got as the person who found the body, I escaped the cafeteria and went outside in the cold to the old smoking pit next to the loading dock. Since smoking was banned at school, the place was mostly abandoned, especially at this time of year, but it was a good place to do some thinking. In the dock, a truck was unloading.

All the speculations ran around in my head and just confused me. I had never actually seen Harper approach any schoolgirl, so what if that wasn't the reason he'd been killed? Dad had said he seemed like an okay guy—just lonely and trying to buy friends with donuts and bread. Seemed like a pretty sad existence to me. And that truck—it could have just been someone who knocked on Harper's front door and who left when he didn't answer.

But that didn't make sense either. Someone coming to call would have done exactly the same thing I'd done and check around the house because all the lights were on. They would have seen Harper face-planted in the bowl.

No, there was a very good chance I'd just missed meeting the killer.

I shivered and stood. If the killer knew what I'd seen, would he come after me? I had to think it was a good possibility, but so far no one knew that fact.

I headed for the cafeteria door and ran right into Jennifer Barbour, the class president.

"It's you." Blonde and beautiful and with an unexpectedly excellent brain to match, she crossed her arms over her chest and looked me up and down. "What's this I hear about you seeing the killer?"

Crap. Clearly Katy or Ron and blabbed that I'd seen something. In search of them, I shoved past her, into the stench of cafeteria spaghetti and garlic bread and the noise of a school full of students with stories to tell. I was pretty sure it was Katy I was going to kill for this one. She never could keep a secret.

There she was, craned forward over a table with a bunch of girls and guys avidly listening. I marched over and grabbed her arm. "We've got to talk. Where's Ron?"

He came strolling up at exactly that moment and I steered them both toward the outside door.

After the heat and smell of the cafeteria, the outside was a smack upside the head. I faced Katy and Ron. "You told. You told everyone that I'd seen the killer."

Ron shook his head. "No way. I wouldn't."

Katy looked at her shoes. "I only told Stacey."

Stacey Joe, the school's resident gossip.

I closed my eyes and turned my face to weak sunlight. "I am so dead. The entire town is going to know by the end of today."

"So?" Katy asked.

"Katy, think about it," Ron said. "If the killer hears it, he could come after Grace-Rose."

I have to say, Katy actually paled. "No. No." She shook her head.

"If I'm killed, remember it's because of your big mouth." I stomped off, suddenly so furious I could barely speak. Katy was to blame for all of this, and she was just too stupid to see it.

I stalked up the loading dock and headed for the road, hugging myself against the cold. I should phone Mom and Dad, but they were probably so tired of worrying about me after last night, that I just couldn't do it.

Call the police?

I ended up in the school bus shelter considering what to do. The thought of talking to Officer LaCroix again didn't exactly appeal to me. No, I was better off just keeping my head down until the police caught their killer.

It was the rattle that caught my attention.

I straightened up as a navy-blue pick-up truck turned into the loading dock driveway. All the little hairs on the back of my neck rose to attention as the truck rolled past me and down to the dock. A single person was in the cab, and as he passed he caught sight of me and smiled and waved.

Mr. Fitzhenry, of Fitzhenry Bakery.

OMG!

I backed up, turned and ran, slamming into the school doors, jamming them open and stumbling into the principal's office.

"I need to speak to Mr. Wilson," I managed to say to Mrs. Guthrie, his receptionist.

"I'm afraid he's not here. Meetings, you know."

"Then Mr. Webb. Please. I know something and I have to tell."

"Goodness gracious, Grace-Rose. You're white as a ghost. But Mr. Webb had a lunch meeting, too. If it can wait, he'll be here by two."

I eyed the clock on the wall. It was twelve-thirty. By two, Mr. Fitzhenry might have tracked me down.

I sank down on a chair and tried out my options. Call Mom or Dad? I could claim I was sick, and Dad would come and get me. That might deal with today, but what about all the days after? Mr. Fitzhenry would still be out there, and I'd still be in danger.

I realized Mrs. Guthrie was still looking at me. "What is it, dear?"

I pulled out my phone. "I—I need to call the police. Can I wait here for them?"

"The police?"

"It's a long story," I said and dialed 911.

It was hard facing Officer LaCroix again and even harder telling him what I hadn't told him last night. I don't think he believed that I'd simply forgotten to tell him when he interviewed me. When I told him that I'd recognized the rattle in Mr. Fitzhenry's truck Officer LaCroix went down to the loading dock, only to be told that Fitzhenry had come inside, heard people talking, and had left again. They caught up with him at his office, and he broke down and admitted killing Harper.

According to the rumors, Harper had been robbing Fitzhenry bakery for a while, stealing the baked goods he'd been spreading around in Big Lake Valley and shorting the orders to Fitzhenry's clients in towns up and down the Cariboo District. Fitzhenry's had been losing clients and when Mr. Fitzhenry figured out what was happening and confronted Harper the night he was killed—well, things got out of hand.

It was sort of fitting that the man responsible for the bread thefts drowned in bread pudding.

As for me, now Mom introduces me as her brave, brave daughter.

I guess it's going to take a while to earn back "good girl" status.

BILLY HOUSTON

Billy Houston lives in the Washington, D.C. metro area with his wife, Elizabeth, and his son, Booker. Born and raised in Memphis, Tennessee, he has always been a fan of all things mystery, horror, and suspense. He keeps busy as a public health graduate student and a stay-at-home dad, but has always aspired to be a writer. This is his first published work. Find him at www.instagram.com/billys_booksandstuff/.

THE PROMOTION

BILLY HOUSTON

Peter Hayes felt a swell of pride when he finished going through the last customer in the database—Mr. Anthony Yates, who signed up for his security system in 1983. A quick Internet search showed that Mr. Yates had died seven years ago, so it was safe to say he was done doing business with Harris Securities or anybody else.

Pete hit the delete key and rubbed his eyes, feeling like he could just lay his head down and fall asleep right at his desk. Either that or have a cigarette. He gave up smoking a few years ago, but after the amount of work he finished it was a cigarette night if there ever was one. Karen, his wife, gave him a hard time about it around the time their daughter Jessica was born. She complained at first, even though he always smoked outside, so Pete agreed to smoke at the end of the driveway. But it wasn't long before that was too close to the house, too. Eventually, Karen refused to let him even have an unopened pack of cigarettes in the house.

It wasn't easy to do, but he gave them up. Not in a day or two, it took some time and discipline, but with Karen's help he managed. In all, Pete counted at least a dozen occasions of having "one last cigarette," but after two years, he was sure he had kicked the habit entirely. It was one of the many ways his life had changed since having a child. He quit smoking, sure, but he also learned to like his job. A younger Peter Hayes hated the idea of sitting in a cubicle and talking to people about how secure they felt their home was, but fifteen years later, he was content. Respectable, even. He worked hard and for that he earned a decent paycheck, good benefits, and a great insurance plan for his whole family. That was better than what a lot of people got.

Pete shut his computer off and took a quick look around the office. It wasn't the first time he saw it so late at night, but it was always a little eerie. The place was empty, the overhead lighting turned down to a soft orange glow. All the computers were turned off for the weekend, the only other source of light coming from the office where Greg Hamilton, Pete's boss, sat and typed away at his own computer.

Pete didn't think much of Greg when he first came along a few years back. He was a transfer from another branch in Michigan and he treated people as if they were children, always talking down to them.

"Are you sure the customer was happy with your service?" was a favorite line of his. They usually were, except the ones who wouldn't be happy unless you gave them the whole damned system for free.

"What did you charge them?" was another go-to for Greg. The same prices everybody else paid for whatever package they got, was the answer, as if that needed to be explained.

There was also the popular, "I don't care what I said before, this is what I'm saying now," on one of those occasions where Greg was caught in a lie or a mistake. This happened at least once a month.

But, as time went by, Pete thought he didn't give Greg enough credit. He cared about the job and doing it right. And what was wrong with that? Maybe it was silly, but the longer Pete worked there, the more he cared, too. Greg wasn't much of a people person, sure, but he knew his job, and Pete could appreciate that.

It looked like Greg saw that in Pete, too. Whenever extra help was needed, he usually asked Pete. When someone had to do some extra work on a Saturday, Pete was the first one on Greg's list. When some time off the clock was needed to play catch-up on paperwork,

Pete always did it. It only took a few hours, and he didn't mind the free labor too much, especially on the occasions he was able to work from home.

"That assistant manager position is getting closer and closer," Greg would tell him each time and Pete believed it. The current assistant manager, Henry Williams, was a good enough guy, but he was also over sixty and due to retire soon.

In short, Pete knew the promotion was in the bag and while he didn't discuss it with his coworkers, he knew that they knew, too. The employees with the skills to do it were few and far between. And the number of people who came and went in the company made Pete one of the senior members of the branch. Besides, nobody else took on extra work like he did.

With the task completed, and a bed twenty minutes away, Pete was ready to call it a night. He'd already punched out for the day at five, so he didn't need to go to the time clock. The labor budget couldn't support overtime, so he was doing it in exchange for more vacation time. A few extra hours of work for another day or two on the beach come summertime seemed like a fair trade. He would remember it for possible future use. Assistant managers needed to know these kinds of money-saving strategies, too.

Pete knocked on the doorframe of Greg's office to say goodbye and get his boss's attention. Greg was about ten years older than Pete, with a slight bald spot on the back of his head. As usual, there was a cup of coffee in his hand, and he didn't look away from the computer until a couple of seconds after Pete knocked.

"Done for the day, Pete?" Greg asked.

"Yep, just in time, too. Any later and my wife would be calling me every five minutes to make sure I haven't been beaten and mugged on the way home." Karen was always concerned when he worked late. The neighborhood Harris Securities was located in was safe enough, but a little further down the road the area was rather sketchy. Crime didn't often make its way up to this part of town, but it did happen on occasion.

Greg set his coffee down. "Well, I hate to keep you longer, but would you mind having a seat for a second?"

Pete took a seat, looking around. Greg's office was somewhat plain, but there were a few things decorating it. There was an American flag at the back of the room, a few business books strategically placed on top of the filing cabinet—for show, more than for reading, Pete thought—and a large bronze eagle paperweight holding down a stack of paper on his desk. There were no family photos, or any other photos for that matter, but the ever-important coffee pot sat on a small table in the corner.

This is it, Pete thought. *I'm getting that promotion.*

"Pete," Greg said, "The business is changing. I've been doing it long enough to see it happen a few times. When there's a shift, we have to do the best we can with what's given to us."

Pete nodded, trying to suppress the grin wanting to form on his face.

"You know there's an app that can send an alert to your phone if your home gets broken into?" Greg asked. Pete did know that, but said nothing. He'd worked with Greg long enough to understand that most of his questions were rhetorical. "Innovations like that are making times hard on the company. On a lot of businesses."

Greg leaned back in his chair, as if thinking of what to say, and that was weird for a man who always had something ready to come out of his mouth.

And then...

"We have to let you go, Pete."

It took Pete's brain a minute to realize the words "let go" were said instead of "promoted." The potential for being fired never crossed Pete's mind, not ever. He said the only thing he could think of at the moment. "But I've been here for years."

"That's why it has to be you. We need to cut some money somewhere and you're the best option. You have one of the largest salaries and benefits packages because of your seniority."

"What about Henry? He's been here longer than anyone."

"Henry's the assistant manager. He does a lot of internal work that's hard to replace."

Couldn't I replace him? Pete thought. Greg had made it seem that way, many times, actually. It was all but a done deal in Pete's mind. Seeing it slip away didn't seem real.

"I know this is hard." Greg walked around the desk and helped Pete out of the chair. "Get yourself home. Put the weekend behind you and collect your thoughts. I haven't pulled up the paperwork yet, so come back Monday morning and we'll get everything straightened out. Your severance package will be more than fair. I'll make sure to answer any questions you or Karen might have."

Pete was outside Greg's office before he realized that Greg was back to typing on his computer. He turned and saw his boss (former boss) sipping coffee. The feeling started coming back to his body and a thought occurred to him.

"What about my vacation time?" Pete asked.

Greg didn't look away from his computer right away. He was in work mode again, the sincere look was gone, and it was back to business as usual. "What's that?"

"I stayed tonight for extra vacation time," Pete said.

"Well," Greg said. "Vacation time is a work perk, not something you get when you leave the company."

"Then what the hell was I doing here tonight?"

Greg stood up. "Pete. Go home. We'll discuss it Monday when you've calmed down."

"No," Pete said, feeling anything but calm. "We'll discuss it now. What kind of compensation am I getting for tonight?"

"We can't afford any overtime. I'm just trying to do what's best for the business." Greg didn't raise his voice, which just made Pete angrier.

"I thought *I* was best for business. I thought I was your next assistant manager."

"I never said that."

"No," Pete said, and could feel himself smiling despite the fury brimming within. "No, you were real careful about that, weren't you?"

Greg was tapping his finger lightly against his coffee cup now. "Whatever you thought, that's on you. We have an assistant manager, and you don't deserve the position *just because*."

Greg ended the sentence there and shook his head. As if Pete had done nothing to earn any recognition. He didn't deserve it, why? Because he was the perfect employee? Because he'd done everything that was asked of him and then some for years? That sounded pretty damn deserving to Pete.

He tried to calm down, not let his anger get the better of him. Stick to the facts, that's what he would do. Choose his words carefully. "I worked overtime, and I deserve overtime pay."

"Did you?" Greg asked. As calm as Pete was trying to be, Greg went the other way now. He set his hands on his desk and leaned forward, inches away from Pete's face. "According to the system you clocked out at five just like everybody else."

"Then I'll take you to court," Pete said.

"And risk losing your severance entirely? It's not worth it, Pete. Go home. Get your résumé together. I'll see you Monday morning."

"You're going to fix this." Pete spent years being shoved around by this company and he was not going to spend another minute being treated like garbage by some asshole who thought he was better than everybody else, just because he had a reserved parking space and an office instead of a cheap cubicle.

"Like I said. I'm going to do what's best for business." Greg smiled, a smarmy, smug know-it-all smile.

It was the smile that really pushed Pete over the edge. He wasn't sure when his hand found the bronze eagle. The paperweight was close by though, and at some point it ended up in his hand. Greg's face didn't change, that know-it-all smile never left, he never knew what happened. One minute he was telling a man he was fired and the next minute the side of his head was being crushed in. There was a soft crunch, followed by Greg's head hitting his desk, and then the thud of his body hitting the floor.

For a long time, Pete just stood there. He wasn't sure when he came back to himself and saw what he'd done. He rushed around the desk to see if he could help, but the puddle of blood pooling around Greg's head, and the teeth sprinkled beneath the desk, told Pete that there was no helping Greg out of this. An all-nighter at the computer wouldn't fix this problem.

Pete paced around the room. He realized the bronze eagle was still in his hand and he quickly dropped it on the floor. He sat back down in the chair. It was a little easier from there. Sitting down he couldn't see the body. Not seeing it helped somehow.

He looked at the wall and saw blood spatter. He'd been standing at an awkward angle when he hit Greg. Pete quickly checked his shirt and hands. No blood. By some miracle, it had all ended up on the wall, the floor, or the desk.

He checked his phone. Karen hadn't called, but she would soon. He texted her, knowing his voice wouldn't sound normal. "Be home soon. Love you."

He could imagine her sitting with the phone in her hand at home, ready to call when his text message came through because she almost immediately replied, "OK, stay safe."

With his wife satisfied, Pete walked out of the room. Not seeing the body wasn't enough anymore. He wanted to be out, away from it. He made his way along the identical cubicles until he came to the one with Gavin Robinson's name on it. Pete looked around in the drawers of Gavin's desk until he found what he wanted. A half-empty pack of cigarettes. There were some matches in the same drawer, and he took those, too.

For a moment, he considered going outside, but then lit the cigarette anyway. He'd just killed a man; smoking indoors didn't seem like a big deal anymore.

He thought of ways to get rid of the body, mostly things from movies that wouldn't work. It wasn't like there was a lake nearby that he could toss Greg into. If he hid the body out there somewhere, somebody would find it eventually. Plus, there was the problem of the blood soaking into the carpet. Pete didn't know how to get a regular stain out of the carpets at home, so this was absolutely above his skill set.

Pete smoked most of the cigarette down to ash. He grabbed an envelope off the desk, tapped the end of the cigarette inside, and crushed what was left on the bottom of his shoe. He considered throwing the butt into the garbage but decided to put it in the envelope instead.

There was no moving the body anywhere safe and if there were, getting Greg out of the building and into Pete's car without looking suspicious or getting blood everywhere wasn't likely.

What if I went to prison? If he called the police and confessed maybe he could get less time. But even an accident—if that's what this was—would probably mean a few years locked up. And that was his optimistic look at it. He could be facing life behind bars. What would that mean for Karen and Jessica? Pete didn't think he'd go to one of those nice prisons that rich stockbrokers went to. No, he would end up in the regular prison with the criminals from down the road.

Then it came to him.

Pete went back into Greg's office. He stepped over the body to get to the computer, an act less cringeworthy, now that he thought there was a solution.

The alarm code hadn't been entered yet and there were no security cameras set up on the property, inside or out. Harris Securities might have an office here, but they didn't own the place. Unless the landlord decided to invest in cameras, it wasn't going to happen.

Pete grabbed Greg's keys out of his pocket, trying not to breathe. He wasn't sure if he was really smelling anything or if it was his imagination, but either way it was making him gag. It only took a second to find the keys, but he was grateful he made it through without vomiting.

He walked downstairs. The double glass doors leading to the parking lot were locked like he thought they would be. Pete unlocked them.

Once outside, he considered getting in his car and leaving. Just be done with the whole thing and hope for the best. Pete held strong, locked the door from outside, and took a few steps back. He could see there were a few rocks in the grass by the moonlight. Pete grabbed the biggest and threw it as hard as he could at the door.

The glass shattered and he walked through the opening, careful not to cut himself on any of the glass that was clinging to the doorframe. He made his way back to the stairs. Midway up a second wind hit him. The fear of being caught didn't disappear, but dulled, hidden beneath the need to make his plan work.

Back in the office, Pete put the keys back in Greg's pocket. For a second, he considered wiping down the office wherever he might have touched something, then decided against it. Yeah, his fingerprints were going to be here. He worked here. Even the bronze eagle could be explained. Still…

There were wet cleaner wipes in his desk and Pete was back with them in seconds. He cleaned the side of the eagle he touched, careful not to touch it with anything but the wipes, picking up some blood and turning the disinfectant wipes red. Pete ran to the restroom around the corner and flushed it down the toilet. He felt a little relief, quickly replaced by panic as he remembered the rock. He charged down the stairs, wiped the rock clean with another wipe, and flushed it, too.

He wondered if he should do more, maybe break some computers and steal Greg's wallet, really make it look like a gang came in and roughed the place up. But he decided to keep it small. He didn't want to overdo it and risk leaving more evidence against himself.

It almost felt like a typical late night when Pete got ready to leave. He got his jacket from his chair, made sure he didn't leave anything he needed out on his desk, and walked out the door. He felt so normal, he was even a little surprised to see the broken glass door. He stepped through the glass and walked to his car.

The fear didn't set back in until he was almost home. *They'll assume it was an employee,* he thought. And he was fired. But Greg said he didn't have the paperwork drawn up yet. It was possible nobody knew he intended to do it.

Pete was so stuck in his thoughts he didn't realize he was already home. It felt like no time had passed, and he remembered none of the drive. He turned his car off, got out, and was met by his wife in the driveway. In the moonlight, it was hard not to see the annoyed look on her face.

"Well, it's about time," she said. Then her expression changed. "What's the matter, Pete? You look terrible."

The look of concern on Karen's face made him try to look more relaxed. He loosened his shoulders and let his arms hang a bit freely before embracing her. "I'm just tired, honey."

Karen smiled. "That's okay. We have the whole weekend to..." She looked him over. "To relax. Drink a couple of beers. Smoke a cigarette."

Pete rolled his eyes. He didn't think about how his breath must smell after smoking. "It was only one. I'm sorry, Karen. It was a long day."

"Better be the last one. What's that in your hand?"

Pete looked down and saw he was holding the envelope he put the cigarette out in. It was folded in half, but open, so when he turned it a few ashes fell out.

"The evidence," he said.

She took it and looked at the crushed cigarette inside. The garbage can was at the top of the drive and Karen walked over to throw it out. Pete considered stopping her, telling her everything right then, but couldn't find the words.

Karen tossed it into the can and turned back. "Ready for bed?"

He wasn't. All he could think was potential evidence was in his trash and garbage day was Monday. But Karen was tired, and Jessica was asleep, so it wasn't long before they were in bed. His head sunk into the pillow, the blackout curtains blocking the moonlight, as the enormity of what he'd done finally hit him.

Like a paperweight to the face.

I'm a murderer. I killed a man tonight and worked damn hard to get away with it.

He wondered if he would. He'd been numb, then afraid, then numb again, and now it was back to fear. He could be sent away for life. Or worse, executed. He was afraid for himself, for his family, for what could happen to them. For the first time in years, he was unsure of what his future would be like.

And yet.

Beneath all the fear, all the doubt that he would get away with it, there was one thing he didn't feel. Regret. If he could go back to that moment and stop himself, he would, of course, but that was because of the possible repercussions. But the truth was...

He almost didn't want to admit it to himself.

The truth was he killed Greg and he didn't feel bad about it. He killed a man who took advantage of him and plenty of other people for years. All for a company that's only concern was the bottom line.

Greg was an asshole, always was. No family, except an ex-wife. God knows how he managed to get a woman to marry him in the first place. No one liked him, no one loved him, and no one would miss him.

A few minutes later Pete was asleep.

MOST OF THE cubicles were full, but few of the inhabitants looked up as Aoki walked by on the way to the manager's office. He'd been a regular fixture these past two weeks, questioning everyone with dogged determination. No one was surprised to see him back.

He knocked on the manager's door, and Pete Hayes looked up from his computer.

"How can I help you, Detective?"

Aoki took a seat, but not before taking a look all along the walls. "Does it feel strange working in here?"

Hayes shook his head. "Nah, it's not like I saw him in here or anything. Besides, they painted and replaced the carpet and almost everything else."

"That was nice of them. Most corporations don't exactly go out of their way to help their people." Aoki pulled out a notepad. "I just have to go over a few things we've already covered."

"Of course."

"The time clock indicated you and everybody else left at five p.m. the day Greg Hamilton was killed. Is that correct?"

Pete nodded. "Except Greg, yeah. I can get you those time sheets and any other files from corporate if you like, but it might take a while for them to give the okay on it."

"That won't be necessary," Aoki said, getting a headache at just the idea of digging through all of that useless paperwork for information that had been confirmed by the entire office already. "And Mr. Hamilton made a habit of working late?"

"Yes, he did."

"Will you be working the same way?"

"Not after this. No, sir."

"Can't say I blame you," Aoki said. "The other employees tell me Mr. Hamilton relied on you."

"I suppose he did."

"Could you recap what that Friday was like?"

Pete frowned. "Hard to remember. They all blend in here, you know? Not much variety. It was a regular day, I guess."

"And the weekend?"

"Pretty normal, at least until Henry Williams called to give me the news. That the cleaning ladies had found Greg. After that..." Pete's voice trailed off, a slight croak in his voice. "My wife used to worry about me working late. But I never thought anyone would break in and kill someone."

Aoki closed his notebook. "The neighborhood's changed, and not for the better."

"Any chance you'll catch whoever did it?"

Aoki lowered his voice. "Between you and me? No. This was a bunch of random low-lifes. They'll probably end up dead before they end up in jail."

"Well, at least it's behind us." Pete stood up. "Let me show you out."

They made it to the stairs and Aoki stopped. "You don't happen to have a cigarette on you, do you?"

Pete hesitated, then shook his head. "Had to quit."

Aoki shrugged. "I probably should, too," he said, and walked down the stairs.

As he got in his car, Aoki wondered if he should try to talk to some of the known local gang affiliates again. He didn't really want to, knowing they wouldn't have much to say, if anything, but it was good to be thorough. Only the best work would do if he was going to get that promotion.

SHARON HART ADDY

Her husband's retirement, moving from her life-long stomping grounds, and building a house forced **Sharon Hart Addy's** inner child to grow up, replacing her inner ten-year-old's spirit of adventure with something a lot less playful and a lot more realistic. Before, she wrote almost exclusively for children, now most of what she writes is for adults. Her published work spans stories for adults—including 'Near Warrenton' in *Heartbreaks & Half-truths*, the second Superior Shores anthology—stories for children, award-winning picture books, and poetry for both children and adults. Sharon is a member of Women's Fiction Writers Association and the Short Mystery Fiction Society. Find her at www.sharonhartaddyauthor.wordpress.com.

THE LIBRARY CLUE

SHARON HART ADDY

For hours, snow flew, fell, billowed, and blinded, covering everything with a distorting layer of white. Just before the power went out, an alert from the library's security system sounded at police headquarters. Grabowski and Tyler were dispatched to answer it.

Grabowski drove slowly, the cruiser pushing its way through several inches of snow, while the windshield wipers pounded back and forth. Nothing seemed to be moving but the thinning curtain of white dancing from the sky.

A strong gust swirled snow across the library's parking lot. "Of all the times to get called out for a burglar alarm," Grabowski grumbled as he parked. "Friday night, during the worst snowstorm of the year. Who would break into a library?"

Tyler reached for her flashlight. "Whoever it is, they're not looking for a book. Not with the power out." She looked at the sky. "The clouds seem to be breaking up."

Grabowski stepped out of the car and aimed his flashlight's beam over the one-story brick building, illuminating the dark windows on the main floor. He moved the beam to the lawn where downed tree branches stuck out of snow drifts. Running the light over the building's foundation, he found a branch half in and half out of a broken basement window.

Tyler tilted her chin toward it. "That's what set off the alarm."

"Probably." Grabowski pulled up his collar to keep the snow off his neck. "We'll still have to go inside and check."

Tyler's flashlight played across the drift between them and the window. "No footprints. The wind could have buried them."

They slogged through the drift to examine the window.

Tyler stooped for a close look. "The opening is big enough to crawl through and there's a table just below it."

Headlights swept across the building as a car pulled into the lot. Grabowski turned. "That must be Mrs. Jennings, the head librarian. She's got the key."

Mrs. Jennings hopped out of her car and hurried to join Grabowski and Tyler. After surveying the scene, she cast a disgusted glance at the oak tree. "I always said that tree should be cut down. It loses branches whenever there's a strong wind, and now it's broken a window. Let's get inside and see how much damage it did." She waded through the snow to the staff entrance at the back of the building, unlocked it, and opened the door.

Grabowski caught her arm before she rushed into the dark hall. He shut off his flashlight, led the way inside, and let the door close slowly behind them. They stood in a short hallway, listening. The wind whispered and whistled as it coursed around the building. There were no other sounds. Dim moonlight seeped through a window, thinning the murky darkness.

Mrs. Jennings leaned close. "The basement steps are over there."

Grabowski caught Tyler's attention. "I'll go. You wait here with Mrs. Jennings."

Tyler nodded. Satisfied, Grabowski crept down the stairs and into the black basement. He inched his way along a central hall, the activity room on one side of him and the children's section on the other. He started with the children's section, and, using his flashlight, alert for footsteps other than his own, checked the rows of bookshelves, the circulation desk, and office.

Finding nothing out of the ordinary, he returned to the hall and put his ear against the door to the activity room, listening. Silence, except for the whisper of the wind. He eased the door open and slipped inside. With his flashlight aimed at the floor, he edged along the walls to the broken window. A fine spray of snow, blowing into the room, sparkled in his light's beam. He looked at the snow piled on the table, then turned his attention to the snow on the floor. He thought he saw something and bent over, directing the flashlight beam at the indentation.

A partially buried footprint.

The size suggested a man's shoe. Grabowski knelt for a closer look. Whoever made it was going out, not in. He headed upstairs, sorting through his questions.

He found Tyler and Mrs. Jennings waiting where he left them. "Does the library have anything valuable? Rare books? Money?"

The librarian shook her head. "We keep a few dollars in petty cash to make change when people pay fines. It's hardly enough to warrant someone breaking in."

"Let's see if it's still there."

Using their flashlights, they moved toward the front of the building. Tyler handed her light to Mrs. Jennings, who slipped behind the circulation desk to the office. After a few minutes she came out again.

"Nothing's missing," she reported, handing the flashlight back to Tyler.

Tyler began checking the rows of shelves.

Grabowski moved to the front of the circulation desk. His toe encountered a pile of books scattered on the floor. He called Mrs. Jennings.

She came immediately. "That's odd. Those books weren't there when I left."

Grabowski ran his flashlight's beam over the books. "Are you sure?"

"Of course, I'm sure." She flipped through the books quickly. "These are from the book drop." She pointed to the slot in the front of the counter marked RETURNS. "Usually, I go through the books for bookmarks and notes, then put them on the book trolley, but the storm was getting nasty, so I left them on the counter and went home."

Grabowski nodded, considering possibilities. Tyler yelped as if she'd tripped on something. Grabowski called out, "You okay?"

"I'm okay," Tyler answered. "But I found something."

"Where are you?"

"By the front door."

Grabowski instructed Mrs. Jennings to stay where she was. Moving quickly, he approached the front entry and nearly stumbled on a man sprawled on his back. Tyler was checking him for signs of life.

Tyler looked up as Grabowski's light centered on the man's bloody face. Grabowski whispered, "Do you recognize him?"

"John Stanton, or someone who looks a lot like him."

Grabowski nodded. "It's John. Somebody hit him with something."

Tyler shivered and scanned the darkness around them. Not far away, a bronze figurine of a child reading lay on the floor. Tyler ran her light over it. "I think I found the weapon." She crouched beside it for a closer look. "It has blood on it."

Grabowski stepped over to her. "That's the statue from the circulation desk."

"It was handy. Lethal, too."

"Whoever hit him is gone," Grabowski said, running his light over the scene again. "There was a footprint in the snow below the broken window downstairs, heading out. The branch was positioned to hide the break-in and escape." He paused. "Let's keep this between you and me for now. Mrs. Jennings is calm. Let's keep her that way."

A blast of wind hit the building. An eerie silence followed.

"Officers?" Mrs. Jennings called. "Is it okay to pick these books up?"

Tyler answered, "Yes," and walked back to help her.

Grabowski called the station to report the body. A minute later, he joined Tyler and Mrs. Jennings at the desk. "Did anything unusual happen at the library today?"

Mrs. Jennings, stood, books in hand, as she thought. "Only one thing. Mrs. Stanton, Clarice, came in near the end of the day."

"She doesn't usually come in at that time?" Grabowski asked.

"Oh, no, she does. Every Friday afternoon like clockwork to return her books. It's just that one of the patrons told me John put a sign in their store's window saying the store was closed for a family emergency. I was sure Clarice would tell me what happened. She's usually very chatty, but she just mumbled something about Mark Twain needing attention, pushed the books in front of me, and left in a hurry. It was all very odd."

"Did you check the Mark Twain?" Tyler asked.

"No. I assumed she'd found a torn page or pencil markings."

Grabowski lifted Twain's Huckleberry Finn off the floor. A folded paper stuck out. He opened it and read, *"Burglars! The money from the register wasn't enough. They took John to the bank to empty our accounts. They'll hold me at the house until they get all the money!"* Grabowski held the note so Tyler and Mrs. Jennings could read it. "Is that Mrs. Stanton's handwriting?"

Mrs. Jennings nodded. "Poor Clarice. If I'd gone through the books like I always do, I could have called the police." She caught her breath. "Clarice knew my routine. She was counting on me and I let her down."

Grabowski called the station to ask for backup at the Stanton house, then asked Mrs. Jennings to stay at the staff entrance to let in an investigative team. With that taken care of, Tyler and Grabowski left for the Stantons'.

Tyler glanced up at the sky. "Looks like the storm's blown over."

"Looks that way," Grabowski said. "And the moon is almost full. It's nice and bright." He turned onto the Stantons' street, cut the cruiser's headlights, and slowed as he passed the Stantons' house.

Candles flickered in other houses, but the Stanton house looked dark and quiet behind closed drapes. Two cars sat in the driveway. Grabowski kept the cruiser moving and parked further down the block. "You go around the back. I'll take the front. Be careful."

Tyler nodded. Grabowski watched her skirt the neighbor's hedge as she approached the house, crouching to duck behind the cars on her way to the backyard. Once she was out of sight, he trudged through the snow to the Stantons' front door.

At the door, he paused a moment, listening. A murmur of voices, a man and a woman arguing, probably somewhere at the back of the house. Hoping his timing was good—that Tyler was in place and ready—he pressed the doorbell. The bell chimed. The voices stopped, replaced by the scrape of a chair, and scrambling noises. Grabowski waited, but no one came to open the door.

He tried the doorknob. It wasn't locked. He heard Tyler shout "Stop," pushed the front door open, and rushed into the living room, where a man stood with his hands held high in the air, Tyler watching his every move. Grabowski cuffed the man as Tyler recited the Miranda warning. As the cuffs snapped shut, the man muttered to himself. "Stupid John. We should be on our way to Jamaica."

"Jamaica?" Tyler asked.

"It doesn't snow there." The man's lips curled into a snarl. "The damn fool went to the library to take the note out of the Mark Twain. I had to stop him. He was wrecking our plan."

Grabowski and Tyler exchanged a glance. "Is that why you hit him with the statue?" Grabowski asked.

"Yes, and I'd hit him again if I had the chance." His stared at them, belligerent. "One good thing, it was so cold I kept my gloves on. You won't find my fingerprints on anything."

As backup arrived and led him away, Grabowski shook his head in disbelief. Gloves or no gloves, he'd already confessed to hitting John Stanton. A muffled sound from the kitchen caught Grabowski's attention. He approached slowly, Tyler behind him, to find Clarice Stanton, bundled in a jacket with a blanket around her legs, tied to a kitchen chair. He pulled the loose gag from her mouth. "How many are there?"

"Ju...just that one."

Grabowski undid the rough ropes around her hands. She rubbed her wrists and let out a long sigh. "Thank heavens you're finally here."

Tyler knelt down to untie her ankles.

"What happened?" Grabowski asked.

Clarice Stanton blinked several times, then seemed to collect herself. "Two men came in the store. They had guns. After they emptied the register, one took John to the bank to drain our accounts. The other one said he was taking me to the house as a hostage. I told him I always return library books on Friday, that Mrs. Jennings would notice if I didn't. He wasn't happy about it, but he agreed to stop. While he drove, I slipped a note in the Mark Twain and hoped Mrs. Jennings would find it. The fellow followed me into the library and out again. I murmured 'Mark Twain,' but I don't think Mrs. Jennings took notice, and I couldn't risk repeating myself. When we got to the house, he tied me up. I've been tied to this chair, sitting in the cold for hours."

Grabowski took her hand and held it as he examined her smooth wrists. He shook his head at her. "That's a nice story, but I'm not buying it." He slapped his handcuffs on her. "It's all a fake —the robbery and you being a hostage—but John *is* dead. We found him at the library."

"John's dead? Charlie said he was, but he can't be. He said he'd be right back. He was only going to the library to get the note." Her mouth dropped open. She shut it when she realized she'd said too much.

Tyler gave her a sympathetic glance. Grabowski was all business. "Who else is involved?"

Clarice Stanton's expression changed from unbelieving sorrow, to twisted anger. "The guy you caught. John's no-good cousin, Charlie. It's all his fault. He talked John into this mess. John wanted to close the business, but Charlie—smart, smart Charlie— thought up this scheme. He said leaving that note at the library would bring the police in and then we'd have proof that we didn't just close the store. Charlie said we'd have the store's money, *and* the insurance would pay off for the robbery." She stared into the darkness of the living room, her shoulders drooping. "How did you know?"

"A lot of little things," Grabowski said. "What I don't

understand is why your husband broke into the library to get the note."

"The power was out. The furnace wasn't working. It was cold in here. I told John I wouldn't sit here in the cold until the power came back on. I said we should call the whole thing off, just move someplace warm. He said we couldn't just leave. We had to get the note first."

Clarice huddled into her jacket. "I just wanted to be warm all year round, so I told John to get the damn note. But Charlie had a fit and followed him, leaving me here to wait. When Charlie came back, he said John was dead and he had to tie me up to make the story stick. That the police would find me and he'd come back for me in a month or so."

She glanced at the handcuffs. "Charlie said it would be easy, that it would solve all our money problems. We shouldn't have believed him." A flash of anger hardened her features. "Wait until I see that Mrs. Jennings. I'll give her a piece of my mind. If she'd done her job properly, I wouldn't be in this mess. She was supposed to find the note and call the police. If she'd done that, I wouldn't have been waiting here, freezing in the dark."

Grabowski helped Clarice Stanton to her feet. "Let's go. The police station has a generator. It'll be nice and toasty there. And the good news is, prison is warm—all year round."

ELIZABETH ELWOOD

A former high-school English and drama teacher, **Elizabeth Elwood** spent many years performing with Lower Mainland music and theater groups and singing in the Vancouver Opera chorus. Having turned her talents to writing and design, she created twenty marionette musicals for Elwoodettes Marionettes and has written four plays that have entertained audiences in both Canada and the United States. She is the author of six books in the Beary Mystery Series; her short stories have been featured in *Ellery Queen Mystery Magazine* and Malice Domestic's 2020 Anthology, *Mystery Most Theatrical*. Elizabeth is a member of Crime Writers of Canada, Sisters in Crime National and Canada West Chapter. Find her at www.elihuentertainment.com.

ILL MET BY MOONLIGHT, PROUD MISS DOLMAS

ELIZABETH ELWOOD

IN MY FORTY years as an English and drama teacher, I have never had a problem with keeping high school principals in their place, but in that blissful unaware-of-what-was-to-come-September before the pandemic took over the world, one appeared who tested my patience to the limit. Half my age, drop-dead gorgeous if it hadn't been for the predatory look in her baby blue eyes, and steeped in current mores of jargon, political correctness, and administrative protocols, Martha Dolmas was determined to root out any staff members who disagreed with her ideology. Furthermore, she considered herself the champion of those young people of today who equate the term, *safe*—which, in my day, meant being free from the prospect of physical danger—with not being criticized or forced to listen to anything they don't want to hear.

Not that I have a problem with the majority of my students, who, once they realize that in me they are facing an immovable object, settle down nicely and take pride in their ability to come up to my high expectations. I enjoy my charges, and like to think they enjoy, at least in hindsight, how well they have come along in my care, even if they find it uphill along the way. Of course, there have been the occasional disgruntled ones in my drama club, teenage divas who did not get the role they wanted, or ones who lost their parts through lack of attendance at rehearsals, but on the whole, my theater students form a great interactive team. Our current preparations for our spring production of *A Midsummer Night's Dream* were going like the dream of the title, a little confused at times, but safely predicted to end well in the final reckoning. What we didn't need, however, was interference from outside.

Not having ever undertaken the challenges of teaching a class—our new principal's pre-admin experience was a few years as a guidance counsellor—Martha Dolmas was unflinchingly certain that she knew everything about what did or did not work in the classroom. Her first visit to my drama room when checking out her new domain resulted in the following observations, thinly disguised as questions:

"Is it not rather irrelevant to do Shakespeare with today's students? Don't you feel an improv program would better enable them to have a free rein to explore their emotions? So much structure is rather inhibiting, don't you think?"

Martha stared complacently through her fashionably streaked blond bangs while she awaited my capitulation.

I replied succinctly:

"Introducing students to Shakespeare in drama is particularly relevant, now that the Bard has been virtually banished from the English curriculum in favor of media studies and world lit in translation. Acting means getting inside other characters' emotions, not letting your own run rampant. As regards to structure, theater is a discipline, and the sooner the students learn discipline, the better off they are, not just for coping with theater class, but for coping with life. So, in answer to your questions, that would be no, no and no."

The baby-blue eyes hardened. "Don't you think you are being, perhaps, a little inflexible?"

"And that would be a no, too. Now, perhaps I can get on with my class."

As you can see, Martha and I did not get off to a good start.

"You really need to watch out for the Ice Queen," my English department head warned me one day over coffee. Peter was a millennial, like Martha, but a bright, well-educated one with an impressive list of literary credits to his name. He was also a kindly young man who, ever since he discovered that I had seen the Beatles live in concert, had treated me as some sort of valuable antique and considered it his duty to look out for me. Today, he seemed to be genuinely worried. "She was grilling the secretaries about your drama room," he explained, "and the frost took on Antarctic levels when she heard how it came about."

I sighed. My drama room was something of a legend in the district, having been borne of a grievance I had filed against a former principal who had buckled like an accordion when a maintenance foreman demanded that the black box theater I had created with my students be dismantled, since it had not been constructed with union labor. My students had rallied their parents to storm a school board meeting to complain about this abominable affront to their offspring's creativity, and the superintendent, who had been taken by surprise and embarrassed in front of the board, had come to the school the next day, lambasted the weak-kneed principal, and asked me what I wanted done to replace the dismantled theater.

Within the week, my classroom black box had been replaced with an upscale version built by the required union workers. Furthermore, it was located in the major portion of an old gymnasium, leaving the smaller part to serve as a dance studio during school hours, or a dressing room when we were performing a play. Thus, I ended up with a much larger theater with many extra goodies attached. After that, my drama room became a prototype, and by now every high school in the district was equipped with a similar facility. However, the legend was a mixed blessing, because although it kept many administrators off my back, it served as a challenge to individuals like Martha who were into power and control.

"What she can't bear," my department head continued solemnly, "is the fact that you have a block of students who are so loyal to you, especially as you're one of those despised Baby Boomers who, in her view, have ruined the world and should be excoriated by all youth. She can't bear the fact that they stick up for you. She sees that as a challenge to her own authority."

"That's because she's undereducated and over-indoctrinated," I said. "Her authority depends on her position, not on any earned merit or respect."

Of course, I knew my department head was right. Martha was just waiting for her first opportunity to cause trouble, and it came in the form of Janine Perry, who had committed the ultimate sin of being absent yet again after a final warning about missing rehearsals. Janine, having been replaced in the role of Helena, wasted no time in running, damp-eyed, to Miss Dolmas and complaining about the trauma she had suffered.

After school that day, I was rehearsing the journeymen in their scene from the final act of the play. Given the small size of the stage-within-a-stage, our resourceful techie had created a brilliant moonlight effect from a single Fresnel, hung from the front-of-house section of the lighting grid, combined with a small, round mirror, high on the night-sky backdrop. Greg Bentley was a short, wiry teenager of few words who sat at the back of my modified English 10 class, quietly staying under the radar there, but coming into his own in the drama club. Here, he found a venue where he could shine and be treated with respect by students who appreciated his practical skills. As agile as a monkey, and always dressed in his techie blacks, Greg created magic with paint and light and sound. He was so proficient that I had recommended him for a summer job with the community theater group that occupied my non-teaching hours. There, he had performed Trojan service doing the lighting for the production of *Little Shop of Horrors* that I had directed for the group. I was fond of Greg, and valued his efforts, though I had quickly realized that the mirror in his *Dream* lighting plot would have to be modified. The moon, at present, was a blinding circle of light that would drive audiences to distraction.

"Where's Greg?" I asked my band of journeymen. "That mirror needs to be coated with hairspray or we'll all go blind."

Ian Hutchins, who played Snug, popped off his lion head.

"Gone to the washroom," he said.

"Smoke break," muttered Rick Patel, alias Flute, who was lounging in the wings, awaiting his entrance as Thisbe.

"Okay, never mind. He can fix it when he gets back. Let's get started. And speak up," I bellowed, so as to be heard over the pounding coming from the adjacent studio, where a dance class, presumably for elephants in tap shoes, had just commenced.

I flipped the switch by the door to turn off the overhead lights, then moved to the foot of the stage area. However, the prologue had barely started when the door opened at the rear of the theater and a shadowy figure marched down the aisle and emerged at the foot of the risers.

The first one to notice Martha's presence was Darren George, the earnest youth who played Tom Snout, the tinker, and Wall in the play-within-a-play. His eyehole was in a direct line with the aisle.

"Watch out, Ms. Hawthorne," he murmured. "Principal at twelve o'clock."

My jaw tightened, but I ignored Martha's presence and nodded for the prologue to continue. Alan King was a solid performer, which was why I'd cast him as Peter Quince, the carpenter, and although he had heard the muttering from Wall, he picked up his cue and carried on. However, he had barely delivered the next couplet before Martha's drill bit tones penetrated the air.

"A word, please, Ms. Hawthorne."

I turned to face her.

"We are in the middle of a rehearsal," I said. "Could this wait?"

Martha pouted irritably, probably due to the fact that she was semi-blinded by the moon beaming at her from the rear drop. She raised her voice to be heard over the nerve-jangling vibrations from next door.

"No, it can't," she said, spite streaking from her squinting eyes like Exocet missiles. "I am going to be forced to cancel this production. I have had a complaint from a student that may end up at the school board, even possibly the human rights commission. Until it is resolved, you are to cease working on this play."

I heard a communal gasp from the area behind me. I turned to the students, who had surged indignantly to the front of the stage, and raised a hand to indicate they should relax and wait quietly. Then I walked over to Martha so we could talk privately. I forced myself to speak calmly and kept my voice low.

"Martha, it would be entirely unreasonable to cancel the production because of a complaint, which, I can assure you, will prove to be unjustified. I assume we are talking about Janine Perry. Janine's dismissal came about through her frequent flouting of rules and her lack of attendance at rehearsals. She continued to skip practices, in spite of being warned of the consequences, and was only replaced after she ignored the third and final warning and failed to show up for an important run through. The other students have worked hard for months to prepare this show, and to punish them for their schoolmate's transgression would be grossly unfair. You cannot disappoint these students this way."

Martha glared at me. She had raised her forearm to shield her eyes from the light. (Yes, our moon definitely had to be muted.) Instead of emulating my quiet tone, she raised her voice so that every word carried to the students who were straining to listen from the stage.

"Do not tell me what I can and cannot do. You will end this rehearsal now and shut down this production until further notice. I shall expect you to report to my office in fifteen minutes to address the situation you have caused. If you apologize to the student in question and restore her position in the play, the crisis can be averted. I expect you to cooperate in this. Only then will your production be allowed to resume."

That was the last straw. It was open warfare. My eyes blazed enough megawatts to rival the moonlight.

"I am most certainly not going to apologize, nor am I taking Janine back into the play. She can take her complaint all the way to the Supreme Court as far as I'm concerned, and if you did your job in backing your staff and pointed out to her that she'd brought this on herself, there would *be* no crisis."

I strode back to the stage and gestured to my students to retake their positions.

Martha's shrill voice flew at my back, rising in decibels to compete with the cacophony from next door. It was as if a banshee had invaded the fairies' forest.

"How dare you speak to me in that tone! I will not tolerate this kind of insubordination. You will do as I requested, shut this rehearsal down, and report to my office now. And turn off that blinding moonlight while you're at it."

Her words were punctuated by a volley of crashes as the number in the adjacent gym reached its finale. At the same moment, as if in response to Martha's decree, the moonlight suddenly disappeared and the theater was plunged into darkness. In the blackout, I heard a thud. Amid bewildered cries from the players on stage, I made my way to the switch and flipped the overhead lights back on.

And gasped. Martha was sprawled motionless in the aisle. A bizarre halo of crimson was slowly developing around her head. Beside it lay the Fresnel, its moonlight as thoroughly obliterated as the objections of my confrontational administrator.

I CALLED for an ambulance right away, sent Lion to the office to let them know what had happened, and dispatched Wall to watch for the paramedics. Then I tried to revive Martha, though it was clear that there was nothing to be done. She had passed on to the happy networking bubble on high, where deceased administrators spent eternity.

Once the paramedics arrived and took over, I spoke with my students to try to make sense of what had happened. They assured me that nobody else had been backstage. No one had entered via the connecting door to the dance studio, nor by the backstage-left door, which opened onto a little-used hall that ran between the main hall and the exit doors to the parking lot. Neither had anybody gone up or come down the ladders to the lighting grid that ran all around the top of the theater.

To make sure no one was lurking in those inky shadows, I

climbed up to see for myself. But the grid was definitely empty. However, I was concerned to see no safety chain on the bar where the light had hung. I had always impressed the importance of safety on my students, and Greg had unfailingly proved to be reliable. Therefore, I was worried as I returned to the ground. My hope that I could question Greg before the police arrived was in vain, because I descended to find we had already been graced with the presence of a stolid RCMP corporal who was bringing everyone out into the front of house so he could take statements from all who had been present at the time of the accident.

When Greg returned from the washroom, reeking of smoke, which explained his lengthy bathroom break, he hung his head and managed to mutter the few words of apology that made us understand what might have happened. Realizing that his moonlight was a problem, he'd intended to return to make an adjustment to the light, so he had not tightened the screw holding the light as firmly as he would have done once he'd made the final setting. He also explained the absence of the safety chain. He had noticed that the wire had been frayed, so he had taken it down with him, intending to replace it with one that was not damaged. He produced the two chains for the investigating officer, who seemed sympathetic to the wiry little teenager who was so clearly mortified with the lapse that had produced such dire results.

This was relief of a sort. When I'd first seen Martha laid low in the aisle, I'd had the horrible thought that one of my students had deliberately sabotaged the light. My eyes had immediately swept the stage to ensure that every one of my players was still in place. Yes, in that quick glimpse, I had seen that all were present and correct. Alan was still rooted to his spot for the prologue, and Mario Boscetti and Rick Patel remained where they had come forth from their respective wings, their bewildered expressions perfect for Bottom and Flute, if not for their Pyramus and Thisbe characters. Lion and Moonshine still hovered at the edge of the stage, the former with his head tucked, Anne Boleyn-style, under his arm, and the latter clutching his rough-hewn crescent. Wall remained within his wall. So, whilst Greg certainly would draw a degree of culpability, which would also reflect on me, it seemed clear that the release of the light had not been intentional.

The corporal took his time exploring the theater and ascertaining for himself whether or not any intruders could have accessed the area. There were thirty tap dancers and their coach to prove that nobody had come through the dance studio door, and the drama students were adamant that the backstage-left door had also remained closed. The corporal was further satisfied after questioning Steve Briggs, a habitually unruly member of my department head's class, who had been banished to the hallway for some delinquency or other. Steve had seen everyone who had come in or out of the auditorium doors. He insisted that only three people had entered: Martha, the policeman, and Greg, in that order. Wall had led the paramedics in by the backstage-left door.

All the same, the corporal climbed up to the lighting grid and plodded around, examining the lights, shaking the teasers, prodding the rolled-up tormentors, and dislodging an extension cord or two in the process. He noted that there were only two ladders up to the grid, and both had been in view by the various cast members ever since Greg had left to go for his break. Therefore, in the absence of any indications of intruders or foul play, he decided it had probably been the vibrations from the dance studio that had caused the screw to loosen and the light to be jolted off the bar. The force of its fall, combined with its weight, would have wrenched the plug from the socket.

The corporal finally concluded that Martha's demise was death by misadventure. He, like me, seemed genuinely concerned about the mental state of the wiry little student who so deeply felt the weight of responsibility for the accident. I was relieved that the policeman was taking the approach that he did, but it was with a heavy heart that I forged on with the play. Much as I had disliked Martha, I would never have wished her that terrible end.

KIDS, much as I love them, can be utterly heartless. After Martha's death, a week lapsed before we resumed rehearsals, but the very next time I entered the theater, I heard a bright, clear voice with impeccable diction delivering a variation on a line from the Bard.

"Ill met by moonlight, proud Miss Dolmas."

The speaker was Jasmeet Laghari, our stunningly beautiful Titania, an International Baccalaureate student with a sharp brain and an even sharper wit. She followed the phrase with a shriek of laughter, which her castmates echoed like a hysterical Greek chorus, only subsiding as they saw me come in. Jasmeet, for all that she was a straight-A student, or maybe because of it, had also had her run-ins with Martha Dolmas.

I was about to utter some words of reproof when Greg Bentley beat me to it.

"It isn't funny, you know," he said soberly. "I'm glad she can't stop the show, but it was really awful that she died."

Jasmeet opened her mouth to say something scornful, then, seeing the look in Greg's eyes, thought better of it and held her peace. There are times the modified students can teach the scholastic ones a thing or two.

After the rehearsal concluded, I gave the actors their notes, then dismissed them. I needed to go through the lighting cues with Greg, so he remained behind and made his way up into the booth at the top of the risers. He slid the glass window open so we could communicate without the use of headsets.

"Bring up the lights for the final scene, Greg," I called. I switched off the work lights and waited in the darkness.

A moment later, the forest emerged from the shadows, a gentle, pale blue wash illuminating the painted trees and making them glow as if lit from within. It was eerie and magical, the realm of sprites and fairies. Greg had an assured future ahead of him if he persevered. Actors might be a dime a dozen, but good technicians were always in demand.

Suddenly, I noticed a flaw in the moon. There was a shadow across it, and I realized immediately what had caused it. The extension cord that had been knocked loose by the RCMP corporal had not been gathered in. It was dangling in a direct line between the Fresnel and the mirror.

"Hold on, Greg. I'm going up to move that out of the way. I'm going to adjust the tormentors, too. They're a little too far in."

I went backstage, watching my own shadow eerily flowing across the silvery forest as I crossed the set. I climbed the stage-left ladder and stepped out onto the grid. I tweaked back the tormentor nearest to where I stood. Then I crossed the backstage section of the grid to deal with the cord that was creating the shadow on the moon. I pulled it up and secured it, then continued across the grid to adjust the stage-right tormentor. As I pushed it back, I became aware of the smell of smoke. It was very faint, but the scent prompted a memory. In the panic and turmoil immediately following Martha's death, I had smelled smoke in that very spot when I had come up to inspect the grid. At that time, the tormentor had been rolled up and secured below the grid, a burly hammock of sturdy fabric, easily large enough to conceal a person, particularly one who was small and wiry. I thought back to that day. I had found great difficulty believing that my star techie would have taken such a long time to replace a defective safety chain. Could he have come back earlier? Was there any moment when the backstage door was clear for him to enter?

And then I realized that there had been such a moment. When Martha had made her first dramatic announcement, my students had all come to the front of the stage. What if Greg had slipped in at that very moment and heard that the play was about to be canceled? He would have been up the ladder and onto the grid by the time I walked over to Martha to discuss her concerns? With the noise from next door, and our focus on the imminent threat, we would have been oblivious to anything that was happening overhead.

Greg was agile as well as wiry. It would have been nothing to him to lower himself off the edge of the grid and into the rolled-up tormentor. In the cavernous darkness, I would never have seen him there. But when could he have come down unseen? It only took me a moment to figure it out. The corporal had brought us all out to the front of house for questioning. The backstage area had been deserted at that point. Greg could have come down the ladder, gone out through the backstage-left door, and come up to the main hall. Then he could have re-entered by the auditorium doors.

I'd wondered at the time why he'd come back that way, given that we knew perfectly well that he'd sneaked out into the quadrangle for a smoke. But it made sense if he'd wanted his late entrance to the theater to be witnessed.

He wouldn't have meant to kill her, of course. But given how passionate he was about the play, how dedicated he was to the one area in school where he had found success, I could imagine the wave of rage and indignation he would have felt. Could he have deliberately dropped the light in the heat of the moment?

I looked across to the booth. It was at eye level from where I stood just below the ceiling of my precious black box. I could see Greg's head clearly. He was sitting at the lighting board. The outline of his spiky, unruly hair made a corrugated silhouette against the gleaming yellow light within the booth.

"It looks okay, now, Ms. Hawthorne," he called to me. "Come down and have a look. See what you think."

He was a good kid, and I knew he was already riddled with guilt over the principal's death. He had enough of a burden to carry, without adding any more. And anyway, all those thoughts going through my mind were pure speculation. For all I knew, they were as fantastical as the Bard's mischievous fairies; as insubstantial as the dream in our play. And I knew Greg would talk to me if he felt the need to unburden himself.

"On my way," I called back.

The RCMP corporal had given the verdict: moonlight and misadventure. Who was I to argue?

M.H. CALLWAY

M. H. Callway's short crime fiction has been published in many anthologies and magazines. Her stories and novellas have won or been shortlisted for several awards, including the Bony Pete, the Crime Writers of Canada Arthur Ellis Award, and the Derringer. Her debut novel, *Windigo Fire*, was shortlisted for the Debut Dagger and the Arthur Ellis Award for both the Best Unpublished and Best First Novel. In 2013, she co-founded the Mesdames of Mayhem, a collective of Canadian crime writers whose work is showcased in their four anthologies. The Mesdames are also the subject of a CBC documentary by director Cat Mills. M.H. is a member of Crime Writers of Canada, Sisters in Crime National and Toronto Chapter, the Short Mystery Fiction Society, and the Writers Union of Canada. Find her at https://mhcallway.com.

THE MOON GOD OF BROADMOOR

M.H. CALLWAY

THE LIFE of a public health inspector is not easy. In college I'd studied to become one, because I yearned to protect the public from danger. But out in the real world, I quickly learned that my approach to fixing health problems guaranteed that I'd remain a junior inspector forever.

For the past year my boss, Rick the Dick, had me logging reports and drafting S.O.A.D letters for his signature.

S.O.A.D. translation: "We don't handle your problem at the public health department so I'm sending it over to [*insert handy department name here*]. Thank you so much for sharing your concerns with us. Now Sod Off and Die."

One steamy August afternoon, my job turned to crap. Literally crap.

Rick dropped a color print-out on my desk. "That's not chocolate ice cream," he said with a smirk.

I stared at the glistening brown image, trying not to gag. I longed to ask Rick if he was proud of his accomplishment, but since I needed my job, I said, "You're showing me this masterpiece for a reason, right?"

"Correct. This one's yours, Liz. So step in it. I mean *on* it."

Two of my colleagues burst out laughing and urged me to tread carefully.

From Rick I'd learned the hard way to avoid inter-jurisdictional disputes like poison. "OK, so a dog took a dump on someone's lawn. That's a local by-law violation. Not our jurisdiction. Therefore, not a public health issue."

Rick puffed up to his full five feet six inches. "Councilor Viola Best phoned me this morning. Personally. She's very upset with the health department."

My heart sank. Councilor Best was a fire-breathing reformer who looked and acted like an African warrior queen. She attacked city hall's old guard at every opportunity—and won. No wonder Rick was sweating like he'd just stepped out of a sauna.

"Fine, I'll bite," I said. "Why does Councilor Best care about your chocolate ice cream?"

"One of her pet constituents, some old lady, filed this complaint with us. Six months ago, Best claims. But I can't find it in our database."

I shrugged. "If it's not in our database, we didn't receive it."

Rick swore. He'd ordered me to file all dog crap complaints directly into our system's Recycle Bin. Now one had risen from the grave to bite him in the butt.

I decided that I really liked Councilor Best—a lot.

"OK, OK," Rick said. "You can track that lost file later. Get yourself down to Old Lady Grump's garden and do an inspection. Show her that public health really cares."

In other words, flood the old dear with warm words, but don't actually resolve her complaint.

I smelled a set-up. "Why send me? Why not someone experienced?"

"You asked for more field experience." Rick bristled. "Now's your chance."

"Fine, I'll do it."

"Good, great. And Liz, remember, don't get carried away. Be discreet, OK?"

Well, I'd see about that.

FREEDOM AT LAST. No more eye-burning computer screens and no Rick hovering and micromanaging.

Field work came with perks: our own official wheels. I happily signed out a city van with Toronto Health Department emblazoned in blue down its sides and punched the old lady's address, 588 Broad Street, into the navigation system.

Google Maps led me to an older neighborhood east of downtown that was lined with worn-out Victorian houses and ancient maples about to drop rotten branches on the unwary. Broad Street turned out to be so narrow that street parking was forbidden. Best's pet constituent, a Mrs. Jack, lived in the Broadmoor Suites, the only apartment building on the street. It was a four-storey, U-shaped red brick fortress that dated from the 1930s. Its two wings, the arms of the "U", embraced a courtyard filled with a straggly lawn.

I parked illegally in front of the building. From where I sat in the driver's seat, I could see that Mrs. Jack had ample cause to complain. The grass was befouled.

Step one, find Mrs. Jack. I climbed out of the van, but couldn't spot the entrance to the building. Now what?

My answer came in the form of an apparition: a chubby, middle-aged man wearing a powder-blue tunic, shiny mauve tights, and a gauzy, iridescent cape.

He emerged from a doorway located in the bend of the U on my right and sauntered down the fractured cement path that bisected the lawn. He stopped just in front of me.

"I see that I have struck awe in your heart," he said. "Don't be afraid."

"Excuse me?"

"I am Thoth, God of the Moon. How may I help you?"

A large brooch, in the shape of a pink rhinestone flamingo, pinned the ends of his cape to the front of his tunic. His stringy black hair badly needed a wash, but his round face looked friendly.

Best to play along. "Nice to meet you, um, Thoth. I seek Mrs.

Jack."

"Ah, yes, the keeper of my earthly home. And what is your business with her?"

"I'm with the health department. Mrs. Jack made a complaint."

"Sad." Thoth shook his head. "So young and already ensnared in the satanic coils of bureaucracy. You will find Mrs. Jack through there." With a sweep of his plump arm, he pointed to the left wing of the U and a small doorway, the mirror image of the one from which he'd appeared.

I smiled, sidestepped him on the path, and went into the building.

Mrs. Jack, an 85-year-old Jamaican lady, worked as the Broadmoor's superintendent. Leaning heavily on her cane, she insisted on accompanying me back outside and showing me the lawn herself.

"Twenty-five years ago, when the late Mr. Jack and I moved in, this was a beautiful garden." Mrs. Jack waved her stick at the dry yellow lawn. "But Mr. Richard, the new owner, hates spending money. Especially on frivolities like flowers. The Broadmoor has become a disgrace."

Together we gazed over a vast tundra of excrement in various stages of returning to nature.

"You're right, it's disgusting," I said. "Does one of the tenants own a dog?"

"No pets are allowed in the building." Mrs. Jack shook her head, then smiled. "Well, if they own a cat or little lapdog, I turn a blind eye. But none of them did this."

Certainly the work of a much larger dog.

I cleared my throat. "A dog poop removal service could clean up this mess for you."

"I'm way ahead of you, girl." Mrs. Jack drew herself up. Despite her advanced years, she had several inches on me. "I already called those doggy-doo people and they blew me off. They won't remove this muck because whoever made it was no dog. That's why I called the health department!"

"Right." I felt sick to my stomach.

What other city department dealt with human waste? The Works Department! They handled water and sewage. I could toss Mrs. Jack's problem over to them, S.O.A.D. But when I suggested this, Mrs. Jack got annoyed.

"I've already been down that road," she said. "The Works Department won't deal with human waste unless it's in the pipes. And I don't see a pipe here, do you?"

"No." I shook my head.

"What does a taxpayer have to do to get you government types moving? Six months I've endured this mess. Mr. Richard doesn't care. He plans to sell the Broadmoor for development. But Councilor Best, she cares. Mm-hmm, she cares a lot."

Trapped, I saw no way to extricate myself from Rick's set-up unless...

"Mrs. Jack," I said, remembering the snow shovel stashed in the back of my van, "I'm going to clean up your problem. Personally. But I'll need garbage bags. As many as you can spare."

"Allow me to be of help," a man's voice said behind us.

There was Thoth, lurking behind us on the path. Apparently he'd overheard our entire conversation.

"Why thank you, Thoth," Mrs. Jack said. "That's real nice of you."

I waited until he vanished back into the building in a rainbow flash.

"Who or what was that?" I asked.

"Oh, that's just Stanley." Mrs. Jack chuckled. "Don't worry, he's harmless. Lives up there on fourth." She pointed her cane at the top floor of the right wing. "He fell down to earth from the moon. Until the cosmos summons him back home, he's doing good works on our planet."

"He told you this."

"All the time."

"And does he always dress like that?" Like a charity store drag queen, I wanted to add.

"Sure. How else would we earthlings know that he's God of the Moon?" Mrs. Jack threw me a wink before she limped back inside.

STANLEY AKA THOTH proved true to his word and showed up with an armful of black garbage bags. He then stood guard while I literally shoveled crap, though he did hold the bags open for me.

The afternoon wore on. The sun grew hotter, but I'd only cleared a quarter of the grass. I leaned on the snow shovel, desperately thirsty.

"You look ill," Stanley said. "May I get you something to drink?"

"Sure, that would be nice." I half-suspected he wouldn't return, but thankfully, he did, and handed me a large plastic bottle of water.

"Thanks." I took a long drink.

"You are welcome. Forgive me for saying so, but you're rather pale and thin. And from your state of tiredness, unused to physical labor."

True, I *was* out of shape from sitting in front of a computer all day. Still Stanley's remark hurt.

"I do not wish to offend," he said. "Merely to offer my assistance."

"Won't your royal robes get dirty?"

"Please, hand me the shovel."

Why not? I passed it over.

This time I held the bags open, while Stanley shoveled. I insisted that we take turns, to which he agreed, though he proved to be far faster than me.

Three hours later, the lawn stood clear, while a heap of black garbage bags rested on the walkway.

Now what? I hadn't thought ahead to disposals.

Stanley was studying his wristwatch, an old-fashioned steel Timex. My grandfather owned one just like it.

"I regret that I must leave," he said. "My astro-chronometer has reminded me of my commitment at the public library."

"You can't just take off. I can't leave these bags lying here." In fact, the whole point of our exertions had been to make the problem disappear.

Stanley considered this.

"Return tonight at ten p.m. and I will assist you."

With that, he departed.

I managed to summon enough strength to drag the bags over to the city van. One by one I hoisted them in, leaving barely enough space for me, let alone my deadly cargo.

Finally finished, I slumped down and sat on the walkway, holding the stained snow shovel like a spear. That's where Mrs. Jack found me.

"My goodness. Let me make you a nice cup of tea," she said, inviting me inside.

Though the city had strict rules about health inspectors accepting gifts from the public, I figured that a cup of tea would be okay. Especially after Mrs. Jack offered me her bathroom to clean up.

The living room of her ground floor apartment was crammed with photos of her grandchildren. Books lined the shelves along her walls and more books were piled everywhere I looked. I moved a stack of sci-fi novels from a pink velvet armchair and sat down while Mrs. Jack wheeled in the tea trolley.

The tea was Yorkshire Blend, strong and aromatic. Mrs. Jack served it in gold-rimmed china cups patterned with cornflowers. When she offered me a slice of what looked like fruitcake, I accepted despite my misgivings.

I took a bite. "This is delicious."

"Ah, you've never had Jamaican rum cake before," she said. "My secret is over-proof rum and lots of it."

Exactly what I needed. I ended up eating three more pieces while I learned why Stanley had left me literally holding the bag. "You mean, they let him read to kids at the library? Dressed like that?"

"Oh, the librarians and the children love him," Mrs. Jack said, sipping her tea. "And he teaches those poor homeless guys at the mission how to read, too."

"Was Stanley a teacher? Before all the Moon God stuff?"

"Maybe. But he's been like this ever since I've lived here. All I know is that he pays his rent on time and doesn't cause trouble. Now tell me about yourself, Elizabeth."

My background was suburban middle class boring, so I didn't have much to tell. Besides, I was growing antsy about the illegally parked van outside. I thanked Mrs. Jack and left as soon as I helped her clear up.

Now what? I rolled down the windows—it was getting ripe inside the van—and drove through the neighborhood scouting out potential dump sites. No luck. I ended up back at the Broadmoor counting down the miserable hours until ten o'clock.

What if Stanley didn't show? I'd probably violated a dozen by-laws, crossed over myriad jurisdictional boundaries, and ensured that a city van would reek of excrement forever.

By 10:30, Stanley had still not appeared. Why, oh, why had I put faith in a false Moon God? I climbed out of the van, stomped into the courtyard, and screamed out Stanley's name.

The answer came in a shower of water—at least I hoped it was water—from above. It barely missed me. I looked up and spotted Stanley on the roof of the Broadmoor, backlit by the rising moon like an overweight superhero.

"Come up. Join me," he called down.

"How?" I shouted back.

"Take the elevator. You will find the stairs to the roof on fourth."

Stanley's wing of the Broadmoor did indeed possess an ancient, creaking elevator. I rode it up to the fourth floor and stepped into a long corridor. Its jaundiced linoleum floor squeaked under my runners as I made my way along.

Halfway down, a gray metal door stood open. It gave onto a set of cement stairs that led up into the dark. Using my cellphone as a flashlight, I went up, opened the door at the top, and stepped outside into a night full of stars.

The moon shone down on the Broadmoor's flat roof, turning it into a lake of silver. Stanley picked his way over to me, his pink flamingo glittering.

"Why did you throw water at me?" I asked.

"Sorry about that. I needed to get your attention. Please, follow me."

He led the way to the edge of the rooftop, the courtyard directly below. This, then, was Stanley's throne room from where he kept watch over us earthly mortals.

Under a blue tarp canopy, he'd set up a pink velvet armchair, the twin of Mrs. Jack's, next to a large, antiquated refrigerator, and a floor lamp with a beveled glass shade. A stack of paperback novels leaned against the armchair.

Close to the roof's edge, I spotted a white plastic bucket, dripping water: Stanley's unorthodox communications system. Next to it stood the small stone sculpture of an owl.

"That is Ibis, my sacred bird," Stanley said, following my gaze.

"I see." First a pink flamingo, now an owl. "Nice arrangement, reading lamp and all," I said. "Good to have the tarp in case it rains."

"The men at the mission presented it to me. To thank me for teaching them to read. I am, after all, god of wisdom and learning."

"Right. I see you have a beer fridge, too. Convenient."

"That is my spaceship."

"What?"

"For the day I return to my home, the moon."

"Stanley, don't climb into that fridge. It's airtight. You'll suffocate."

"I do not breathe air like you humans. You forget that the moon, my home, has no air."

Enough of this. "Did you forget that you promised to help me?"

"Not at all. But I have more to show you."

I followed him across the roof to the opposite side.

"Behold," he said, waving at Toronto's spectacular, shimmering skyline.

"Beautiful," I said, impatient to get going.

"Do not be beguiled by their beauty. They are the Crystal Blades, the relentless destroyers. Already they plan to devour my earthly domain."

"You mean the condo towers?" The name "Crystal Blades" sounded similar to a monster from *Star Trek*.

"The Crystal Blades enslave thousands of your fellow humans in order to reproduce. Once they take root in the earth, they capture thousands more. Seal them in a hive and drain their bio-energy."

"Like *The Matrix*." I dreamed of owning a tiny apartment in a downtown Crystal Blade. That's why I was still living at home with my parents trying to save up for one.

"You do understand. Now let us depart."

THE FETID ODOR in my van didn't bother Stanley, who cheerfully strapped himself into the passenger seat. He assured me that he knew where I could safely dump the bags.

He directed me to drive west toward the city lights. Soon we arrived at a huge construction site for a thirty-story condo tower. He guided me over to a spot where an oversized dumpster leaned against the chain link fence.

I parked, jumped out of the driver's seat, and unlocked the back cargo door. Stanley followed. He seized a bag of offal from the van, and with a powerful swing, tossed it over the fence into the dumpster.

"Good shot," I said.

He continued this way without needing my help. But halfway through, he raised his hand.

"We must move on from here."

"Why did someone see us?"

"I wish to distribute our message equally."

I was too tired to argue. We drove to a second condo construction site where he lobbed the rest of the bags directly into its cavernous excavation.

Three o'clock in the morning found us at a 24-hour DIY car wash where Stanley watched me scrub out the van. We blended in perfectly with the other eccentric night people.

BACK AT WORK NEXT MORNING, fuzzy-headed after only two hours sleep, I was blindsided by Rick's verbal onslaught.

"You took a city van without authority. Junior inspectors use their own cars or take the bus. And where's your report? Councilor Best is asking for it."

My bleary brain stopped focusing on the lies I needed for my report. "Mrs. Jack's lawn doesn't have a problem anymore. Somebody cleaned it up."

"Please, tell me that somebody wasn't you."

"A volunteer?" I ventured. That sounded better than Moon God.

"You had no authority to enlist a volunteer. What if the volunteer injured himself? The health department would be liable—"

"There she is!" a woman's deep voice rang out.

Councilor Best strode into the office, an entourage of aides in her wake.

"You, Elizabeth, are a hero," she declared, towering over my desk. And Rick. "Mrs. Jack can't say enough good things about you and the health department. That's what this city needs, workers who solve problems."

Rick moved from condemnation to preening at warp speed. "Yes, indeed, Councilor. Elizabeth is one of my finest inspectors."

"I'll say she is," Best said. "Keep up the good work, you two."

But my good fortune didn't last. Friday morning, a week later, Rick's signature smug smile was back in place. Mrs. Jack had called the office: her problem was back. But Rick refused to let me look into it.

"Those reports, they're your priority," he told me.

Now what? The minute I left work, I grabbed an Uber to the Broadmoor. I asked the driver to wait while I inspected the lawn.

I almost burst into tears. Once again, the Broadmoor's grass was polluted with stuff that belonged in the sewer. The thought of doing yet another clean-up felt crushing.

I looked up at the roof, but saw no sign of Stanley. Then I remembered: no moon tonight.

Think outside the box, I urged myself. The only way to stop this outrage would be to catch the perpetrator in the act. I couldn't camp out at the Broadmoor for days on end, but there was another digital alternative.

On the way over, we'd passed a spyware store with a comical neon sign: a cartoon cat peering through a large magnifying glass. Cyber Cat, that was the store's name.

My Uber driver ferried me back to Cyber Cat. The owner, a young man named Tony, couldn't stop laughing after I explained my problem.

"I love a challenge," he said. "What you need is a spy cam."

I didn't have a clue how to install a spy cam, so when Tony offered to do it for me, I gratefully accepted. Besides, Tony was pretty hot, so that was a bonus.

Tony drove us and his equipment over to the Broadmoor in Cyber Cat's van. He wrinkled his nose at the disgusting mess on the lawn, his dark eyes scanning the Broadmoor's façade for the best spot to install the spy cam. "I recommend there, behind the bird." He pointed to the entrance into the wing where Mrs. Jack lived.

There above the lintel squatted a stone owl, the twin of Stanley's stone "Ibis" that resided on the roof of the other wing.

"Good thing I brought my ladder," Tony said.

In twenty minutes, he'd set up the spy cam and got it running. Even better, he offered to drive me home.

"I'll take it down for you on Sunday night," Tony said on the way. "I can't wait to see what turns up."

My anxiety that weekend was off the chart. Finally, on Sunday evening, Tony knocked on my parents' front door, carrying his computer and the precious camera tape. My mother insisted he stay for dinner, but I could hardly eat, I felt so wired.

Afterwards Tony set up his computer and together we viewed the tape. Lots of people entered and exited the Broadmoor, but none of them acted suspiciously.

Then Tony laughed. "Oh, man, is this Thoth, the Moon God?"

There was Stanley striding out of the building in colored splendor. Judging by the time of the recording, he was off to the library.

Night fell, the tape wound on. Stanley returned home. Then a short man trotted into Mrs. Jack's wing. When he left, he was carrying a loaf-sized parcel. As he crossed the courtyard, a stream of water hit him from above. He stopped, swore, and shook his fist at the roof.

There was something awfully familiar about him.

"That guy really looks like my boss, Rick. Can we zoom in?" I asked.

Sure enough, the man was Rick. But why would he be visiting the Broadmoor? And why was Stanley dousing him with water?

"Liz, take a look at this," Tony said, interrupting my thoughts. He pointed to the screen. The time was after midnight.

A wild-haired man appeared. He looked around, dropped his pants and unloaded on the grass. Shortly after he'd finished, another disheveled man showed up and repeated the performance. And then another and another.

Tony and I were grossed out, but we quickly pieced together what was happening. I had my answer and, hopefully, the solution to Mrs. Jack's problem.

When Tony left for home, he refused to let me pay him. Instead, he asked me out.

Of course, I said yes.

MONDAY MORNING BACK AT WORK, Rick seemed unusually cheerful. I found out why at the end of the day, when he called me into his office and closed the door.

"You took a bribe," he said, smug smile in place. "Mrs. Jack told me. Councilor Best will be so disappointed in her star employee."

"What, tea and rum cake? That's not a bribe."

"Oh, but it is. That's why you took such a personal interest in her case. Don't bother denying it."

"And what about you? I have a tape that shows you collecting an entire rum cake from Mrs. Jack. Because you own the Broadmoor Suites, *Mr. Richard*."

Rick's face turned scarlet, from the top of his bald head down to his tight shirt collar.

"And you're selling it to a developer," I went on. "If that isn't a conflict of interest, I don't know what is."

"Urban development is a completely separate jurisdiction from public health," Rick declared. "Prove there's a conflict of interest. I dare you. Meanwhile I'm calling Councilor Best. You can quit or get fired, your choice."

He pulled out his cell phone and started punching numbers.

And I'd believed that truth mattered. Rick's mastery of city by-laws had outwitted me completely.

I slammed out of Rick's office, gathered up my things and rushed outside. In little over a week, I'd gone from glory to epic fail. I was going to lose my job in disgrace, but Rick would remain in the clear.

How would I tell my parents? And Tony? I wandered aimlessly through the downtown streets, searching for a brilliant solution, but none came to mind. Darkness fell. In the end, I could think of only one meaningful task to accomplish before I vanished into ignominy.

But first I needed to speak to the Moon God.

THE NEW MOON WAS RISING. I found Stanley on the roof, seated on his pink velvet throne, his floor lamp lit against the dark, a book in his hand.

"Mrs. Jack says that your name is Elizabeth," he said as I approached. "But your true name is Diana."

Diana, goddess of the moon. Great.

"Stanley, we need to talk. Last week my friend and I installed a security camera to discover who makes the mess on the Broadmoor's lawn."

He closed his book and sighed. "I thought so. I watched you

from the window of my earthly dwelling. You defiled Ibis's twin."

"The tape shows you throwing water down on my boss, Rick."

"Ah, yes, Mr. Richard, Harbinger of the Crystal Blades. Your boss, you say."

"Yes, he is, or rather was, my manager at the health department. Look, throwing water on Rick won't stop him selling the Broadmoor. Nor will asking your friends from the mission to take a dump on the lawn."

Stanley smiled. So I'd guessed right.

"Please ask them to stop. Don't upset Mrs. Jack anymore."

Stanley stood up, shaking out his shimmering cape. "I am Thoth, god of justice. On the one hand, Mrs. Jack is my friend and lends me books. On the other, she bribes Mr. Richard with rum cake."

"She's only trying to stay on Rick's good side. To keep her apartment."

He moved over to the roof's edge and knelt down beside the stone owl, resting his hand on its head. "Perhaps it is time for me to return home." He gazed up at the faint sliver of moon.

"Councilor Best is Mrs. Jack's friend. She'd be a powerful ally for you. If anyone can save the Broadmoor from the developers, I mean the Crystal Blades, she could."

"I understand nothing of your earthly politics." He shook his head. "Behold, here comes the Harbinger now."

He pointed down at a dark figure strutting down the Broadmoor's pathway. It was Rick all right.

Stanley's hand groped for the bucket of water, but somehow he missed. It toppled over the roof's edge, bounced down on the grass and narrowly missed Rick, though it doused him with water.

Rick stared up at the roof, furious. "You nearly killed me, you lunatic!"

"You are trespassing on my earthly domain," Stanley declared. "Be gone. I order you to depart."

"You're the one who's leaving. You're a danger to this building and everyone in it. I have your eviction notice right here." He patted his shirt pocket.

Stanley seized Ibis the owl. "I am Thoth, god of justice and death!"

"Stanley, no!" I shouted.

With the same powerful swing that he'd used to hurl the garbage bags, he set the gargoyle in flight.

It arced down. Rick's head vanished in a mist of red.

I was too shocked to scream. In the ensuing silence, I heard only Stanley's heavy breathing as he stared down at the courtyard and what he had done.

"Stanley?"

He gathered up his book, turned off the lamp, and retreated back to the roof stairs. I followed him.

"Thoth, Great One, listen to me. We have to call the police."

"No." He shook his head. "Mr. Richard was your boss. They will accuse you, Diana. You must leave this place."

"No, I can't do that. But I'll help you with the police, Stanley, I promise."

"Please, Diana. Thoth, your god, commands you to leave. *I* will call the police."

With that he turned and went down the stairs with me behind him. I watched him walk down the corridor on the fourth floor and disappear into a suite at the far end.

By the time I reached the courtyard, I heard the first police siren.

FORTUNATELY, the police believed my story: that Rick and I met up at the Broadmoor after work to investigate Mrs. Jack's ongoing lawn problem when out of the blue, the gargoyle fell from the roof. I never mentioned Stanley.

And he didn't mention me when he made a full confession to the police.

The crown attorney wanted to charge him with murder, but his public defender argued that Rick's death was a terrible accident.

While Stanley's case dragged on, Mrs. Jack and I crowdfunded his bail money.

Councilor Best turned Rick's ownership of the Broadmoor into a juicy scandal. So, I'd been right after all. Rick's secret deal with the developers *was* an egregious conflict of interest.

Councilor Best also offered me a place on her team, but I politely declined. I'd had enough of politics for a lifetime. In fact, I left the health department because I'd found a better way to help people.

LATE ONE EVENING, a year later, the phone rang at Cyber Cat.

"Elizabeth, do you remember me?" an elderly voice asked.

"Why, hello, Mrs. Jack. Of course, I remember you," I said.

"Councilor Best said you work at Cyber Cat now."

"Yes, Tony and I got married."

Mrs. Jack took a deep breath. "I hate to bother you, but I'm worried about Stanley."

"Has something happened?"

"Maybe," Mrs. Jack said. "I haven't seen him in quite some time. Could you come over?"

How could I refuse? Tony was out visiting a client, so I texted that I'd meet him at home afterwards. What would Stanley say if I told him that our new home was a condo in one of his hated Crystal Blades?

I drove over, the full moon rising, its pale blue light turning Broad Street into a river of ice. The Broadmoor Suites looked the same except for the sign planted on its withered lawn: NOTICE OF DEMOLITION.

Mrs. Jack was waiting for me in the courtyard. Her cane was gone, and she leaned heavily on a walker. I tried not to be shocked by how greatly she had aged.

"Thank you so much for coming," she said. "I'm moving into the retirement home tomorrow. It's time."

"I saw the demolition notice," I said. "I'm so sorry. The Moon

God's mortal enemies, the Crystal Blades, have won after all."

Mrs. Jack sighed. "Yes, indeed. Turns out Mr. Richard had already sold the Broadmoor to the developer. Things just took longer with his estate and the scandal and all."

"How's Stanley taking it?"

"How do you think? I'm worried about him. He's due in court tomorrow and his lawyer can't find him. He's not answering his phone."

She pressed a wrinkled hand over her heart. "If I give you the key, would you check his apartment? It's beyond me now. If he's there, he might listen to you. He really liked you, you know."

Cold dread tracked down my spine. "Sure, okay."

I accepted the passkey from her and rode the battered elevator up to the fourth floor, though every cell in my body warned me not to look. But when I started down the long corridor, I remembered the stairs to the roof.

I pulled open the metal door to the roof stairway. The door at the top stood open. Moonlight spilled down the cement steps in a ghostly waterfall.

"Stanley? Thoth?"

No answer. I climbed up.

Moonlight bathed the rooftop in silver, but Stanley's throne room lay in ruins. The tarp had blown away. Rain had turned the pink velvet armchair into a sodden mess. The lamp stand had tipped over and shattered. But the fridge still stood there, immovable.

I became aware of a rattling sound. The fridge's motor was running.

Moving closer, I saw that its door wasn't quite closed. Through the gap, the moon shone down on a blue, frozen face, the eyes like white marbles.

"Oh, Stanley," I said.

He'd roped the door, held it shut, and slowly frozen to death on his journey back to the moon.

Thoth, god of wisdom, justice and learning.

Thoth, god of death.

JUDY PENZ SHELUK

A former journalist and magazine editor, **Judy Penz Sheluk** (editor/author) is the author of two mystery series: the Glass Dolphin Mysteries and the Marketville Mysteries. Her short crime fiction appears in several collections, including *The Best Laid Plans* and *Heartbreaks & Half-truths*, which she also edited. Judy is a member of Sisters in Crime National, Toronto, and Guppy Chapters, International Thriller Writers, the Short Mystery Fiction Society, and Crime Writers of Canada, where she serves as Chair on the Board of Directors. She splits her time between Alliston and Goulais River, Ontario. Find her at www.judypenzsheluk.com.

STRAWBERRY MOON

JUDY PENZ SHELUK

THE U.S. BORDER guard looked at me with barely concealed contempt. I had the feeling he enjoyed his power a little more than he should have. I made an effort to summon up a winsome smile.

It didn't win him over.

"Lose the shades," he said, and pointed, as if I wasn't quite bright enough to catch his meaning.

I'm a lot of things, but not bright isn't one of them. I pushed my sunglasses to the top of my head, hoping he wouldn't notice my black eye. I'd done my best to cover it up, but an observant individual might still be able to spot the burgeoning bruise beneath the makeup and mascara. I figured border guards were trained to be observant.

If he noticed, he didn't comment. Instead, he studied my passport photo, his eyes flicking back and forth from my face to the picture. Apparently satisfied that I was the woman in the photograph, he began asking the usual questions.

"Citizen of what country?"

"Canada."

"How long do you intend to stay in the United States?"

"A few hours."

"Purpose of your visit?"

"I want to see the freighters." I smiled at him. He didn't smile back.

"Where do you live?"

"Toronto." I pronounced it Ta-ronno, the way folks do who come from there.

"Lake Superior's a long way to travel to see some freighters. You don't have freighters in Lake Ontario?"

Truthfully, I had no idea. I'd thought up the freighter story after listening to Gordon Lightfoot's *The Wreck of the Edmund Fitzgerald* for the fourth time in as many hours, Sault Ste. Marie radio stations feeding off the long-ago local tragedy.

"I've been camping at Pancake Bay Provincial Park."

That netted me an arched eyebrow. "A man has been reported missing in Pancake Bay. Just found his aluminum fishing boat. There's been no sign of his body." He favored me with a glacial stare. "Yet."

Yet. I felt my black eye twitch. "Is that so?"

I must have passed the test, twitchy eye and all, because his expression almost passed for a smile. "Almost" being the operative word. I glanced in the rear-view mirror, took note of my flushed cheeks, the dilated pupils. The first could be attributed to the heat. The other? Drugs, though I knew I was clean. Anxiety? Surely it was normal to be anxious in an interrogation. Because that's what this felt like. An interrogation.

At least the concealer was holding. Small mercies. I took note of the growing line of vehicles behind me, winding far out of view. I could imagine the cursing going on inside those cars, the mindless conjecture, and prayed that the guard would wave me through.

No such luck. Maybe I needed to pray on a more regular basis to make it work. If I got out of this mess, I might consider it.

"Were you camping alone?" Assessing me. Any hint of a smile erased.

Was camping alone something he could check up on? Maybe. Probably. Who knew? I mentally cautioned myself to keep it simple.

I had a bad habit of saying the wrong thing. Especially when my eye started twitching and my mind drifted off.

I BLAME it all on the Strawberry Moon. My astrological sign is Cancer, which means I'm heavily influenced by the moon and all its phases. Before you dismiss that as a lot of nonsense, consider that the ocean wouldn't have tides if it weren't for the pull of the moon. Being a Cancerian may not be a defense, but at least it's an explanation.

But I digress.

This year's Strawberry Moon was extra-special—it was the first time since 1967 that the full moon coincided with the summer solstice in the Northern Hemisphere. It would be another forty-seven years before it would occur again. Think about it. Forty-seven years. I'd be seventy. Ben would be seventy-five. Assuming we'd still be together.

Or alive.

And, so, I'd planned this camping trip. I simply had to see that amber-rose moon in a sky unfettered by high rises and streetlights. The sun at its highest, the moon at its lowest, shimmering over Superior like a beacon of hope.

Hope. I'd had that once, with Ben. Before he lost his job. Before he started drinking. It was the reason I'd invited him to join me. As if a Strawberry Moon would magically transform him back into the guy I once thought could be "the one." Never mind my know-it-all sister's dire predictions, my friends' well-intentioned warnings. I could do this. *We* could do this.

Except. It was quickly apparent that Ben's idea of camping and mine were vastly different. While I pitched the tent, unpacked, started a campfire, and got dinner underway, he sat, his back to me, drinking beer and watching the waves crash against the shore. He finally turned around after his fifth beer, crushed the can in his hand, and belched.

Belched.

"Beans and wieners for dinner?" he'd asked. "That's the best you can come up with after a nine-hour drive?"

Part of me wanted to drive the smirk on his face into next week. After all, *I'd* been the one doing the driving—with his stupid aluminum fishing boat in tow—but I wasn't about to let him ruin my Strawberry Moon. Forty-seven years, I reminded myself. Forty-seven years.

"I thought we might make s'mores for dessert."

The idea of s'mores seemed to placate Ben, though he continued to drink, switching from beer to vodka shots while I sipped on a single glass of Australian chardonnay. Maybe he didn't care, but I wanted to experience that moon sober.

The sun set at nine thirty-three, exactly as forecast, unveiling the Strawberry Moon in all its full splendor. By then Ben was passed out cold in our tent. I might have been able to deal with that, but his chainsaw impression was insufferable. Here I was, in one of the most beautiful places in the world, witnessing one of the rarest full moons in almost five decades, and I had to listen to his snoring as background music.

I slipped into the tent and attempted to turn Ben over on his side to stop his snoring. He resisted, arms flailing. The next thing I knew, his right fist connected with my left eye. I swore under my breath, knowing it would be black by morning.

And then, something inside of me snapped. Thinking. Remembering...

Two years of "seriously" dating. One year of waiting for an engagement ring. Six months of driving him everywhere because he'd lost his license in a DUI. I knew I'd wasted the last three-and-a-half years of my life, and yet, until that moment, I'd had hope.

Delusion can be a wonderful thing.

Until it isn't.

I held my pillow over Ben's face and ignored his pathetic struggling until I was positive there was no movement. Dragged his lifeless body and hoisted it into the trunk of the car. It's amazing how strong you can be when adrenaline courses through your veins and the moon is full.

The boat came next. I waited until an hour before dawn, then I tossed Ben's empty beer cans onto the floor, poured a bit of vodka onto his PDF, and pushed that baby into the water, watching as the waves pushed it out, farther and farther from shore, shining in the last light of the Strawberry Moon.

THE BORDER GUARD stared at me with narrowed eyes, still assessing. "I asked if you were camping alone."

I thought about Ben in the trunk, getting stiffer and smellier by the minute. It was a hot day by June standards, and it wouldn't be long before the smell started permeating the car, and the air around it. I needed to get him as far away from Pancake Bay Provincial Park as possible. Crossing the U.S./Canadian border was supposed to give me the alibi I needed when Ben's empty boat was discovered thrashing about Superior. Who would have thought they'd find it so soon?

As for Ben's body, there were plenty of isolated spots in Michigan's Upper Peninsula where no one would look. Except the coyotes and bears, of course.

"I'm sorry. I was worried about the vehicles behind me and got distracted." My eye twitched again, and I resisted the urge to tug at it. "I was camping with my boyfriend."

Was, not *am*.

The border guard finally cracked a smile.

"Pop the trunk."

THE LINEUP

K.L. Abrahamson
www.karenlabrahamson.com

Sharon Hart Addy
www.sharonhartaddyauthor.wordpress.com

C.W. Blackwell
https://twitter.com/CW_Blackwell

Clark Boyd
www.twitter.com/clark_boyd

M.H. Callway
https://mhcallway.com

Michael A. Clark
www.reverbnation.com/michaelaclark

Susan Daly
www.susandaly.com

Buzz Dixon
www.BuzzDixon.com

Jeanne DuBois
jeanne-dubois.com

Elizabeth Elwood
www.elihuentertainment.com

Tracy Falenwolfe
www.tracyfalenwolfe.com

Kate Fellowes
http://katefellowes.wordpress.com

John M. Floyd
www.johnmfloyd.com

Billy Houston
www.instagram.com/billys_booksandstuff/

Bethany Maines
www.BethanyMaines.com

Judy Penz Sheluk
www.judypenzsheluk.com

KM Rockwood
www.kmrockwood.com

Joseph S. Walker
https://jsw47408.wixsite.com/website

Robert Weibezahl
https://robertweibezahl.wordpress.com

Susan Jane Wright
https://susanjanewright.ca/

THANK YOU FOR READING
MOONLIGHT & MISADVENTURE

If you enjoyed this collection, please consider checking out the first two Superior Shores Anthologies:

THE BEST LAID PLANS: 21 STORIES OF MYSTERY & SUSPENSE

Whether it's a subway station in Norway, ski resort in Vermont, McMansion in the suburbs, or trendy art gallery in Toronto, the 21 authors represented in this superb collection of mystery and suspense interpret the overarching theme of the best-laid plans in their own inimitable style. And like many best-laid plans, they come with no guarantees.

Stories by Tom Barlow, Susan Daly, Lisa de Nikolits, P.A. De Voe, Peter DiChellis, Lesley A. Diehl, Mary Dutta, C.C. Guthrie, William Kamowski, V.S. Kemanis, Lisa Lieberman, Edward Lodi, Rosemary McCracken, LD Masterson, Edith Maxwell, Judy Penz Sheluk, KM Rockwood, Peggy Rothschild, Johanna Beate Stumpf, Victoria Weisfeld, and Chris Wheatley.

HEARTBREAKS & HALF-TRUTHS: 22 STORIES OF MYSTERY & SUSPENSE

Whether it's 1950s Hollywood, a scientific experiment, or a yard sale in suburbia, the twenty-two authors represented in this collection of mystery and suspense interpret the overarching theme of "heartbreaks and half-truths" in their own inimitable style, where only one thing is certain: Behind every broken heart lies a half-truth.

And behind every half-truth lies a secret.

Stories by Sharon Hart Addy, Paula Gail Benson, James Blakey, Gustavo Bondoni, Susan Daly, Buzz Dixon, Rhonda Eikamp, Christine Eskilson, Tracy Falenwolfe, KateFlora, John M.Floyd, J.A. Henderson, Blair Keetch, Steve Liskow, Edward Lodi, Judy Penz Sheluk, KM Rockwood, Peggy Rothschild, Joseph S.Walker, James Lincoln Warren, Chris Wheatley, and Robb T. White.

CPSIA information can be obtained
at www.ICGtesting.com
Printed in the USA
LVHW020544090621
689685LV00003B/105